Always Hope

Always Hope

Mia Stadin

This book is a work of fiction. Any references to real people or real places are used fictitiously. The characters, incidents and dialogues in this book are of the author's imagination and are not to be construed as real. Any resemblance to actual events or persons, living or dead, is entirely coincidental.

Cover Design by Lucy Holtsnider, lucyholtsnider.com

Back Cover Photo by Tina Tang, Parris Blue Photography, tinatang@
parrisblue.com

ISBN 978-1-7378146-1-0

Published by Victory Vision Publishing & Consulting, LLC

www.victoryvision.org

Dedication

To John Stadin, for all your help and support in making this book a reality. With your expertise in the logging industry, the truth about environmentally sound logging, and your critiques all those late nights, you are forever appreciated and loved.

Acknowledgments

My sincere thanks to Joyce Mochrie, the best copy editor and proofreader out there. Without her magnificent, first-rate expertise, this book would still be sitting on my shelf. She was very thorough and precise and helped me see things in this novel that I could not see, even having polished it myself numerous times.

Also, many thanks to Lucy Holtsnider, my amazing formatter, who helped turn this into the real thing.

Thanks also to my writing peers and critique groups over the years, whom I spent many hours with going over and over rough drafts. One exceptional reader who stands out to me is Giselle Albertson for giving me courage, reading my drafts, and keeping me going when I wanted to give up. Also, a special shout out to Laura Carter for being my favorite and best critique partner ever!

I also want to thank R.E. Vance, my book coach, for helping point me in the right direction. Your quick wit, boundless energy, enthusiasm, knowledge, and humor kept me inspired. You ROCK!

And finally, Dear Reader . . .

If you're reading this, miracles do come true. I was told many times it would never happen, but it did. Persistence paid off. Finding that tiny bit of confidence when the majority was nowhere to be found. Saying over and over in my head, "I can do this." It's about never giving up. It's about holding true to your dreams.

From my heart to yours, enjoy.

Hugs and belief in yourself,

Mia Stadin

Chapter One

She could smell the alcohol on his breath from five feet away.

Monet Allen rose from the couch where Shane sat, slumped, a bottle of beer in his hand. She stood directly in front of him and, in a controlled voice, said, "Shane, I'm asking you nicely to leave."

"Yeah, right." He shrugged. "I've heard it all before."

"It's over, Shane." Dixie Cup, Monet's orange tomcat, chose that moment to wind his tail around her calves as if to say, no worries, it'll all work out.

"You don't mean it. You never do." Shane shot to his feet. "I know you, Monet."

Telling Shane that she was through was one thing, but his believing it was another. It had happened too many times before. Being in a relationship with him for two years was like going the wrong way down a one-way street. It couldn't work. “I do mean this.” He adjusted his crotch and wagged a finger at her. “Fine, but you’re making a big mistake. Don’t forget it.”

“Then I’ll deal with my mistake.”

“I love you. Doesn’t that mean anything to you?”

“You don’t love me, Shane.”

“What will it take for you to see that I do?” He swayed, putting a hand on the wall to steady himself.

“You’ve been living rent-free for the past two years. Come on, I think it’s time for you to go. Maybe you should get help for your drinking.”

Shane hurled his beer can against the wall. “You think I have a drinking problem?” The can exploded and fueled the air with fumes.

“No comment.” Disgust hit her—hard—not so much from his outburst, but from the realization that she’d put up with his empty promises for two years.

“Look, I’m sorry.” Shane closed the distance between them, whispering in her ear, “I want you.”

She smiled as if she found his remark amusing. “It’s too late, Shane.”

She retreated toward the kitchen, while watching him stagger to the bedroom door, jerk it open, and disappear inside. She expelled a breath. Hopefully, he’d start packing his things.

In the short silence, she scanned the almond-colored appliances in her tiny kitchen. The black coffeemaker and calming, blue Formica countertops brought out the contrast in colors. She forced her mind from interior design back to Shane. If she expected him to drive away, he needed to sober up. She set the coffee to brew, inhaling the pleasant, Irish cream flavor.

Moments later, Shane trudged from the bedroom, limp duffel bag in hand, and scooped up some of his rap CDs from the coffee table.

Monet quickly filled two coffee mugs. "Here, sit down." She gestured at the kitchen table, pulled out a chair, and took a seat. "Drink this. You'll feel better."

He fell into a chair. "What do you care?"

"I'm not a bad person, Shane." She took a sip of the warm, flavored coffee. "Besides, it'll help to sober you up."

"Fine, but it's not like I'm going to be sober anytime soon."

Monet took a deep breath, quieting her frayed nerves as she eyed his bag on the floor. "Your bag looks nearly empty."

"It's a start. I'll get more of my stuff later." He slurped some coffee and wiped a hand across his mouth. "This shit's hot."

Determinedly, she drew herself up. "Shane, I'm serious this time."

"Yeah. Yeah, right. Whatever." He nodded. "Hey, I was thinking that ... um ... maybe we could ... uh ... you know, have a little fun before I leave."

His offer shot her right out of the chair. "I don't think so."

"Come on, it might change your mind." Shane rose and

sidled up to her. "And I thought maybe I could … uh … use your car to get you something … you know, to show you how much I care about you."

Humorless laughter slipped from Monet's throat. "I'm not going there."

He tipped the coffee to his mouth, swallowed several times, then handed her the empty mug. "Here, you happy?"

"If you'll leave."

Shane chuckled at her remark. "Now, let me show you how much I've changed." He held a hand out. "Your car keys, please."

"You've got your own car." She took his mug to the sink and picked up her own.

"Yeah, but it's not a Lexus."

"Well, I worked hard for it. I'm not going to continue to let you abuse it."

Her words were met with an icy glare. In a huff, Shane grabbed his bag, his car keys, and left.

Shortly after, she heard tires squealing, but she didn't care where he was headed. This time, he hadn't taken her heart with him.

Monet set her coffee on the counter and crossed the living room to the window, where her Lifecycle was strategically placed. She burned calories here while taking in the view of Seattle's skyscrapers. Emotionally, she felt like she'd been riding that cycle nonstop for the past two years. Shane's constant financial demands had depleted her. She wondered how she'd ever gotten herself into this, or better yet, how she'd fallen for it.

Minutes later, the door flew open and Shane stormed across the threshold. Her heart slammed to a stop.

"I refuse to believe it's over between us." Shane closed the distance between them and wrapped her in his arms.

Monet broke free, stepped back, and took in his close-cropped hair, baggy gangster jeans, tank top, and well-muscled arms. "Start believing it."

"I don't think so." He chuckled low in his throat.

"Really." She whirled away to gaze out at the sparkling view of water and buildings against Seattle's skyline, trying for a sense of calm. She sensed he wouldn't just walk away.

"You think you can get someone better than me, is that it? That's it, isn't it?" His lip curled in disgust. "You're a gold digger."

"What? I think you've just described yourself, and as usual, you don't know what you're talking about."

"No, Monet." He pointed a finger at her. "You're the one who doesn't know what you're talking about."

She spun around to face him. "Come on, Shane. Just try to understand where I'm coming from. I have goals and a future I need to think about. I can't do this anymore."

He blinked hard. "Do what?"

"Be a part of your life. I want to start school in the fall."

"For what?"

"Interior design."

He laughed.

Monet refused to let his ridicule hurt her. "How many times have I told you this?"

"Sorry, it's just ... I don't know. I really can't see you doing anything else but dancing."

"Is that right?"

"You've been dancing forever. Why stop now?"

"I can't stop now. I need to support myself. I'd like to start going to school, too, which means, I need to make some lifestyle changes."

"When you do stop dancing, how are you going to keep supporting your leech of a mother?"

"Look who's talking. Worry about yourself, Shane, not others. That's what you're good at, isn't it?"

"Whatever." Shane suddenly grabbed her shoulders. "I know you don't mean this."

Monet broke contact and hauled in a much-needed breath, all out of words.

"I'll be back." His eyes narrowed to slits. "Don't worry."

"Yeah, only to get the rest of your stuff."

Then he whipped around so fast, she felt a whoosh of air before he stomped out the door, slamming it shut.

"We'll see about that," she called after him, her body jolting from the impact of the door.

Collecting herself, Monet turned to the oval mirror on the wall and took in her golden hair that fell well past her shoulders. It looked limp, lifeless, much like she felt.

Dixie Cup meowed and rubbed up against her, instantly easing her shattered nerves. She scooped him up and grabbed her coffee off the counter. As she sank into a chair, she closed her eyes, took a deep breath, and reached inside herself for calm.

Coffee gone, she turned to her cat. "You think I should call Cameo?"

The cat purred. She took that as a yes.

Phone in hand, Monet dialed the number. "Cameo, hey, it's Monet. You ready for this?"

"Ready for what?" Cameo asked.

"How about you come on over and I'll tell you."

"No problem. I'm on my way."

True to her word, Cameo arrived fifteen minutes later in chic jeans and an orange tank top. The scent of rose, peach, amber, and musk filled the apartment.

They headed straight to the couch in the living room and plopped down on the cushions.

"I told him to move out," Monet began.

"Did he?" Cameo searched Monet's face. "He didn't, did he? The prick!" Gold, hoop earrings jangled from her ears as she tossed her head in disgust.

"Not to worry," Monet said with more conviction than she felt. "He'll move out. He already took a few of his things, but then he came right back, and, you know, the usual. Can you believe this has been going on for two years?"

"It's called never giving up."

"I had feelings for him once. There's just only so much a person can take. But hey," she said and shrugged, "can't say I didn't try."

"That's an understatement." Cameo touched her hand. "Maybe you stayed with Shane to punish yourself."

"Do you think I have father issues?"

"How could you not? Your father abandoned your mother before you were born."

"I guess I feel like my mom's problems are my fault. Perhaps if I hadn't come along, she'd still be with my father and wouldn't need me so much."

"You know what I think?"

"What?"

"I think you analyze too much. Quit blaming yourself and feeling guilty. Your mom's a grown woman who should be able to take care of herself."

"You know I know you're right." Monet smiled. "You're always right."

"How about this then," Cameo said, twirling a strand of plentiful, brown hair around a finger. "Let's get out of here for a while. Maybe go get some munchies or something."

"I could go for that."

"Let me freshen up first."

"You got it." Monet rose from the couch and crossed the room to gaze out the window at the glossy view of Elliot Bay. In the evening light, the water lay smooth as tinted glass.

"You ready to go?" Cameo asked, emerging from the restroom.

Monet caught a whiff of cotton candy lip gloss. "Yeah, let's go."

"You know, I'm really glad you ended it with Shane." Cameo spread more gloss on her lips, rubbing them together. "You just don't need the trouble."

"Who does? Besides, I can't wait to finally start putting money away for school."

"I know what you mean. Do you still have your heart set on interior design?"

"Definitely," Monet said, closing the blinds. She tucked her oversize T-shirt inside her jeans and gathered up her purse. "Come on. Let's go splurge."

She locked up before they headed out on foot.

At the supermarket, they strolled through the bakery department and got the last two apple fritters in the glass case, then headed to the chip aisle for a bag of Classic Lay's potato chips.

"Ice cream's turn." Monet started toward the freezer section.

"Wow." Cameo whistled softly, stopping dead in her tracks, Monet right beside her. "Look at that. Where did he come from?"

Monet stared at a guy with eyes the color of molasses and a goatee that matched his thick, jet-black hair. A diamond stud flashed in his left ear. Nice. Leave it to Cameo, even though she had a beautiful, black boyfriend, to always notice a hot guy.

"Alex," a young woman said, tugging at his arm. "Come on."

He was taken. Good. Monet released a thankful sigh. She really didn't need to be thinking about men right now.

Before she could pull her eyes away, they locked with his. She couldn't get herself to blink. She caught a glimpse of faded, snug Levi's and a royal-blue shirt outlining a well-sculpted chest.

Cameo elbowed her in the side. "Monet, what kind of ice cream do you want?"

"Huh? Oh yeah, Rocky Road." Monet inclined her head at Cameo while shifting her glance to the woman with Alex. A body that women envied and men wanted was encased in a red dress, barely covering a curvy figure. Her russet-colored hair was wavy, thick, and tumbling about her shoulders. She reminded Monet of Angelina Jolie with red hair.

Monet's attention caught at the thump in the shopping cart and another nudge from Cameo. "So, are we done then?" she asked.

Cameo nodded. "We're done. Let's go."

The sexy couple disappeared from the aisle.

"Wait." Monet stopped Cameo. "Let's make sure we're not forgetting anything."

"Okay. Donuts, chips, ice cream." Cameo counted off with her fingers.

"I'd really hate to get home and have to come back," Monet said, "but maybe not if Alex was still going to be here." She wouldn't even know his name if the woman hadn't said it.

"Oh, you. Now think hard." Cameo rolled her eyes. "And not about him."

"Do you think they're together?" Monet whispered.

"Who?" Cameo's eyes widened with confusion.

"That couple who looked like they could be on the cover of a steamy romance novel."

"I don't think they're brother and sister, if that's what you mean. Of course they're together. Don't even think about it. I'm glad you're a free woman, but I wouldn't mess with that. They're definitely attached. She couldn't get any closer to him without being on top of him."

Monet knew she didn't need more heartache. "I know. Come on, let's go." But something electric just beneath the surface called to her.

Monet and Cameo dashed around to the next aisle. Seconds later, the same couple appeared.

"Oh no," Monet whispered.

Under her breath, Cameo said, "Damn."

With the woman leading the way, the young couple drew toward them. They stopped within a foot of Monet and Cameo. The flashy redhead gave her hair a toss and asked, "Don't I know you from somewhere?" Her sharp, green gaze addressed Cameo.

Monet looked at the woman next to Alex, then at Cameo. What was going on here? Then her eyes fell on Alex, who completely stole her train of thought.

"I don't believe so," Cameo finally answered.

Monet detected something. Did she and Cameo know each other?

"Well, for a minute, I thought I might." The redhead shrugged and draped an arm around Alex's waist. "See you later then."

As they walked away, a sense of longing settled over Monet.

"She's pathetic," Cameo said, referring to the woman with Alex.

"She's definitely full of herself," Monet added, following Cameo to a checkout line.

When she heard the deep-timbered voice behind her, Monet angled around and locked eyes with Alex.

"Hello again," he said.

The same gorgeous woman stood at his side. Her face now blended well with her hair.

Hope spread through Monet at the sight of him again. Maybe the woman was just a clingy ex.

"Hey Ruby," Alex suddenly said. "Why don't we introduce ourselves?" He flashed Monet a bright smile.

"What for?" Ruby fired back. "We need to go."

Monet blocked out Ruby's demand, taking in the sight of Alex. She noticed his sun-browned complexion, and when their eyes met and locked, he raised his brows and flashed Monet a charming grin. His diamond earring sparkled against his black hair. She felt her heart skip a beat.

"Fine, Alex." Ruby rolled her eyes, then pinned Monet with a dark glare. "I suppose we could introduce ourselves."

Monet had a bad feeling about this.

"I'm Ruby, and this is Alex, my … uh … well?" Ruby sidled up to Alex. "Should we tell them we'll be getting engaged soon?"

Disappointment slid through Monet. She should have known it was too good to be true.

"Screw that," Alex told Ruby.

Ruby turned evil eyes on Alex.

Anticipation mounted.

"Ruby and I are friends, nothing more." Alex grinned at Monet.

She smiled back. It was obvious he wasn't too into Ruby. Hope sprang back to life inside her.

Cameo cleared her throat. "I'm sure the ice cream's melting. We really should be going."

"Yeah," Ruby snapped, "we should, too. We have some business to take care of," she said as she steered Alex away.

Monet's thoughts jumbled together. What was wrong with this picture? Was it she and Shane in reverse? As Shane's image appeared in Monet's mind, she blinked it away. She wished Ruby had given her a chance to introduce herself to Alex.

Ten minutes later, after Monet and Cameo made it through a checkout line and whirled out the automatic door, Monet couldn't stop thinking about Alex. Where was he?

"I was hoping I'd catch you before you left." Alex appeared just as they turned the corner for home. "I didn't get your name," he said to Monet.

Amazed excitement stopped her. "It's Monet."

Cameo nudged her. "I'll take the groceries back if you give me the key."

Monet rooted out the key to her apartment and slipped it into Cameo's hand. "I'll be right behind you," she promised.

Cameo's eyes widened. "See you soon, okay?"

"Of course." She nodded her agreement, then found herself fiddling with her hands, forcing her eyes back on Alex. "Where's Ruby?" she finally asked.

"She's in the car, parked around the corner." He gestured with a hand. "I told her I forgot something, hoping you hadn't left. I figured I'd go back in and grab a beer. You live close, huh?"

"Yeah, just a few blocks away. So, is Ruby your girlfriend or what?" She was desperate to figure him out.

"No." He chuckled. "She's married to someone else." Then he leaned into Monet. Lowering his voice, he said, "And when I saw you, I liked what I saw and said to myself, 'There's an angel in disguise. She can help me outta this mess.'" He wiggled his brows. "I don't have long, though. She's still waiting for me."

Through her confusion, Monet focused on what he'd said. Ruby was married to someone else. So, what were they doing out together? It didn't make sense. The whole situation seemed one-sided. Maybe Alex was looking for a way out. She had to know before another second slipped past. "What's this thing between you and Ruby?"

"I already told you." He raked a hand through his hair. "She's married to someone else, not me."

Something was really wrong here. "Then why did she want to say you two would be getting engaged?"

"Because she's a pathological liar."

"So why are you with her?"

"We had some business to take care of."

"I see. Must be important." Monet nodded. "It seems Ruby mentioned that."

"Well, hey, it's you and me now."

She slanted a brow. "Is it?"

"Yeah."

Their gazes locked. The early summer evening slowly slipped away. Even though it was still warm out, a chill crossed over Monet's skin. She couldn't get her eyes to leave his. "So, what do we do now?"

"How about I get your phone number and we start by seeing each other?"

"How about I get yours instead?"

"No problem. You got paper and pen?"

"Sure." Monet rummaged through her purse and handed him a small piece of paper and a pen.

He drew a Camel cigarette out of a jean pocket, lit up, then scribbled his number down and handed it back to her.

"I have to get out of this thing with Ruby," he said, exhaling away from her. "Her husband is my boss."

Puzzled, Monet squinted up at him. "Your boss?"

"Yeah, it's a mess. Call me, and we'll go from there."

"I will." This web Alex had spun piqued her curiosity.

"She's got something over me and won't let go." Alex flicked his cigarette and disappeared.

When Monet got herself to move, she started home with questions plaguing her.

How could Ruby do this to her husband with the guy who worked for him? And why would Alex mess around with the wife of his boss? Was Ruby blackmailing him? That had to be the problem. Did Ruby's husband suspect anything? What kind of person was he? When she called Alex, she'd find out.

When she arrived back at her apartment, she knocked a few times.

Cameo swung the door open. "It's about time."

"I'm sorry." Monet flashed an apologetic smile. "But just wait till you hear what Alex told me."

"What?"

Monet slipped inside.

"Yeah, get in here and get some of that Rocky Road ice cream before I eat it all."

"That woman, Ruby," Monet began, "is married to someone else."

"Oh, boy. The plot thickens. Here." Cameo gestured toward the ice cream on the table.

Monet took a spoon from a drawer and joined her.

"So, did you get a number?" Cameo dug into the chocolate ice cream. "Wait a minute. You couldn't resist, right, even though he's out with a married woman?" She wagged her spoon at Monet.

"It's not what it looks like," Monet said, defending Alex. "She's married to his boss. I have a feeling she's blackmailing him."

"Even so, he was with her tonight."

"I agree, but what if you were being blackmailed?"

"I just don't know. It seems odd." Cameo sat back and folded her arms across her chest.

"But interesting."

"What about Ruby? She didn't seem to be on the same page with Alex. I don't know about you, but if it were me, I think I'd stay away."

"This blackmail thing, though. Maybe I can help him," Monet said.

"Yeah, okay, possibly. Hey, what does he do for the guy anyway, besides screw his wife?"

"I don't know, but he wants out."

Through a mouthful of ice cream, Cameo asked, "Are you going to go out with him?"

"I'd like to." Monet swallowed a bite of roasted almonds, marshmallow, and chocolate.

"Yeah, help him take his pants off." Cameo rolled her eyes. "Just be careful. Remember, Shane was definitely in need of help, too, and still is."

"How could I forget? Besides, the situation with Shane is entirely different."

"How's that?"

"He wasn't being blackmailed."

Cameo arched a brow. "I suppose you have a point. By the way, what is it with you rescuing guys, anyway?"

"No way. Me?"

"Yeah, you."

"Okay, I admit I'm attracted to guys who—"

"Need something."

"God, what am I doing?" Monet ran both hands through her hair. "I see a hot guy and right away get his phone number. I'm like a bitch in heat."

Cameo chuckled. "Hey, if it's just sex you want, bang away. I just don't want you hurt again. I guess what I'm trying to say is, I hate to see you fall into the same trap, only to be used again."

"It's not going to happen. Don't worry, I'll be smart."

"Good. I'm holding you to it."

An hour later, not long after Cameo left, Monet had the

kitchen all tidied up. She returned to the living room, put her Alicia Keys' CD on at a low volume, and sank down onto the couch. She skimmed through her *Vogue* magazine. Within seconds, Dixie Cup jumped up and settled himself into her lap. She stroked his back. "What do you think of all this?"

Her cat answered with a purr.

"I know I should probably forget about Alex for now and concentrate on work and figure out school, that sort of thing, but there's nothing wrong with helping Alex out."

Dixie Cup stretched out and curled up into a ball.

"Thanks for listening."

While Monet prepared for bed, she wondered if being raised without a father had something to do with her *need* for men, as well as her fear of being without one.

The next day, those thoughts and her curiosity urged her to call Alex. Retrieving his number, Monet punched in the digits.

After the third ring, Alex answered, "Hello."

"Hi, Alex, it's Monet from the grocery store."

"Oh, yeah, cutie, what's up? I'm glad you called."

Her pulse jumped as she cradled the receiver between her ear and shoulder. "I'd really like to get to know you."

"You wouldn't happen to have a boyfriend, would you?"

"If I did, why would I have called you?"

"Maybe you want to get laid by a real man." Alex chuckled. "Hey, it's cool, but I can certainly arrange it, though."

"I'm sure you could."

"So, let's hook up."

"By the way, I just ended a relationship."

"You're on the rebound then."

"Not at all. He supposedly moved out yesterday."

"Yesterday?" Alex said. "I think you are on the rebound."

"Okay." Monet sighed. "To make a long story short, for two years, we've been splitting up and getting back together, but it's finally over."

"Well, I'm glad."

"That makes two of us. So, how about filling me in on your situation. What do you do?"

"You sure you want to know?"

Her blood pressure plummeted. What does he do for the guy, sell drugs? "Yes."

"I drive a log truck."

Relief washed through her in waves. "How long have you been doing that?"

"About four years. It's easy to remember because I'd just turned twenty-one when he hired me."

"You're only twenty-five? I'm six years older." She paused, wondering if he'd think she was too old. "You like your job?"

"Women in their thirties are more experienced. And yeah, sure, the job's cool."

"So why are you seeing your boss's wife?"

"She's blackmailing me."

That explained it. "Would it be too forward of me to ask how she's blackmailing you?"

"Nope, but I'd rather tell you in person."

Monet let a beat pass. "Do you get along with your boss?"

"Yeah, sure. Look, maybe you could help me figure a way out of this mess, huh?"

The urgency in his voice played havoc with her heart. "Then you need to tell me about the blackmailing."

Alex sighed into the phone. "In person."

"You mean right now?" What did she have to lose?

"Sure, that sounds great. My place or yours?"

This was too new. "How about if I come to your place?"

"Great. Let me give you directions."

Monet jotted them down.

After she cradled the phone, she quickly showered, threw on black jeans and a cap-sleeved top, and went straight to her car before she could change her mind.

On the drive to his house, Monet had a chance to think about their conversation. It intrigued her. Maybe she really could help him end it with Ruby.

By the time she made it to his place and was on his doorstep, her heart pounded like a beating drum.

Was she making a mistake?

Then the door opened.

Alex stood there looking sexy as hell in worn Levi's and a dark-gray shirt. The diamond stud earring in his left ear added to his allure. She hadn't forgotten how well his tight jeans fit. Nice. "Hi, Alex."

"Well, hello there, cutie. Come on in." He moved aside to let her enter.

As she stepped inside, she inhaled his masculine fragrance, a cool breath of citrus and herbs, mellowed by the scent of warm, sensual wood. "So," she said, taking in her surroundings, "how long have you lived here?"

"Too long." He chuckled. "About four years, as long as I've worked for Jay. It's not a mansion, but it works for me."

"It's not bad at all," she said, even though the place could use an extra coat of paint, maybe off-white to lighten up the beige-colored walls.

She inhaled Alex's fragrance, which helped to drown out a hint of stale tobacco in the air, and followed him to a well-used, brown, vinyl couch in the living room.

"How about a Corona?" he asked.

"Sounds great." She nodded. "But only one. I have to drive home."

"You sure about that?" Alex winked. "You never know, you might want to spend the night with me." He turned and headed for the kitchen.

Monet gazed after him, admiring his loose, gaited walk.

Seconds later, he emerged with two open bottles of Corona Extra.

"Thanks." As he handed one to her, their hands grazed each other.

"No problem, anytime." He situated himself beside her about a thigh length away and lit up.

Monet sipped the imported beer. It slid down her throat smoothly, warming her insides. "So, tell me about Ruby." She set the bottle down on the newspaper-lined coffee table, ready to listen.

He took a pull of Corona and a drag off his smoke. "It has to do with her seducing me in the heat of the moment. Like an idiot, I gave in. When I tried to break it off, she threatened to tell her husband and get me fired. I don't like being in the middle of this shit."

"Well, I'm here to help," she reassured him.

"I'm through with her." Alex took another chug of beer, followed by an inhale of nicotine.

Monet picked up her bottle. "How long have Jay and Ruby been married?"

"Three years, but he's had his business a lot longer than that. I'm hoping Jay divorces her and that the bitch doesn't get half his money like she thinks she will. She really doesn't deserve him. Can you believe he bought her a ZR1 Corvette for a first-year anniversary present?"

"Wow, one of those Corvettes with all the horsepower. Sounds like Ruby's pretty lucky."

"I'll say. Well, hey, enough about her. I want to know more about you."

Monet swallowed some beer. "Tell me a little bit more about this thing with Ruby first."

"I caught her taking money after hours. She seduced me. What can I say? It's as simple as that."

"Where did this happen?"

"In the office next to the house. When I started to leave, she stopped me and said if I told Jay anything about her stealing, she'd tell him what we'd just done."

"You're in a tough spot."

"Yeah." Alex took a drag off his smoke, a pull off his bottle, and drained it.

She reached over and lightly squeezed her hand around his. "We'll figure this out."

He removed a container of wintergreen Tic Tacs from a shirt pocket and offered her some.

"I'm still working on my beer, but sure, why not."

He slipped a few into her hand, then put the Tic Tac container to his mouth and poured.

She popped them into her mouth and heard him chew, then swallow.

Then his mouth was inches from hers.

His fragrance mingled with wintergreen, tobacco, and beer. The thought of kissing him enticed her, but she turned away instead and said, "Alex, I want to know more. Keep going, don't stop."

"I wish you were saying that under different circumstances." He wiggled his brows. "I was thinking once we got started, we wouldn't be able to stop."

"You could be right."

Then he leaned into her and brushed his lips across hers.

"Alex." Her stomach tingled.

"You want me, I want you," he said, parting her lips with his. He pressed his erection against her leg as if to prove his point.

"I ..." She felt his tongue slide over hers in a caress that left her craving more.

And then their mouths came together in a hot tangle of tongues and moans. She wrapped her arms around his back and ran her hands through his hair.

He deepened the kiss, moving her closer into him until he was nearly on top of her. He began working at the buttons on her jeans.

She took his hand, like a customer at the club, moved it away, and said against his face, "We don't have to rush, you know. We should get to know each other."

He moved away, and with a shrug, said, "No problem."

She picked up her beer and finished it.

"Ready for another?"

"Thanks, I'm okay. Now, where were we?" She fought to get her emotions under control. A part of her wanted to let him drive right into her, right here, right now, fast and furious.

"Yeah." Alex took a pull on his beer. "Where were we?"

"Oh, you were telling me all about Ruby and how you got into—"

"Ruby's a lying bitch," he said, plowing a hand through his hair. "How can I believe she'd tell Jay what we'd done? I don't trust a thing she says."

"She's manipulating you."

"Yeah, and get this. Ruby told me she doesn't care if Jay finds out. Pretty contradictory, wouldn't you say? She plans to divorce him, take half of what he has. She says he'll probably give her more than half." Alex shook his head. "She really doesn't know him. He's not like that."

What was he like? "She sounds psycho."

"She is. Her lies don't even jive, but you never know what she might do. Just make sure you watch your back around her."

Sympathy for Jay stole over her, even though she didn't know him. "I will."

"I need someone who's nothing like her."

"I'm not."

"Good. Okay, then, tell me more about yourself. What do you do?" Alex's gaze held hers.

Not sure she wanted to end this conversation, Monet felt it was only fair. "I'm a dancer right now."

"No kidding? Do you dance on tables?"

"Not exactly." She laughed, enjoying his sense of humor. "We dance alongside them, though. And I'm hoping to start college in the fall to study interior design. It's what I really want to do."

"And dancing's not?"

"Let's just say it's not something I want to do forever."

"I don't blame you."

"So," Monet said, wanting to know more about him, "where's your family?"

"In Oregon. I didn't want to work for my dad, so I came up here."

"What does your dad do?"

On a sigh, Alex said, "He owns a dump-trucking company."

"Wow, more trucking. How come you didn't want to work for your dad?"

"We don't exactly get along." A sharp edge lined his voice.

Monet wouldn't push. "I'm sorry."

Alex seemed to relax. "Where's your family? What does your dad do?"

Monet's heart took a dive. She swallowed, and in an unsteady voice, said, "He left when he found out my mother was pregnant with me. I've never known him. My mom lives by herself."

"That's rough."

Silence stretched between them.

She wasn't searching for pity, but she couldn't easily forget the lonely nights as a child doing her homework and eating dinner alone while her mother was out trolling for men.

Alex's voice brought her back. "Hey, I know if we started seeing each other, neither one of us would regret it."

"You think so?" Monet was grateful for the distraction.

"I know so. Besides, I could show Ruby I have someone else."

"I suppose that would be a good start to ending it with her. Does Jay suspect any of this?"

"Not that I know of."

"Is Ruby unhappy about being married to him?"

"Ruby's never satisfied. She's mixed up, spoiled, and unpredictable. She acts like her looks can get her whatever she wants."

"As I saw last night."

"She's a taker and a user. And you know what?"

"What?"

"Jay married the wrong person. Yep." Alex shook his head. "He married the wrong woman."

Monet felt bad for Jay. "Does Jay seem happy?"

"Not like he was when he first met Ruby. Sometimes I think he realizes the kind of person she really is."

"I wonder why he stays with her."

"He's loyal, he's responsible, and he doesn't give up easily."

It would be really great if Monet could find someone like Jay. Could Alex be the right guy for her? Inexplicably, she felt a chill. "Is Jay able to keep you working year-round?"

"Pretty much. Even though logging has slowed down some, he runs an environmentally sound operation, which these days you really need in that line of work. Plus, he has a good reputation and is very particular about the kind of work he does. It makes a big difference."

"That's good." Ruby had to be an idiot not to appreciate him.

"Where do he and Ruby live?"

"In Maltby, not too far from here. It's handy for me."

"I'll bet. Jay sounds like a terrific guy to work for. Look, we'll work this out together."

"I look forward to it." He gathered her in his arms and set his mouth on hers.

Monet reveled in the softness of his lips. The minty taste of his tongue against hers sent sparks through her. Heat generated between them. He explored her mouth, and she slid her tongue over his smooth teeth, telling herself to stop.

She broke the kiss before her hormones spun out of control and she straddled him right there on the couch. "I want you." She touched his face. "But, really, we're in no hurry," she said as she rose to leave.

"I know." Alex pushed to his feet and stood directly in front of her. "I can't wait to see you again," he said, brushing her cheek with warm lips.

"I'd like that." She looked up at him, at least seven inches taller than her five-foot-five frame. "I'll call you and we'll arrange a time."

"Sounds good." Alex drew in a deep breath. "Monet," he said on a mint-flavored exhale.

"What?" Sweat pearled between her breasts.

"I can't help this." He leaned into her, and his mouth slowly closed over hers—again. His hands slid to her waist, and lower to grip her buttocks, pulling her hard into him.

She felt his arousal and savored his lips on hers, loving the feel of his hard body against her. But even so, she broke the contact. "Look, how about I give you my number?" She dug out pen and paper from her purse and jotted it down. "Thank you for the beer and great company. I mean it. Call me, or I'll call you." She slipped the piece of paper into his hand.

Alex stuffed it in a front jean pocket and searched her face. "I enjoyed being with you tonight."

"That makes two of us." She slid her lips across his.

Alex walked her to the door in silence. "I'll call you."

"I'll look forward to it." She smiled encouragingly, slid out the door, and retraced the steps to her car.

There was always next time.

Chapter Two

Jay finished washing the black Peterbilt, his number one truck of two, then stood back to admire his handiwork. Perfect timing. Darkness had just started to fall. Summer nights made it easy to stay out later and get things done.

He hopped in the truck and ran it into the shop. After locking up, he made his way to the house. Corner quoins and keystones above the windows gave the one-story home a touch of old-world charm. A dark house told Jay that Ruby wasn't home yet.

Anger churned in his gut. Where was his wife? Things had changed with Ruby. She was such a warm person at first, but lately she'd become cold. Jay couldn't pretend anymore to be happy, but he'd be damned if he'd let their marriage fall apart. He'd made a commitment and he intended to honor it by trying until he was sure he'd given all he had. He felt he owed Ruby that.

After a quick shower, Jay slipped outside to enjoy a bit of fresh air. He took in the property, surrounded by cedar and fir trees. A breeze whispered through the trees. He stared out at the expansive lawn and breathed in deeply. Moonlight created a glow in the otherwise darkened sky. Jay wouldn't trade living out here for anything. He only wished to have his loving wife back to the way she'd once been.

As he strolled to the area intended for a future kid's play space, sadness squeezed his heart. Lately, every time Jay brought up having kids with Ruby, she changed the subject. When they'd first gotten married, he'd made it clear that children were part of his plans. She seemed to be all for it then and had said to wait a few years. What had changed? He longed to raise children the same way he'd been raised.

Jay found himself wandering toward the shop. Best to think about other things, like work, to keep his worries from spiraling out of control. Owning a successful, environmentally sound timber and land management company at thirty-eight, he should feel pretty fortunate. He certainly appreciated his driver, Alex, and liked having someone who took care of the truck. Jay couldn't complain about his other employees, either. Overall, he had a great crew. He knew he had a lot to be thankful for. Then why did he feel this emptiness inside?

Something was not right with his wife. What was she up to?

* * *

Through his kitchen window, Alex watched the red Corvette tear out of his driveway, wishing it was the last time he ever had to deal with Ruby. But he knew better. Even after he stopped the affair, he would still have to deal with her. She made out his paycheck, unless he got fired.

Shit! He slammed his fist into the wall at the thought. That's all he needed. A great piece of ass wasn't worth his job, but now he had Monet to think about. If he could start seeing her, he wouldn't give Ruby a second thought. He might have to work to get in her pants, though, but that's just what he needed.

He grabbed a bottle of Corona from the fridge, opened it, and chugged. He couldn't stop thinking about Monet, with her long, blonde hair, tiger eyes, and that luscious, little frame he'd love to have his way with. God how he'd wanted to do her right there on the couch. Next time, he'd have her moaning his name. He had to admit he was weak when it came to turning down hot women. What man wasn't?

His stomach suddenly growled, sending him to the refrigerator again. He searched its contents for something to eat. Not a lot to pick from, other than beer, bread, a little mayonnaise left in a jar, and some cheese. He'd have to get pizza delivery again.

He grabbed the phone, punched in for delivery, and ordered his usual—a small pepperoni and black olive pizza, a side salad with Thousand Island dressing, and a two-liter bottle of Pepsi.

While he waited for his meal to arrive, he crossed to the living room and fell onto the couch. He took a long pull on his beer. He liked the thought of Ruby seeing him with Monet. Jay had invited him to dinner plenty of times. Alex would take him up on it now, if Monet would go with him. He couldn't wait to see the look on Ruby's face when he walked in with her. Would she do something drastic? Ruby was such a bitch that he wouldn't put it past her. That thought left a bad taste in his mouth. He cleared his throat and grimaced at the aftertaste of Ruby still on his tongue, drowning it out with the last of his beer. He eyed the clock, noting he still had about twenty minutes to wait for his meal to arrive. Restless, he jumped up from the couch, fetched another beer, and went outside.

The square taillights on Ruby's 'vette were long gone. Stars blinked everywhere in the night sky. Tomorrow promised to be a good day. Alex tucked his thumbs through his belt loops, rocked back on his heels, and thought more about how to get out of this mess.

* * *

Ruby's temper raged as she drove her car at breakneck speed. The five miles from Alex's home to hers usually took a good ten minutes because of the slower country roads. She'd made it in five, lucky a cop hadn't nailed her for reckless driving. She sped into the driveway, hit the automatic garage door opener on the visor above her head, and pulled into the three-car garage.

Her thoughts slammed into each other as she brought the car to a stop. *Why had Alex been so distant tonight?* They'd had sex, but he'd acted as though he were somewhere else. Ruby could see no other reason than that bimbo at the grocery store with Cameo. Ever since Alex had first seen her, he'd acted differently. Why? What could he possibly see in someone like her? Besides, Ruby constantly reminded Alex that they could live comfortably together. She took care of her husband's books for a reason and had been stashing away money from the start. And when she divorced Jay, she'd go for all she could get. But it looked as if she'd run into a problem with Alex. The bastard was attracted to someone else.

She took her time from the garage to the kitchen. Jay would no doubt start bitching at her the moment she walked in.

"Where are the groceries?" Jay asked, meeting her just inside the doorway.

She rolled her eyes. She was always right. "I … uh … forgot," she said, trying to wriggle herself out of trouble.

Jay laughed without humor. "You forgot? Then where have you been?"

"I ran into an old friend," she stated, her tone flat, "and we got to talking, and—"

"You could have at least called." Jay shook his head and folded his arms across his chest. "Ruby, don't lie."

Sweat trickled between her breasts. She couldn't act nervous. Not now. He couldn't know she was lying. "I'm not lying." Her voice quivered. "I saw a girlfriend I used to go to school with. So, instead of grocery shopping, I went out with her for coffee and we talked about old times. I told her what a wonderful and great-looking husband I have. Can you believe I even described you, saying how your hair was always combed back so perfectly, and that you had the dreamiest, bluest eyes I'd ever seen? Huh ... well, you know what? I wish I hadn't said anything about you, especially if all you're going to do is accuse me of lying." She spun away and attempted to flee from the room.

He called after her. "It seems like the more I try to please you, the more you despise me. I'm not done yet. Don't walk out on me."

"Fine," she yelled, angling around and stomping back to the kitchen. She stopped ten feet away from him, shoved her hands on her hips, and shot him an icy glare. "What?"

"I thought that if I just gave you more, I could make you happy. Apparently, I was wrong."

Ruby sniffed. "Why do you say that?"

"You just don't get it, do you?"

"Whatever are you talking about?" Ruby scrunched her face like a child who hadn't gotten her way.

"How's the bookkeeping class? Keeping up your skills?" Jay turned his back on her and retrieved a pitcher of water from the fridge, got out a glass, and filled it.

Anger and anxiety roiled in her stomach. "It's going great." She barreled past Jay to the fridge for her wine, glaring at him as he took a seat at the kitchen table. She drew a deep breath, anticipating the long night ahead. Usually, he didn't bother when she went away in a huff. Did he know about Alex?

"Look, Ruby, is it so bad that I want to spend some time with my wife?"

She poured herself a glass of wine, took a hefty drink, and joined him at the table. "That depends on if you're nice or not."

"It goes both ways. Look, why do you insist on doing your grocery shopping so late at night after class?"

"Why the interrogation?" She picked up her wineglass and tossed back the remainder of the contents. "Just because I didn't bring home any stupid groceries. Wow, you know what? I think you need to switch to beer."

"Ruby, what I want is a real partner, someone to share every evening with. But it seems that lately, all you want to do is be away from me. I want to know what's going on."

"Nothing." Her voice rose and fell. "Are we done?" She bolted from her chair and felt dizzy.

Jay dropped his face in his hands.

"Now what?" Desperation crept in. "Jay, I'm sorry. It's just that I don't know why you're being so hard on me. I didn't do anything."

"You know what? You're right." His voice took on an edge. "You didn't do anything. I'll be out in the shop."

"Fine." The slam of the door pierced her ears. Jay would probably go fiddle with his truck. Good. She didn't want to be around him anyway.

Ruby was used to getting her way without questions.

Beginning in childhood, she had made a big noise and others would back down. She would see to it that the pattern continued.

Craving comfort, she sashayed to the bedroom to change. She slipped free of her heels and nylons, then out of her tight dress. She carried them with her to the large, walk-in closet, set them on a hamper, and searched the closet for her silk-and-lace lingerie. She chose a turquoise teddy with a matching, short, silk robe.

How could Alex not want her? She had curves in all the right places, unlike some people who appeared to have none at all. Thinking again of the blonde with Cameo, revulsion spun through her. She gave her hair a toss, added a splash of her warm, oriental-flowered, scented fragrance, then headed back out to the kitchen where she helped herself to another glass of white zinfandel, sipping while she stood. She enjoyed the crisp, fruity taste on her tongue while she contemplated what to do. Like a best friend, the alcohol would help her decide. Having a pretty good feeling Jay might be in the shop for a while, she thought it would be a good time to call Alex and pry some answers out of him. Had he had a bad day? Had something gone wrong at work today? Had Jay been hard on him?

She pulled up a chair at the breakfast nook to face a nice stand of trees secluding the twenty-acre property. Enjoying the solitude, she refilled her glass, drained it, then refilled it again before reaching for the phone to call Alex. She paused. What if Jay suddenly walked in on the conversation? Who could she tell him she was talking to? She'd think of someone.

She punched in the numbers. Four rings. Where was he?

"Yeah." Alex sounded irritated.

"You're not in bed already, are you?" If he was, he'd better be alone.

"What do you want?"

"I just called to tell you I miss you already. Jay and I had an argument. He's out in the shop, so it's safe to talk." Ruby drummed her nails against the counter. "And I wanted to ask you about those girls we ran into the other night at the store."

"What about them?" Alex grumbled.

"Do you know them or something? Why were you acting so interested in the blonde one?" She wouldn't tell him she knew Cameo. They went back a ways, but that was her business.

"What's it to you? You're the one who's married, not me."

"Yeah, but don't you remember our plan?" Ruby bit her nails. "You and I together soon?"

"That's your plan, not mine. I'm sick of doing this to Jay,

and if I want to see someone else, it's none of your business. If you had any heart at all, you'd be sick of it, too."

Ruby swallowed back a storm of nasty words. "Come on, Alex. I have a heart, and it's all for you. How could you forget so soon?"

"I haven't forgotten a thing. That's why I'm sick of us. Look, I gotta go."

"Are you alone?"

"Maybe, maybe not."

Asshole. He had to be alone, didn't he? "Okay, Alex, I'll let you go. Dream sweet dreams about me, okay?"

"Yeah, whatever."

"Don't hang up, please," Ruby begged.

"What?"

Without the alcohol calming her nerves, Ruby's temper would have broken like a dam. How could he treat her like this? She'd thought they really had something between them. Now that little bitch had suddenly appeared out of nowhere and turned him sour toward her. "Can we talk again when you're not in such a bad mood?"

"Sure."

Ruby had a feeling he'd agreed just to get her off his back.

She heard the door. "Jay just came in," she whispered. "I have to go." The dial tone greeted her before she finished. She hung up. She'd make that bimbo sorry she'd ever seen Alex. Whether Alex believed it or not, he was hers. He just had to get over his guilt trip. Ruby was sure sex with him couldn't have been so good if he didn't feel something for her.

"Who was on the phone?" Jay asked.

"My parents," Ruby said and left the room.

Why not treat him like he'd treated her? He'd gone outside and left her. Maybe his truck was more important to him than his wife. Good, because that's all he'd have left soon. She had a plan for him ... and it wasn't pretty.

Chapter Three

In a black, lace push-up bra, thong bottoms, and black thigh-highs trimmed in lace, Monet danced for a young man to "Gettin' Jiggy wit It" by Will Smith. He was seated on a padded bench seat that stretched most of the entire length of a wall. Beside him, a small table held Monet's mini handbag, two glasses of soda, his cigarettes and lighter, and an ashtray.

She moved in front of him, graceful yet teasing, as she hooked her fingers in the sides of her bottoms, moving them high and low. She watched his smile widen before she turned around and slowly bent over. As the song ended, she brought herself back up and whirled around to face him.

"I'm on stage next. I have to go pick a song."

"Can you come back after? I'd like a couple more dances."

"Sure." She nodded her agreement.

She grabbed her handbag and crossed to the jukebox. Leaning over the glass, she chose George Michael's "I Want Your Sex."

When the song ended, she reached for the microphone to announce the dancer on stage.

"That was the gorgeous Cheetah," Monet said as the slinky, black girl stepped down from the stage.

Now it was her turn. She headed to the stage for her dance. Carefully stepping up the couple steps, she put her mind in mode, letting herself feel the music, taking in the sexual lyrics and the beat of the song. When she was up on stage and dancing for customers, she was someone else—someone who showed the customers love, much like an escort. She didn't have to feel it or give it, but when she was here, it was all about entertaining them.

With a sensuous roll of her hips, she crossed to the pole in the upper right-hand corner and wrapped a black, lace-gloved hand around it. She twirled around before grinding against it. Then, still grasping the pole, she bent over backward until her hands met the floor of the stage. When just her lace-covered crotch touched the pole, she slowly brought herself back up to begin another seductive grind.

She locked eyes with various customers, playing no favorites, except the ones sitting closest to the stage with a better view, whom she gave more attention to, hoping to convey with heated looks, sexy smiles, and body language that she'd rather be nowhere else in the world but here, doing what she was doing ... as if she loved this more than anything else.

She gracefully slithered up the pole. When she came down, she did a slow, sensual spiral, feeling like she was coming down from the ceiling, and ending up in the splits to begin a floor show—her favorite part.

She loved straining her muscles to the limit, using her flexibility sexually, suggestively, and taking full advantage of what she could do, except when it caused customers to look at her as though they could easily take her home and fuck her just because she did this. That certain sureness in their eyes, somewhat piercing, had her looking away more often than not.

From the splits, she rolled onto her stomach to grind the floor of the stage with the most delicate part of her body, as if it were a lover, to the words, "Sex is best when it's ... one on one." Then she slid up onto her knees and bounced in place, tossing her long mane of hair all around her before bending back and into a backbend to feel the dizzying rush and exhilaration whirl through her. She brought her upper body up again to begin a slithery crawl across the stage. In the middle, she stopped to flatten her upper body against the floor with her arms straight out in front of her, and she stuck her ass up in the air like she was getting it from behind, one of her favorite poses.

Then pushing herself up with her hands to bring her upper and lower body together in a bent-over position, she wrapped her hands around one ankle then the other, loving the feel of the stretch.

She finished her show back in the splits on the floor of the stage in one direction, then easily on one bounce, switched to the other while the song played its last words, "Have sex with me. C-c-c-c come on."

With her mind still in mode, Monet stepped down from the stage and rejoined her previous customer.

"Damn, you're good." He nodded in amazement. "How about a dance to the next song, and maybe just for the rest of the night?" He patted the seat beside him.

She wiggled in next to him. "Sounds good," she said and set her handbag down.

"I like your name, Monet. Is that your real name?"

She smiled. "Yeah. I don't know why, after all these years, I haven't come up with a stage name."

Her customer's eyes narrowed in puzzlement. "After all these years? How long you been working here? You must be what, twenty-two, twenty-three?" Still studying her, he lit a cigarette.

She reached for her soda. "I'm thirty-one, but thanks. That's a nice compliment."

He pulled hard on his smoke, exhaling away from her. "You sure don't look it. So, you've been here, what—"

"About thirteen years, on and off," she said and sipped her soda. "I got certified and taught aerobics for a while, so I did that full time, too."

"Really?" He nodded with interest. "That's why you're in such great shape."

She chuckled. "I don't know about that."

"Well, you're an awesome dancer. You make pretty good money then, huh?"

"As long as I work hard and don't blow it all." Monet noticed a dancer across from her grinding on her customer's lap, his hands all over her.

"How many times a night do you dance on stage?" He tapped his cigarette in the ashtray, staring at her through a haze of smoke.

"Usually around six to eight. It depends on how many girls show up for work."

He gestured at her fishnets. "What's with the thigh-highs?"

"It's one of the rules here." She adjusted the lace band on her leg. She also liked wearing dainty garter belts and sheer stockings.

"Well, they're pretty sexy."

"Which do you prefer? This"—she snapped the top of her thigh-high—"or the garter belt and stockings?"

"Hmm," he said as he swiveled his gaze between a brunette wearing a garter and Monet. "Both, but you look way better than her."

"You're too nice." She chuckled.

A dark brow sketched upward. "You are."

"So, we're even." She smiled at him. His interest and

innocence kindled a desire to stay with him the rest of the working night. She truly enjoyed customers like him—young, nice-looking, yet fresh and a bit naïve, like a little boy.

"You know," he said, "I noticed quite a bit of difference here compared to other clubs. Like the jukebox instead of a DJ booth, these thigh-highs, and the girls never take anything off."

"It's not your average strip club, I know. It's pretty uncommon, but it works for me."

"This is my first time here. It's really cool. It leaves something to the imagination. And your floor show … wow! Anyway, Fantasy's is a good name for it. So," he said as he sipped his soda, "where did you teach aerobics?"

"At Bodies in Motion, a health club downtown."

He toyed with his cigarette. "Was it harder work than this?"

"That's a good question." Monet searched her mind and finally said, "Just entirely different."

"By the way," he said, inhaling off his smoke, "my name's Paul." He exhaled twin streams through his nose.

"Nice to meet you, Paul." She smiled. "I really like your company."

"Likewise. I'm enjoying you, too," he said, desire clear in his dark eyes.

Monet looked up to find a waitress at their table. "How about a couple more sodas?"

Paul glanced at Monet, his brows curved in question.

She nodded.

"Two more Sprites would be great," he said.

As the waitress left with her pert wiggle in a tight-fitting miniskirt, Monet thought of Ruby, which led to thoughts of Alex. In the morning, she'd call him. She couldn't wait to see him again.

After some more conversation and soda, Monet got up to dance for Paul again.

"I love this song," she said, as Bon Jovi's "Wanted Dead or Alive" started to play.

"And I love looking at you." His gaze coasted over her body in delight.

She carefully nudged his knees apart, knelt down in the space between his legs, and trailed a finger between her breasts before pressing them together with her hands. Slowly, she slid back up his body, rubbing it lightly with hers.

As she blew in his ear, he whispered, "You're awesome."

She moved just in front of him, her hands sliding up and down her body, suggestively, squeezing her breasts together with her forearms. Then she took her left leg and brought it all the way up past her shoulder.

He let out a soft whistle.

She whirled around. Just as she was about to bend over, Cameo sidled up to her and said in her ear, "Guess who's here?"

Monet took in Cameo's white, leather bikini glowing against her tanned skin in the darkly lit club. "Let me guess."

"Just thought I'd warn you," she said, and left.

Monet continued dancing for Paul.

As she finished the dance and sat back down, her eyes met Shane's across from her. She slid in closer to Paul, determined not to let him spoil her night.

When Nick Gilder's "Hot Child in the City" began, Monet saw Princess, a petite, black-haired beauty, dancing for Shane, grinding away on him. She wasn't jealous. Her feelings for him had faded. She only wished he'd been honest about always being broke.

Paul continued buying dances for Monet the whole time he stayed. So, a couple hours later, after he left, Monet was able to catch Shane alone.

She stood in front of him. "What are you doing here?"

"What does it look like I'm doing here?" He blinked several times. "And what's it to you, anyway? You dumped me, remember? Speaking of which, that's the real reason I came. I figured out you need me." His voice grew seductive. "I want us to stay together. I love you."

"You don't know what love is."

"Do you?"

She ignored his question and sank down beside him. "Come on, Shane, you need to get the rest of your things out of my apartment, and preferably tonight. That way, all our ties to each other will be over."

"What happened to you? I gave you a couple days to

make you realize how much you missed me. Monet, we've been through this enough times to both know it's not over."

"I'm sorry, Shane. I gave you plenty of chances. Now really, I have to work." She got to her feet and went back to hustle customers.

At two thirty in the morning, when Monet slid the key in the lock to her apartment, total exhaustion hit. She swung the door open and slipped inside, hitting the light switch by the door to bring the rooms into focus. Dixie Cup greeted her. She set her stuff down and picked him up. At least she could count on him. She hoped he adjusted to wherever she moved.

To save enough for school, she'd given notice here and needed to find a roommate somewhere else. Then, she would sell her Lexus and buy something less expensive. The thought brought on a pounding in her head to collide with the pounding of the door.

Shane. She could hardly believe he'd done what she'd asked and come by for his stuff. Or had he? Her heart skipped beats as she crossed to the door.

"Monet, open up. It's Shane."

At his confirmation, she swung the door open. "Thanks for listening to something I said, but please hurry and get your stuff. I'm tired and I'd like to get some sleep."

Shane hurried inside, grabbing her arm. "Wait, just hold on. I thought maybe we could have some coffee and talk."

"What?" She pulled her arm free.

"Monet, just hear me out."

"What can you say that you haven't said before?"

"What's wrong with you?"

"I guess I finally realized you weren't going to change."

"I'll change now." Shane pressed against her and whispered in her ear. "I said I love you. Doesn't that mean anything to you anymore?"

"It used to." Monet leaned back into the cupboards, struggling to keep a voice of finality. He smelled of alcohol. He'd obviously left Fantasy's to drink the real stuff. "Please, just get your stuff and go so I can get some rest."

"I know I still mean something to you."

"Shane, my feelings for you gradually disappeared as I began to see through you."

"I don't want to go."

"Yeah, but I need you to."

"Fine." Shane yanked out a tall, kitchen garbage bag from under the kitchen sink and stormed into the living room. Monet stood in the kitchen, keeping him in her vision, watching as he carelessly tossed CDs and videos into the bag.

When he disappeared and headed to the bedroom, she followed. She had a feeling his temper would flare, and if so, she'd like to keep an eye on him.

He spun around to shoot her a glare. "Give me some space."

"Shane." She pulled in a breath. "I have a right to be in my own bedroom."

"Yeah, whatever," he said, and turned his back on her. He began throwing her *Vogue* magazines to the floor from a closet shelf.

"What are you doing? Please don't throw my things around like that." She fought to keep her voice down. "Besides, some people are trying to sleep."

"I'm trying to find my shit," Shane growled, continuing to toss her magazines off the shelf.

Monet backed into the wall and told herself he couldn't hurt her magazines. She took deep breaths and silently prayed he'd find what he was looking for soon. She'd make it easier on herself if she just stayed calm and in control and didn't harass him.

Several minutes later, he turned to face her. "There, I'm done. But don't worry, I'll be back."

Anger crowded her throat, stalling her words. "I've already given notice here."

"Is that so?" He chuckled. "What are you going to do, move to some fancy high-rise downtown since you don't have to support me anymore?"

"Yeah, right. Hardly. I'm going to start saving instead of spending."

"Good luck. Too bad you can't dump your mother like you dumped me," he said right in her face.

Monet watched him head to the door, fighting to keep herself intact. How could she have ever had feelings for him?

After he slipped out, she sprinted to lock the door. Dixie

Cup rushed out, apparently from under the bed. She scooped him up to comfort him.

She and Shane were over. She had to keep believing it.

The following morning, she poured over the classifieds for used cars and roommates wanted. She outlined some ads until her eyes caught the clock on the stove. Nine fifty-five. Time to call Alex. She took a deep breath and ran over in her mind what she would say.

With his number in her hand, she pressed the buttons.

Her heart pounded harder with each ring. She was about to hang up when he picked up.

"Yeah," Alex said.

"Alex, it's Monet. I hope it's not too early to call."

"No, not at all. I'm glad you called. What's up, cutie?"

His voice grew warmer with each word, causing her insides to warm as well. "I'd like to see you again," she said, "but I'm sure you're busy tonight."

"Nope, as a matter of fact, you couldn't have called at a better time. The boss invited me to dinner tonight and told me to bring a date. I just laughed. But if you'd go with me, it'd be cool."

Tempted to say no because of Ruby, she found herself saying, "I'd like to go with you, Alex, but I'm not so sure Ruby will like the idea."

"Tough. I'm sure Jay will be fine with it."

"If you really think so, I'll go, but I don't want to cause

any problems." Monet heard the click of a lighter, a steady inhale, then an exhale.

"You won't." He laughed. "Trust me. And if you do, we'll worry about it then. How does that sound?"

"Sounds like a plan." Monet felt her palms sweat at the thought of going on their first date to Ruby's home. She'd get to meet Jay, though, who sounded like a great guy.

She gave Alex directions to pick her up at her apartment at five.

When she hung up, she wondered why she was more anxious than excited about seeing him. Most likely, it was because it meant she had to see Ruby, too. Should she call back and cancel? No. She'd told Alex she'd help him ditch Ruby.

Restless, Monet picked up Dixie Cup. She nuzzled him to her and made her way to the window to gaze out at the bay and savor the sun's reflection off the crystal-blue water. The scene calmed her.

"What a view, huh, Dix?" she said.

Her cat purred in agreement.

Through the cat's vibrating purr, the shrill of the phone drew her attention. What now? Monet set Dixie Cup down and thought hard about not answering. Was it Alex calling her back? She'd better get it.

"Hello," she said.

"I need money."

"Mom." Monet swiped at her damp brow. "We need to talk."

"I know, that's why I'm calling."

"But there's something important I need to tell you first."

"I'm listening," Lucy snapped.

Monet swallowed the familiar pain. "I'm changing my life, so I won't be able to help you out like I have been."

"You're still working at that sleazy club in Ballard, aren't you? I just need some money one more time."

"Mom, it's not sleazy."

"Huh. I know what kind of stuff goes on at those clubs. They're just a cover-up for prostitution."

"You don't know that. It's just what you believe. Anyway, look, I'm really trying to save my money now."

"I still need six hundred dollars."

"Mom, I just can't."

"What?" The loud shrill of her mother's voice vibrated through the phone line.

"You'll have to get a job again or figure something else out."

"Excuse me? What?" The last word came out two syllables.

Monet nodded, then realized her mother couldn't see her. "I said—"

"I heard what you said," she yelled, cutting Monet off, "but I don't believe it." After a pause, she said, "Let's talk about your lousy boyfriend then. You still with him?"

Keep your cool. "We split up."

"Aha, I get it. You decided to be selfish now and only think of yourself. You've gotten rid of him, so now it's time to get rid of me."

"I'm not getting rid of you, Mom. I just can't support you like I have been."

"Close enough."

"Mom, you're wrong." Monet nearly lost her temper. "It's not like that at all. You're the one who's always telling me I should end it with Shane. So, you should feel good about it. I finally took your advice."

Silence greeted her ears. Monet wondered if the day would ever come when she and her mother got along. "Look, I'm just trying to get my life in order, and I hope to move soon."

"You're what? Wait a minute, slow down."

In a voice thin with exhaustion, Monet said, "I plan to go to school in the fall, and I said, I'll be moving, too. I'm trying to find a roommate to move in with."

"So that's how you'll go about finding a new man? Huh, I hadn't thought of that. Maybe you'll do one thing right for once."

Wound tight, Monet's nerves were about to snap. "Mom, don't do this. I need a roommate to help lower my monthly expenses so I can put money away for a change. Now, how about you? Have you been thinking of your future lately?"

"What kind of question is that?" her mother hurled.

"An honest question. I really would have thought by now we could get along, or that maybe, as time went by, I could buy your love, but I can see you'll always blame me for Dad leaving you."

"What's gotten into you?"

Monet's throat tightened with emotion. "You."

"Well then, I'm hanging up. I don't have to take this from you. You're trying to make me feel guilty. If you won't loan me some money to keep me from being evicted, don't bother calling."

Who's manipulating who. "You're the one who called me," she said and ended the call.

Sorting through her anger, she hated feeling as though her mother's eviction was her fault. Should she help her mother just one more time?

Chapter Four

Jay finished his outside chores and got cleaned up in plenty of time before Alex and his date arrived. He looked forward to meeting her. Maybe Ruby would enjoy visiting with her … and maybe she wouldn't. Around the wives of his crew, Ruby acted like she was better than everyone else. He only hoped tonight would be different.

Jay crossed to the kitchen to find Ruby stuffing potato chips into her mouth. "Hey," he said with concern. "You need some help yet?"

She jammed the large bag in a cupboard as if to hide evidence. "You're a little late," she snapped. "It's just a good thing I wasn't waiting on your help." She took the flour tortillas from the counter, clicked the oven on, and set them inside to warm.

To calm his rising anger, Jay breathed in the scent of bell

peppers, onions, steak, and chicken, sizzling in two different pans on the stove. "I told you yesterday I'd do anything to help. You said don't bother, so don't start with me now."

"Fine." Ruby rolled her eyes. "Now we wait for the tortillas to warm up. I figured we'd eat buffet style. It's easier. If whoever Alex is bringing doesn't like it, tough."

Jay ran a hand through his gelled hair. "Hey, calm down. Let's try and enjoy ourselves." He reached out to lay a hand on her bare shoulder. She stepped back. "Have you got something against Alex bringing someone?"

"It's just . . ." She sighed. "I guess I'm a little nervous, is all."

"Try not to be, okay?" Jay said softly. "You've done great. Everything looks superb and smells exceptional, including you." He stepped forward and nuzzled her cheek.

She pulled away. "Good. I sure went through a lot."

Why was she so on edge? He thought just maybe it'd be nice for her to have someone to visit with for a change. "Ruby, what's bothering you? If this makes you that uncomfortable, I wish I'd have known sooner. I definitely would have made other arrangements."

"Really?" She arched a brow and crossed to the fridge. Wine in hand, she asked, "Would you like some?"

"No thanks." He watched her pour herself a generous amount and take a long drink. He had to admit she looked incredibly sexy in the short, white dress she'd chosen.

Glancing around the spacious kitchen, he said, "Look, Ruby, I really appreciate all this." He closed the distance between them to graze his lips across her cheek, inhaling her warm, oriental scent … anything to dissolve the tension between them.

Suddenly, the doorbell sounded, jolting them apart.

"Would you like to get it?" He held her intense, green gaze.

"That's okay." She turned away from him and drained her glass. "You can."

Jay crossed to the door, determined to have a pleasant evening.

He swung it open and prayed that was the case.

"Hey, Jay." Alex inhaled around a smile. "Something smells good."

"Yeah, come on in." Jay stood aside to let his guests in. "Ruby made fajitas." He did a quick scan of the woman with Alex. She was shorter and slimmer than Ruby, very petite looking. She wore a long skirt and sleeveless blouse that exposed well-toned arms. Jay wondered why he was comparing her to his wife. He shut the door and shook his head to clear it.

Inside the doorway, Alex made the introductions. "Jay, I'd like you to meet Monet. Monet, this is Jay, my boss."

"Nice meeting you, Monet," Jay said, touching her hand in greeting. A chill raced up his spine. What was it about her? Her hair, much like the gold of a cottonwood leaf in autumn, matched her eyes. "Ruby," Jay called out to switch gears.

Ruby emerged from the kitchen and froze. "Well, they're here," she snapped.

Jay watched her look Monet up and down in distaste. It was going to be the evening from hell.

"Hello, Alex." Ruby fixed him with a glare, then narrowed her eyes on Monet.

"Hi, Ruby, this is my friend, Monet. And Monet"—he grinned and wound an arm around Monet's shoulder—"this is my boss's wife, Ruby, who makes great fajitas."

"Nice to meet you," Monet said.

In a cool voice, Ruby replied, "Nice meeting you, Monet."

Had Ruby and Monet met before? Jay wondered. He and Monet exchanged a brief glance. The eye contact sped up his heart, causing a pinch of guilt. He swallowed, looked away, and made his way to the kitchen.

Once there, he asked his guests, "How about a drink before dinner?" Then, before anyone could reply, he turned to Ruby and asked, "Have you and Monet met before?"

"No," she said on a laugh.

"A drink would be great, thanks," Monet replied.

Alex had an arm draped around her, holding her firmly against him.

Longing for their closeness, Jay got some Sprite out of the fridge. A bottle of Crown Royal and glasses adorned the counter. He held up the whiskey. "Will this work?"

Alex turned to Monet, who nodded her agreement. "Perfect," he said.

Mixing the drinks, a tight feeling filled Jay's throat. He swallowed hard, trying to block out his wife's cool welcome. "Ruby, would you like one, too?"

She frowned. "What do you think? You know me, I like my wine. Don't be silly." She retrieved her wine from the counter and poured a generous glass. "You know," she said, turning to Monet with an evil glare, "I was thinking you looked familiar, but I'm sure it's just a coincidence." She tipped her head back and drained the glass.

Reeling in words better left unsaid, Jay started for the living room. "Why don't we take our drinks in here for a bit before we eat?"

"Sounds good," Alex said, steering Monet toward the living room.

Ruby's snide attitude perplexed Jay. She wasn't just acting like she was better than Monet. She was being vicious. He noted that Monet handled herself well, appearing unfazed by Ruby's hostility. He liked that about her. Was that all? He put the question out of his mind, like a fire before it spread.

He crossed to the chair next to the couch and glanced at the Mariners' game on TV. Garret Anderson hit a home run to put the Angels on top. As he slid into the chair, he eyed Monet. There was something about her expression that aroused his curiosity. When she and Alex settled onto the couch, he asked, "How long have you guys known each other?"

Alex smiled at Jay, tossing an arm around Monet. "Not

long. She drew me in like a magnet," he said and cut Monet a wink.

Monet returned a warm smile.

Ruby suddenly emerged from the kitchen. "Let's eat, otherwise it'll be cold."

Like you, Ruby, Jay thought. "You better get them while they're hot," he said to his guests, then jumped to his feet and headed to the kitchen with his drink, finishing it off on the way.

Once in the kitchen, he found Ruby dishing up fajitas for herself. Inches from her, he stopped. "Don't do this. It's embarrassing."

She gave him a hard stare. "Do what?"

"You know what."

Seconds later, Alex and Monet entered the kitchen.

Being polite, the only way he knew how to be, Jay let his guests dish up first. Even with Alex between him and Monet, Jay was very aware of her spicy, floral fragrance.

He forced his attention from Monet to Ruby, who strolled to the table, her plate piled high. Her green eyes, flowing red hair, and perfect body never failed to arouse him. He only wished she was as sweet as she looked.

"These look great." Alex heaped sizzling chicken, flank steak, peppers, and onions on top of a giant flour tortilla.

Monet dished up beside him. "I agree."

"There's water and soda in the fridge. As you can see, all the dips are out," Ruby said harshly, gesturing to the guacamole, sour cream, and salsa in serving bowls on the counter.

Jay swallowed a knot in his throat before whispering in Ruby's ear, "Why don't you get the beverages for them?" Anger at Ruby's rudeness and embarrassment for Monet and Alex clashed inside of him.

"Let them get it," Ruby fired back, attempting to fit an oversize tortilla chip smothered in sour cream into her mouth.

"I'll get the water. Who else would like some?" Monet asked.

"I'd love some," Jay answered with a smile. He saw Ruby head to the table and join Alex, already devouring his meal. Jay felt at ease standing next to Monet.

Monet set her plate down, got out the pitcher of water, took it to the table, and filled glasses before returning to the food.

"Thank you," Jay said.

"You're welcome."

As Jay dished up beside Monet, their arms brushed lightly. A shiver rippled through him. He needed to get a grip. He topped off his plate with condiments and made his way to the table to slide in beside Ruby.

"So," Ruby said after Monet joined them at the table. "Let's hear all about what you do, even if it's not worth mentioning."

Jay lightly squeezed Ruby's thigh in warning.

Monet cleared her throat, and before she could speak, Ruby cut in. "What's the matter? Ashamed of what you do?"

"Ruby, please," Jay said, fighting off saying more.

"I'd really like to know what you do," Ruby said with contempt. "Heck, who knows, maybe you're a ballerina."

Monet managed a smile. "I wish. Ballerinas are so talented. By the way," she said, changing the subject, "this food's fabulous. Your husband is lucky to be married to such a wonderful cook." Her eyes touched briefly on Jay. "To answer your question, Ruby, I vary between teaching aerobics and working at a nightclub."

"A nightclub, huh?" Ruby said with haste.

Jay watched Alex inhale his food as if unaware of the rising pressure in the room. Or was he? What was going on here? A tortilla with salsa from Alex's plate suddenly slipped to the floor.

"I'll get it." Monet flew out of her seat, using her own napkin to carefully clean the floor. Then she tucked her hair behind an ear and laid a hand on Alex's shoulder.

Jay fought to ignore the sensual gesture. "I'll get some more napkins." He pushed back his chair, shot to his feet, and retrieved a bundle of napkins from the counter. He handed one to Monet. Their hands skimmed. He felt a warm, tingly sensation at her touch. This had to stop. He swallowed hard and thought of something else—Ruby's attitude. It was at its peak. If it climbed any higher, he saw no choice but to say something to stop it from snowballing.

"So, what exactly is it you do at this nightclub?" Ruby asked, resuming the conversation. "Table dance? Or just degrade yourself by stripping on a stage?"

"Ruby, come on now," Jay said, shaking his head. "Act decent."

"Excuse me?" She fluttered her lashes. "What did I do?"

Jay ran a slow gaze over Monet's face. Uneasiness lingered. "It's apparent you're making our guests uncomfortable. Would you like to leave?"

"I'm not leaving this room!" Ruby sprang from her chair to refill her wine glass. "Especially since I went to all this trouble. All I did was ask Monet a simple question. I can't help it that she chooses to degrade herself in front of a bunch of horny men."

Hypocrite, Jay thought, flashing Ruby a silent warning.

"Fine. It's obvious I'm not wanted," she said in a huff and fled from the room with her glass of wine.

"I'm sorry," Jay told his guests as he accepted the fact that Ruby had ruined the evening. What was he going to do about her?

* * *

Ruby hurled herself through the door to the master bedroom, anger burning her up inside. *Fine*, she thought. She didn't need any of them. She'd cooked an awesome dinner, thinking of Alex the entire time. She loved to cook in other ways for him, too. A wicked smile curved her lips at the thought. Plus, she'd made her favorite chocolate brownie cheesecake. Maybe later, she'd devour the whole thing herself. Screw them all.

Not to mention the fact that Ruby disliked Monet the more she saw her, especially the way she treated Alex, like they were lovers. Something would certainly have to be done. She couldn't let the bitch steal Alex. And Jay … he'd had the audacity to kick her out of the kitchen. Who did he think he was?

Ruby emptied her glass of wine and felt it start to work on her frazzled nerves. She fell back on the pillow, mentally calculating her next move. She had to get Monet alone, but first, she needed to go back in the kitchen, say she's sorry, and then hopefully the guys would go out to the shop and find something to do.

As Ruby headed toward the kitchen, she overheard Jay telling Monet about his job. She rolled her eyes. Why would Monet care? She certainly didn't. And if he said something about his logging company being environmentally sound, she'd puke. After hearing him tell plenty of people on the phone about it, she'd heard it often enough.

"It's about a two-hour drive to get to our current jobsite where two log loaders yard and load logs onto the trucks."

"Where do you take the logs?" Monet asked.

"To different mills and log yards, anywhere from Everett to Tacoma." Jay's eyes met Ruby's and looked away.

Fine, ignore me, Ruby thought, then she forced a smile as she began. "Look, I apologize for being rude. I'm just really tired from doing so much today. Here I was, worrying about having everything perfect for tonight, and I'm the one who ruined it. I truly am sorry," she lied.

"No problem." Monet got up from the table. "Let me help you clear these dishes."

"Thanks, then we'll get out dessert. I hope you all saved up," she said with a smile. This was tough, but she'd get through it. Anything to get what she wanted. It would be well worth getting Monet alone after dessert to tell her that Alex had a serious girlfriend. Welcome to the real world.

Ruby hurried to help Monet. Soon enough, she'd get Monet alone. Excitement whipped through her just thinking about it.

When they were both at the sink, Ruby turned to Monet and whispered, "I'm dying to know, are you a stripper?"

"Something like that."

"Well, you look really good." Ruby hated kissing ass, but it was needed. "How is it you stay so slim? Everything I eat seems to go to my hips."

"Your body couldn't get any more perfect." Monet gave Ruby the once-over. "I sure wish I had your problem."

Ruby smiled and ran her hands down her sides. "What exactly do you do at this nightclub?"

"Table dance, dance on stage, but we don't take anything off."

Monet had to work at Fantasy's. It was the only place Ruby knew of where the girls didn't strip. She'd worked there, too, before she'd met Jay, fortunately, when Monet hadn't. "So, you enjoy it?"

"Sure. It's great money."

"I bet," Ruby said on a chuckle as she crossed to the fridge and brought out the brownie cheesecake.

She and Monet gathered plates and forks and served the dessert to the four of them. Afterward, it would be time to break the news to Monet that Alex would toss her away like a used Kleenex.

"This is really good, Ruby," Monet said after the first bite. "You made this?"

"Yeah. It's not easy."

"I agree. This is great," Alex added.

Ruby's eyes flew to Jay. Where was his compliment about this fucking cheesecake that she'd busted her ass to make? If she'd spoiled his evening that was just too bad. He hadn't even thanked her when she set his plate in front of him.

"Tastes good, Ruby, thanks." Jay patted her leg and slid her a smile.

"You're welcome." She clutched his hand underneath the table. "I'm glad you all like it. Anyone for seconds?" She eyed Monet. "You could eat the whole thing and still look good." Ruby needed to show Jay she could be pleasant.

"I don't think so." Monet smiled. "I've had plenty."

"Me, too. Thanks, Ruby," Jay said.

Alex added, "Yeah, I'm stuffed."

Ruby devoured her slice of cheesecake, longing to finish

off the rest of the whole thing. After scanning the empty plates, she pushed back her chair and began clearing again. "Hey, Jay, you got anything in the shop you and Alex could keep busy with for a while?" She used her sweetest voice.

Jay angled around in his chair at Ruby standing beside him. "Why?"

"Well, I was just thinking that Monet and I could get better acquainted."

"Alex and I could go in the other room and watch baseball."

Not what she'd been hoping for.

"Yeah, but I think the Mariners have lost," Alex said. "They played Garret Anderson, remember? Hey, I know," he piped up. "Did you happen to pick up any more of those chrome goodies for the dash in your truck?"

"Yeah, I got a few more," Jay answered.

Alex jumped up. "Cool, let's go put them on."

"Why not."

Ruby hauled in a deep breath. She didn't miss Jay's and Monet's brief eye contact. What was it about? Nothing, she was sure. Besides, she didn't need to worry about her husband and Monet. Alex was plenty.

As she and Monet cleared the table, Ruby watched the guys slip out. Alex's tight ass in faded, black Levi's looked good. If she had her way, she'd do him right now, but there would be plenty of time for that later. If Alex behaved, they had their whole lives ahead of them.

"Here, let me. I'll do the dishes." Monet started rinsing plates and sticking them in the dishwasher.

Ruby stood aside. "Fine, if you want to. I won't stop you." Monet's politeness was starting to piss her off.

A few minutes later, Ruby filled the dishwasher with soap and turned it on. Then she asked, "How close are you and Alex?" She rushed to fill a glass of wine from the fridge and toss it back. "Want some?" She gestured with her glass. "It goes down smooth."

"Water would be just fine, thanks. Actually, Alex and I just met recently, as if you didn't know." Monet arched a brow.

Ruby threw open a cupboard to get Monet a glass. She filled it with water from a pitcher in the fridge and handed it to her. "That's not what I asked. How close are you and Alex?"

Monet shrugged off the question but nodded her thanks as she took the glass.

Ruby took a hefty sip of wine. *Fine, bitch, don't answer me*, she thought as they made their way to the table and sat down.

"So," Ruby began. "I hate to be the one to tell you this, but since I'm the one who signs Alex's checks, and he and Jay are pretty close, I know a lot about his personal life, too."

"I bet. And—"

"Alex is already involved." Ruby tossed a lock of hair behind her shoulder.

"Oh? With someone besides you?"

Anger ripped through Ruby. "Have you slept with him yet?"

"That's none of your business." Monet's eyes held Ruby's.

"Well, he's a player, and as good as he looks, it isn't difficult for him to attract women. You see, when he gets restless, he plays around. I'm sure it's never anything emotional with him. He's been seriously involved for a while now, yet he does this all the time," Ruby said as she drained her glass.

"If he's so involved, why did he bring me to dinner? He must not feel as serious about you as you apparently think he does."

About to slap Monet, Ruby flew out of her chair for more wine. "How about some more water?" she asked, emptying the bottle of wine into her glass.

"No, thanks. Maybe he's in the process of breaking off this serious relationship," Monet said with conviction.

Ruby felt her cheeks heat. She was supposed to make Monet miserable, not the other way around. "Trust me, he's not." She rejoined Monet at the table, leaned across, and whispered softly, "You want to know something?"

"Sure." Monet leaned back in her chair and crossed her arms.

"He's using you, filling your head with lies."

"It seems as if you know him quite well," Monet taunted, "so why don't you concentrate on your marriage and leave Alex and I alone?"

"Excuse me?" Ruby tightened the grip on her wine glass. "Who are you to give me orders?"

Monet shrugged. "Just a little friendly advice."

"Well, I don't need your advice."

Monet straightened in her chair. "Let's talk about marriage, okay?"

Appalled, Ruby asked, "What?"

"Just to see where you're at in yours."

"Excuse me?" Ruby blinked repeatedly.

"I think respect and friendship are key elements."

"Who's asking you?" Ruby gestured with her glass.

Monet held up a finger. "Just listen. Communication and understanding are a must."

Struggling not to ring Monet's neck, Ruby said, through clenched teeth, "I don't give a flying hoot about your stupid-ass beliefs!"

"You care about your husband, don't you?"

Ruby got up so fast, her chair skidded out from underneath her. "You little bitch," she bit back, fighting to regain her balance.

"Not a nice thing to say to your guest."

Through her alcoholic haze, Ruby fought for control. She glanced out the window at a cedar tree outlined in shadow. "You'll be sorry you ever got involved with Alex," she said, dropping back into her seat. "I'm sorry. Look, I'm just trying to warn you. Don't get too involved with him. It'll save you a lot of heartache."

"That's for me to find out."

"Well, good luck." Ruby's tone was laced with bitter sarcasm. "You'll need it." Maybe they hadn't slept together. If she had her way, they never would. "I just wouldn't get too serious if I were you."

"Thanks for the advice. So, how about you. Tell me what you do."

Ruby drummed her nails on the table. "I do my husband's bookkeeping for his business. It keeps me busy."

"I'm sure it does. That's great that you help him out. Anything else?"

"What are you getting at?" Like a wishbone, Ruby snapped. "I thought we were being civil. Guess I was wrong." Then a wave of dizziness washed over her as she fought to stay balanced in her chair. "Just concentrate on your table dancing and forget about Alex."

"What is it to you who Alex sees, anyway? You're married."

Before Ruby could say or do anything, the door from the garage to the kitchen opened. The sight of Alex and Jay was a nice distraction, although she was still fuming from Monet's remark. If Monet wouldn't take her advice and leave Alex alone, something would definitely have to be done.

"You'll need to get one for the toggle switch," Alex told Jay.

"Still talking about chrome goodies?" Ruby said sweetly.

"Yeah," Alex answered.

"You ready to go?" Monet asked Alex.

Alex cut Ruby a glare, then said to Jay, "Hey, it's been nice, but I think we'll get going."

"Okay then," Jay said. "Drive safe."

"Ten-four." Alex tossed an arm around Monet and steered her toward the door.

Ruby rushed to catch up with Jay, who followed Alex and Monet to the door. She exhaled as she watched them leave. *Believe me*, she silently warned Monet, *Alex will be tired of you by tomorrow.*

Since she was good and drunk, she'd seduce her husband, maybe pretend he was Alex. The thought produced a giggle. She suddenly whirled around to find Jay gone. Where was he?

"Jay," she called out, weaving to the bedroom. She switched the light on. Nothing. Then she swayed to the living room. No one there, either. The thought of him in the shop with his truck frustrated her. Wasn't she as exciting as a damn truck? What was wrong here? Her head was spinning. She reeled out of the house and toward the shop, trying not to stumble. Sure enough, the lights were on. She pulled the door open.

"I don't want to be around you right now." Jay was inside his truck, the driver's door open. "Please leave."

"Screw you, too," she said, and staggered back to the house.

Chapter Five

Alex slid Monet a glance from the driver's seat of his black Bronco. "Ruby was torched, huh?"

"You think?" she said on a laugh. "After you guys went outside, she started asking me personal stuff about us."

"Like what?"

"How close we were and if we'd slept together. She also said not to get too involved with you because it would save a lot of heartache."

"She's so full of it. I'm sorry you had to deal with that." Then, whispery soft, he said, "I hope you told her we'd slept together many times."

Monet grinned at his humor. "I was honest."

"I like that about you." Alex reached over and placed a hand on her leg, squeezed, then let go. "Ruby's just jealous."

Their eyes locked before his returned to the road.

"I don't know what she is." Monet chuckled. "And I can't believe the way she treats her husband."

"I don't think they'll last."

Delight spread through Monet. Did it have something to do with Jay? "It seems like Ruby has life made."

Alex shrugged. "Yeah, but she doesn't appreciate it. She expects it."

"I know exactly what you mean."

"Oh, yeah, that's right."

"Shane is over, but my Mom … it's like she expects me to take care of her because she has no one else, and to a certain extent, I feel obligated. I feel guilty if I don't."

He met her eyes with an apologetic smile. "That must be rough."

She returned his smile. "I'll get through it," she said and absorbed a bit of silence.

"Hey, do I get to come in when we get to your place?" he asked.

After a slight hesitation, she replied, "That depends."

"We'll just have to see about that." He drew out a container of wintergreen Tic Tacs and tossed some into his mouth.

Monet watched him. Her mind raced. Her body tingled. Was tonight their night? Would she let him take her to dizzying heights? And why couldn't she get Jay out of her mind?

Alex tossed her a heated look. The contact made her suck

in a breath. Then reality focused her. Alex was available. Jay wasn't.

As the SUV swallowed up the freeway heading south, Monet relaxed into her seat. "I think Ruby gets off on control."

"It's one of the many things she gets off on." Alex bobbed his brows.

Monet winced at the thought of them together.

"Hey, don't take offense."

"Alex, it's clear to me that you're not interested in her anymore. Otherwise, why would you have taken me tonight?"

He gave her shoulder a pat. "Just so you believe it."

"I believe it," she assured him. "Guess what else she mentioned."

"What?"

"She said you have a serious girlfriend."

"Yeah." He chuckled. "And according to her, it's her."

"I thought so. Just had to ask."

"Ruby's good at lying," Alex said. "She should make it her profession. Maybe then she'd be successful."

"I like that," Monet said, enjoying the way his eyes did a quick sweep of her body. "Did you ever care about Ruby?"

"No, but I think I'm starting to care about somebody else."

Her mouth went dry. "Oh, really?"

"Really."

In anticipation, she directed him to her place.

Upon arrival, he parked, cut the engine, and pocketed

the keys. Then he turned to face her, cradling her chin in his palm. "Are you going to invite me in?"

Monet blinked. "Sure."

"Cool," he said. Alex slipped out and met her at the passenger door.

His elbow brushed her side, shooting a tingly sensation up her spine.

"Hey, I suppose I owe you big time for going with me and putting up with Ruby."

She shook her head. "You don't owe me anything."

"Don't worry." He winked. "I've already got something in mind."

She shivered in response.

"At least you got to meet Jay."

At the mention of Jay, her heart picked up speed. "I'm glad I went." She had to stop these thoughts of Jay. He wasn't her business, and she couldn't save him from Ruby.

"Me, too."

As they made their way to the door, Alex drew an arm around her and pulled her close. Once there, Monet fished out her key, slipped it in the lock, and they stepped inside.

Before her next heartbeat, Alex set his mouth on hers. Heat pooled in her belly. He traced his tongue slowly around the inner edge of her lips, slipping deeper. The kiss was on fire. Monet tried to catch her breath and caught his instead—hot and flavored with wintergreen.

Her head spun. She arched against him, losing herself

in him, in this moment. She tangled her hands in his hair. A hungry, raw desire swelled inside of her, pushing aside everything but the hardness of him against her, the softness of his warm tongue inside her mouth. She pressed into his erection, hard, like a slow grind on a dance floor.

Alex shoved her apartment door closed, backed her up against the wall, and forced her skirt up over her hips.

Then he broke the kiss and whispered in her ear, "I'm going to make you scream my name until you beg me to stop."

Already, she moaned. "Alex."

"You can't wait," he said low and rough, pushing her panties aside.

"I know." She was drowning with need.

He slid a finger up inside of her, working it around and probing deeper.

"Oh, Alex," she said on a quick intake of breath.

"See how ready you are?" He pulled his finger out and put it into her mouth. She deep-throated it, running lazy circles all around, imagining something much bigger.

"You're so wet," he groaned, removing his finger from her mouth.

She quickly worked the snaps on his jeans free. She couldn't wait. She stroked her hand around his solid length, wanting it. Wanting all of him. Now.

"Alex, please give it to me," she begged.

He reached for a condom from a pocket and shoved his

jeans down to slip it on. Then he took her hands and pinned them above her head.

She wrapped her legs around his waist and held on tight, her inner muscles clenching in anticipation.

Their mouths came together hard, tongues working furiously.

She felt him rub himself just at her entry, where she was hot, and then slowly work himself inside of her.

"Deeper." She moaned, as he continued to tease her.

He said roughly against her face, "You asked for it."

And then … he thrust into her, deep.

"Oh God," she cried out, her sex twitching hungrily around his.

He worked into her good. "Damn, you're tight."

"Fuck me, Alex."

He pumped deeper, harder, faster. "You like?" he asked into her ear. "Does it go deep enough? Huh?"

"Yes, oh yes. Oh, Alex, yes. Yes … don't stop."

Their parted mouths met, tongues intertwining, feasting on each other. The friction heightened, and she continued calling his name. He swallowed her moans with his and made them his own.

And then … she felt him carry her over the edge and into a mind-blowing inferno of sexual bliss.

Chapter Six

Three hours after Alex left, Monet was still wide awake. In the kitchen, scrubbing the counters spotless, she reflected on the whole evening, from dinner and Alex to . . . Jay. Even though Alex had more than sated her sexually, she found her mind stuck on Jay. That was plain ridiculous. The sex had been her drug tonight. She'd wanted to escape unwanted feelings of finding Jay so damn intriguing, charming, pleasant. It had worked when Alex was way up inside of her. She could think of nothing else but screaming his name.

She glanced at the clock. Cameo would be here soon. She'd go into it with her.

When she heard the phone, she figured it was Cameo. Maybe she'd gotten off work early. With the kitchen sponge still in one hand, she picked up the phone with the other. "Hello."

"Is Alex there?" Ruby drawled.

The voice jarred her memory. There had been plenty of hang ups on her answering machine earlier. Monet assumed Ruby went to bed with Jay at a decent hour. She must have assumed wrong.

Just hang up, she thought, but said, "Sorry, he left. How did you get my number?"

"I have my ways. When did he leave?"

Monet set the sponge down. "That's not your concern."

"Oh, yes it is. Did you sleep with him?"

"Sure."

"Well, that's just great. Apparently, you're not following any of my advice."

"Nope, guess not. And orders, you mean."

"You might want to rethink things a little. Just stay away from Alex."

"Alex isn't yours. You just wish he was. All you do is sign his paycheck. If I were you, I'd worry more about Jay finding out about you and Alex. I'm not the one who has to worry. You're the one with problems," Monet said.

"What's it going to take to make you stay away from Alex and realize he's taken?"

"When you divorce Jay and put a ring on his finger."

"I know the way bitches like you think." Ruby's voice rumbled with rage. "You strippers are all alike. You always want someone else's man. Don't even think about Jay because messing with him would be like playing with fire."

Monet experienced a jolt of weakness. "I'm not like you, Ruby."

"This is not a game. Don't take me lightly. Okay, maybe you're thinking you can have Alex if my relationship with my husband is back on fantastic terms. Wrong. If I find out you're still seeing Alex, believe me, you'll regret it."

"Alex thinks for himself. You don't decide who he sees. Don't you ever worry about your husband finding out about you and Alex?"

"That's my problem, not yours," Ruby said sharply.

"What if I were to tell your husband about you and Alex?"

"You won't," Ruby said with certainty. "Besides, I won't let it happen. I know people who owe me favors. I grew up in a tough neighborhood and kept in touch with a few people over the years. Let's just say some are violent. Keep your mouth shut, and stay away from Alex and my husband. Is that clear?"

"Why should I make you that promise? Just because you're having an affair with Alex doesn't mean you have him on a leash, too. And you don't have to worry about me stealing your husband. I don't do married men," Monet said and hung up.

Two hours later, Cameo tapped on her door.

Monet opened it and said, "Hey, guess who called to check up on me?"

"Who?" Cameo stepped through the door, clutching a

paper sack to her side. She set it on the kitchen counter, turned to Monet, and said, "Alex?"

Monet nodded. "Ruby."

Cameo pulled out two bottles of Seagram's coolers from a four-pack, set them in the fridge, and joined Monet at the kitchen table with the other two. She handed Monet one and took a drink of hers.

"What did she want, to compare notes on Alex? Look, I'm sorry. That's not the most pleasant thought."

"It's reality. Besides, Alex is through with her." Monet tipped the bottle to her mouth and filled Cameo in on the rest of the call.

"Not a polite conversation. It's clear she's got problems. Don't worry about her threats because I guarantee that's all they are. Doesn't she ever sleep? And I mean with her husband. Hey, speaking of that, tell me all about Alex. Ever since you called me at work after he left, I've been dying to hear. That's why I brought coolers. You let him nail you, am I right?"

Monet smiled. "Did I ever! God, Cameo, it was awesome."

"Oh, man." Cameo took a drink. "Tell me everything."

"Right after we stepped through the door, it was like I could think of nothing else. I needed him. I craved him. I had to have him. He shoved me against the wall and we went at it."

"Did you let him raw-dog you?"

"No, he came prepared."

Cameo raised her brows. "Sounds like it. Since you're on the pill, just thought I'd ask."

"Maybe as we get to know each other better, then—"

"Gotcha. There's nothing like it."

"I know." Monet enlightened her on the rest of the details with Alex.

Cameo took a long drink and said, "Now, tell me all about the evening at Ruby and her husband's house."

"Okay." Monet sipped her cooler and kept the bottle near her lips. "It went well, except Jay told Ruby to leave in the middle of dinner."

"What did he do, find out she was banging his truck driver?"

"Not quite," Monet said around a smile. "She was just being rude."

"You mean like at the store?"

"Close enough. Hey, get this. Ruby came back in the kitchen a little while later and apologized. Then we served dessert together and she acted like we were long-lost friends … until the guys disappeared to the shop."

"Oh, please." Cameo rolled her eyes. "Who needs friends like her?"

"Anyway, listen to this. After the guys left, Ruby was back to her usual self, threatening me about Alex … blah, blah, blah … and I totally threw her off by talking about an article I read in *Vogue* last month. I pretended like I was an expert on marriage. Me, of all people." Monet laughed. "I think it rubbed her the wrong way. She can dish it out, but she sure can't take it."

"I think everything rubs her wrong except Alex's dick. Speaking of him, even though he said they were just friends that night at the store, it didn't seem like that's what she thought."

"You're too funny, and I agree. It's like she lives in her own make-believe world where she has complete control."

"Exactly."

"Her attitude started when Alex and I first got there. Jay asked if we'd met before."

"What did she say?"

"That maybe I looked familiar, but that we'd never met. She couldn't very well tell Jay that she met me when she and Alex were together. I honestly don't think Jay suspects anything. If he did, I think he'd do something about it."

Cameo grinned. "So, tell him."

"No way. Get Alex fired and hurt Jay? Nuh-uh."

"You'll just have to wait and see what happens. Maybe Jay will find out somehow. What's he like, by the way?"

Monet smiled, remembering everything about him. "He's not arrogant."

"Well, that would be the opposite of Alex."

"Speaking of that, if sex is so damn off the hook with Alex, why can't I get my mind off Jay?"

Cameo's eyes widened. "What?"

"I found myself unable to stop thinking about Jay before

you came over. It's like ... I don't know." Monet shrugged. "Alex is awesome, but Jay is so—"

"Not your problem," Cameo said as she drained her cooler.

"Even so, tell me more about him."

"He has this way about him that's just"—Monet nodded—"he's gentle, yet sophisticated. He's charming, pleasant to be around. It's hard to describe."

"Okay, then describe his looks."

"He's got awesome dark hair, blue eyes, a gorgeous smile, and he looks really fit."

"So do a million other guys. Hopefully, Ruby at least appreciates that."

Monet arched a brow. "Apparently not."

"But she's still his wife, and it's not your job to fix their marriage."

"I need to stop thinking about him, I know, and focus on Alex."

"No doubt. It sounds like Alex has got plenty to focus on anyway."

"You know something else? When I was thinking about the way I was with Alex tonight, it reminded me of how I am at work."

Cameo raised her eyebrows in surprise. "Oh?"

"It's almost like I'm another person, totally uninhibited."

"How did being around Jay make you feel?"

Monet let a beat pass. "Special. It's the way he talks, so

kind-spoken, and the way he listens, like you're the only one in the room."

"Is that how he treated you, like you were special?"

"Not exactly. He was just very polite. He's just that type of guy." She drew in a deep breath. "I don't know what else to say."

Cameo drained her cooler and jumped up from the table. "Girl, just enjoy the hell out of Alex. That's how it started out with Tyrese and I, and look at us now. I'm in love with his black ass."

"You always give me hope," Monet said.

They finished off the other two coolers before Cameo left.

Close to five o'clock in the morning, Monet's thoughts still wouldn't shut off and let her find sleep.

She wondered about Alex—and if they'd get serious and become long term—and Ruby and her refusal to leave them alone. Maybe it was just a losing situation with Ruby in the picture.

She drew in a sharp breath.

Right now, she longed for a father whom she could talk to, but obviously, her father didn't want to be a dad. She thought if she didn't think about him, it'd be easier. That was far from the truth. And now, when she needed him most, who could she turn to?

And then … there was Jay.

Chapter Seven

Dammit! Monet had gone and slept with Alex.

Desperation gripped Ruby's throat. What had she expected? Alex was the kind of guy who could get a woman to drop her pants with just a look. But the thought of him riding Monet, or vice versa, shook her to the core. Besides, she thought she was different. No one compared to her.

She clutched the steering wheel tighter, driving the Corvette harder as it ate up the ribbon of freeway at a fast clip.

Her destination was the Mexican restaurant at Totem Lake where she'd worked with Brianna when she'd first met Alex and Jay. After three years, they still kept in touch. Ruby would confide in her, explain her own personal problem, except say it was a friend. That should work.

Ruby thought back on her life and the situation she was in. She'd grown up in the Central District in Seattle with parents who fought non-stop and barely scraped by. She learned to fend for herself and become street smart at a young age. Her dad used to physically abuse her mother. She didn't think her parents would last, but the dumb bitch had stayed with him. They lived just north of Woodinville, about twenty minutes from her and Jay. She'd prefer for them not to be so close. Her dad hauled steel for some local outfit, and her mom was just a boring housewife. Ruby forced herself to visit them once in a while and hated it. Her mom would always hound her about having kids. She'd take one look at her mother's body and cringe. No fucking way, so she'd lied to Jay about having kids someday.

She supposed she should feel fortunate to be married to him. He spoiled her and worked hard to be successful, but she wasn't happy unless there was turmoil in her life. She liked bad boys, deception, and sin. That's why she liked Alex. So, she stole from Jay while planning to live happily ever after with Alex. Now, thanks to Monet, it all seemed like a crock of shit.

She put her car in sixth gear and flew.

Fifteen minutes later, she walked into the restaurant to inhale fresh, warm tortillas being made just inside the door.

A familiar face greeted her. "Ruby," an older, Spanish woman called out. "Nice to see you here." She handed her a tortilla. "How have you been?"

Ruby accepted the tortilla. "Thanks, I've been great," she

lied and took a bite. Her eyes traveled to the big, indoor fountain, then the bar to her right. "Is Brianna in the bar?"

"Si," the older woman said.

"Great, I'll pay her a visit," Ruby said and wandered into the bar.

At Ruby's entrance, Brianna dashed over and threw her arms around her. "Hey, how's married life treating you?"

"Wonderful," she lied again.

"How goes the bookkeeping?" the petite brunette asked, waving Ruby over to the empty bar. "I'll bet you're an expert on figures by now."

Ruby slid into a stool. "Getting there. What I like, though, is making my own hours, except when it's payday. No one wants their check a minute late. But it's certainly not like having to hold down a regular job."

"You're lucky." Brianna set chips and salsa in front of Ruby. "What would you like to drink?"

"A margarita sounds great." Ruby took a chip from the basket and brought it to her mouth, watching Brianna whip her up a drink. As she thought about what she would say, she pictured her and Alex in Hawaii, lounging half naked on a warm, sandy beach, being waited on and letting the fresh sea breezes tease their senses.

Brianna whirled around to set a margarita in front of Ruby. "Even though I have to work a regular job," she whispered, "I'm having fun being single."

Ruby hitched a brow. "I bet." She glanced at two older

businessmen, just leaving. When they wouldn't stop staring at her, she ran her tongue suggestively over her lips.

"She's married," Brianna said to the men, laughing.

"I'll be right back," she told Ruby and went to see them out.

She returned a minute later. "They're my favorite customers. And married, too. We're always joking around. Anyway, what brings you here?"

Ruby eyed the place. "Since we're momentarily alone, would you mind giving me your opinion on something?"

"Not at all," Brianna said, making her way around the bar to slide in beside Ruby.

"Okay, there's this friend of mine who's having problems." Ruby sighed heavily.

With concern in her eyes, Brianna said, "Oh, no."

Ruby nibbled on a chip and nursed her margarita. "She's married, right, and having an affair." She leaned closer toward Brianna. "And the guy she's having an affair with is seeing someone else."

"I take it he's not married."

Ruby's heart pounded like a jackhammer in her chest. "No."

"What does your friend expect, for the guy she's having an affair with to be loyal to her when she's the one who's married?"

Ruby flinched. "Yeah."

"That's pathetic."

"I know. Can you believe it?" Ruby reached for her margarita and nearly broke her straw sucking so hard.

Brianna shook her head. "No, I can't. I think you should tell your friend to either leave her husband or get together with this guy. It could be she's just a booty call and he doesn't really care about her." Brianna shrugged. "What it really comes down to is the individuality of the situation."

Ruby's chin snapped up. "You're right."

"Is your friend planning to leave her husband?"

Ruby picked up another chip and chewed thoughtfully. "Who knows."

"How's Alex?"

Ruby nearly choked on the tortilla chip.

"I'm only asking because he's so damn hot. Remember how he used to tease me about dating my customers?"

Relief washed over Ruby. "Yeah, he's fine." She thought back to when Jay and Alex used to frequent the bar on Friday nights ... before she and Jay were married.

"Sure it's not you?" Brianna asked, breaking into her thoughts.

"Excuse me?" Ruby said and swallowed hard.

"I'm only asking because of your situation. It would be easy, with Alex working for Jay, for you two to—"

"Oh my God," Ruby said, exasperated. "I can't believe you'd even think such a thing."

"There's just something about Alex that makes a woman want to do him."

"Did you?"

"No." Brianna's eyes met Ruby's. "I was involved at the time. Look, Ruby, I'm sorry. I just … I just sense that something's bothering you."

"Well, Jay and I are doing awesome. How about you?" Ruby asked before she smacked the concerned look right off Brianna's face. "Anyone special in your life?"

"Yeah, a twenty-one-year-old."

Envy shot through Ruby right along with the rage already boiling. "Really?"

Brianna got up from the bar. "I've got a customer. Be right back," she said and scurried away.

Screw Brianna and her stupid opinion. She didn't need anyone. She suddenly felt all alone in the world.

When Brianna returned, she asked Ruby, "Are you okay? You look sort of pale."

"I'm fine." Ruby pushed her empty glass toward Brianna. "How much do I owe you?"

"It's on the house."

"Thanks," Ruby said and left.

Who could she turn to? Now her only friend was onto her. It seemed as if she'd run out of people to count on.

Chapter Eight

"Hi, Mom," Monet said when her mother answered the phone. She'd called to try and get her mind off Ruby's threats, Alex, and Jay. "Just thought I'd check and see how you're doing."

"That's nice of you. How're things?"

Monet heard ice rattling in a glass. "Okay, I guess. I'll probably be moving real soon."

"Really? That comes as a surprise."

"I told you I was going to move in with someone to lower my monthly expenses. Tomorrow, I'll be meeting with a couple different people to find out for sure."

"Oh, yeah ... that's right. You wanted a female roommate, if I remember right. You should find yourself a rich, successful man and let him take care of you."

I'm not Ruby. "I'd like to take care of myself. Anyway, I met someone. His name is Alex. He's real nice."

"Does he have money?"

"There's more to men than money."

Lucy snorted. "Sometimes I'm not so sure."

"I guess what happened with Dad sort of soured you on men, but then, everybody's entitled to their opinion. The thing is, I think I've found a great guy."

"What does he look like?"

"He's tall, dark, handsome, and young."

"How young?" her mother asked.

"Six years younger than me."

"Well, now. Sounds like you got yourself a good catch. If only he was well off."

"I'm not worried about that."

"What does he do?"

"He drives a log truck."

"I'd hoped you could do better than that."

Monet pulled in a breath. "He works for a guy with a successful company. Don't put him down when you don't even know him."

"That's not the point. Why don't you think about going out with the guy who owns the business?"

A chill went through Monet. "He's married."

"That doesn't stop some people."

"I know," Monet said, "but it's not for me." She felt torn between Jay and Alex.

"Look." Her mother cut into her thoughts. "I wanted

to thank you for helping me out again. You saved me for another month."

"That's good to know. You're welcome."

"And guess what? I started back to work at that convenience store."

"Wow, that's great."

"I don't know if it is or not. We'll see. But I'm not really worried about it because I met someone who works for Microsoft in the upper management level. He's gorgeous and young, too, but he's loaded."

"Where'd you meet him?"

"On the Internet."

"What's a guy like that doing on the Internet?"

"How am I supposed to know? I'm just lucky to have found him. I'm not going to analyze about where I met him. Besides, it lets a person get to know someone a little before they actually meet."

"Good point. The other way is usually all about looks," Monet said, thinking of herself. Uncomfortable, she changed the subject. "So, how do you like work?"

"Not so great, and it hasn't even been a week."

"Give it time. You'll get used to it."

"I'm hoping this man from Microsoft works out. Maybe then I could quit work and be happy doing what I love."

"And what's that?" She was dying to know.

"Taking care of someone who deserves to be taken care of."

The pain nearly paralyzed Monet. If so, her mother could have done that with her years ago. "What really happened with Dad?" She had to ask.

"What?" Her mother's voice rose a notch. "I already told you a long time ago, he left right after I told him I was pregnant with you."

"Yeah, but didn't you ever try to contact him?"

"What for?"

"So I'd have a father."

"I figured you wouldn't want a father like him."

"What was he like?"

"Oh, boy, now you're going to make me think."

"Come on, Mom, I really want to know. Tell me what he was like."

"Really?"

Monet's heart tripled in beats. "Yeah."

"He was a selfish bastard."

Monet closed her eyes and swallowed the grief. "Then why were you with him?"

"Because he was extremely good-looking."

"Sometimes that'll do it." She didn't want to make the same mistake with Alex. "Okay, Mom, I can tell it's too painful to talk about Dad."

"It's—"

"Okay. Listen, I'm glad you met someone and that you're working again, but I really won't be able to help you out like I have been."

"It's not like you've been paying my rent every single month."

Monet bit back a rude reply. "I'm going to start saving up to go to school. I'd like to be an interior designer."

"Why?"

"It's what I'd really like to do."

"Well, if you're sure."

"I'm sure," Monet answered quickly.

"I'm not too worried about money now, anyway. If my job falls apart, I may have a new man to fall back on."

"Well, that should be less stressful."

"Can't you act just a little happy for me?"

"I am, Mom. Quit drawing the wrong conclusions."

"Okay, but you know what?"

"What?"

"Watch it with this truck driver. Don't let him walk all over you like you let the last one."

That wasn't exactly the truth, but her mother would never understand a drawn-out explanation. "Not a chance. Well, I suppose I'd better go." Her mother's mood swings frustrated her.

"Okay, we'll talk later," her mom said and ended the call.

Talking to her mother wasn't the easiest thing to do, but she felt it had to be done. Just like showing Ruby she had no control over her. The thought produced an idea, one that Monet could thank her mother for reminding her to do—not to let Alex walk all over her. She needed to solve the same issue with Ruby.

She would go see her at her house, catch her off guard. If Monet was lucky, she'd be there. Jay had to be working, didn't he? Sure, Alex was.

Before more in-depth thought, Monet began getting ready. She chose a yellow, linen skirt, matching tank, and high-heeled sandals.

Dressed, she crossed to the bathroom, added mascara, lip gloss, a dab of spicy, floral fragrance, and examined herself in the mirror. Confidence in place, she was prepared to face Ruby.

Then realization dawned. She had only been to Ruby and Jay's house once. Maybe Alex could help her out.

She tried him on his truck cell phone. His voice mail came on. She flipped her phone shut. She was on her own. Could she find it? Sure. Her memory was one of her stronger points.

In concentration, she headed out, going over in her mind the way Alex had gone.

She hopped on the interstate that took her to a bridge on the East side. From there, she went on another freeway that brought her to the highway leading into the town of Maltby.

Nearly an hour later, after a few wrong turns and fifteen minutes of being lost, she finally found the familiar street that led her to Jay and Ruby's driveway.

Exhaling in relief, she followed it all the way to the house. As she pulled up to the three-car garage, she admired the one-story home with corner quoins and keystones above the windows. The covered porch at the entrance added to the allure.

She forced herself to slip from her car and walk up to the porch, considering different scenarios. Her stomach jittered. Jay could answer the door. Ruby could answer but shut the door in her face. Uneasiness mounted. She took a deep breath and rang the bell, her nerves strung tight.

Then, what felt like an hour later, the door opened. It wasn't Ruby. She drew a quick, indrawn breath. Dressed in dark slacks and a pale-blue shirt that matched his eyes, Jay stood before her.

She was speechless. Anxiety pulsed through her as she stumbled across. "Hello. Is Ruby home?" She worked her purse from hand to hand at her waist.

Jay hesitated before saying, "Actually, she's out."

The smartest thing Monet could do was leave right now. However, she couldn't get herself to budge.

"She's at an accounting class." Jay continued. "I don't know exactly when she'll be home. Would you like to wait for her?"

Monet's already-racing heart picked up speed. "Sure, I guess I could wait around for a bit." She smoothed her skirt. "That's right. Ruby mentioned she does your bookkeeping. It must be nice having your wife do it."

He stood aside to let her in. "It's handy."

Monet moved through the doorway, taking in the inside of the house, her love for interior design in full swing. But she couldn't *not* think of Jay—the slight lines at his eyes when he smiled, his thick, dark hair neatly combed back and gelled to perfection, and the clear but deep, polite tone of his voice.

"Is it your day off?" Jay asked, heading toward the living room.

His voice shot a tingle of awareness through her. "Yeah, it is." She thought of Ruby. Some women couldn't see a dream if it hit them in the face. Should she tell Jay everything? No. Instead, she studied the living room, painted in a custard cream that offset the pale, damask furniture. Gilt-framed mirrors and modern artwork added dimension to the room and spoke of wealth.

Next, she strolled to a double sliding glass door, breathing in the sensual scent of jasmine. Oval leaves with little, white flowers produced a sweet and pleasant aroma through the screen. Directly behind the ample cluster of jasmine was a patio retreat. She gazed out atoff-white and teal British Isles patio furniture. A table with four chairs, two lounge chairs, and two chaises angled away from an immaculate BBQ.

"Make yourself comfortable."

Jay's voice brought her back to him.

"Would you like something to drink?" he asked.

"Sure, if it's easy."

He smiled. "There's a variety of soda to choose from in the fridge if you'd like."

"Sounds good." Monet trailed him into the kitchen.

When he opened the fridge, she peered inside. She scanned the different cans. To hide her nervousness, she took her time deciding.

When she settled on Orange Crush, Jay said, "I'll get you a glass with some ice."

"That would be great, thanks." Emotion made her voice husky.

When he set a tall glass under the ice dispenser, the shatter of ice hitting glass was music to her ears.

He poured her soda and handed her the glass. Their fingers grazed. The warmth of his touch sent shivers through her body. She should get out of here. But somehow … she couldn't. She sipped her soda, swallowed, and watched as he took a soda and glass for himself.

"Why don't we wait in the living room," he said.

"Okay." Monet crossed the room with him and sank down onto the love seat.

Jay chose a seat across from her on an over-stuffed couch. "I'm sorry for the way Ruby treated you the other night."

"It was no big deal, really." Monet crossed her bare legs and sat back.

Jay skimmed her legs with his eyes. "Are you sure you two don't know each other from somewhere? It's just, Ruby acted especially strange that night, and I felt like there was something she wasn't telling me."

Tense, she hesitated before answering. "We don't really know each other. I guess I just looked familiar to her."

"I see." He rubbed his jaw.

"I just thought it would be nice to get to know her better so that maybe we could all have dinner again without the uneasy feelings," Monet said as she sipped her soda.

Jay set his glass on a round end table. "The thing about Ruby is that she has a hard time getting along with certain people." He leaned forward, resting his elbows on his knees. "She's real … let's just say she can be stubborn."

"Can't we all?" Monet paused. "You have a very beautiful wife."

Jay smiled. "Thank you." He shifted on the couch. "So, how are you and Alex getting along?"

"We're doing fine." With Alex, it's lust. With you, it's … Monet sipped her soda and set her glass down on the coffee table in front of her. "Was it a slow day at work or day off for you, too?"

"Actually, it was a slow day, just a one-trip day. Alex and I got home early. Our log production was down due to the rain we've had up in the mountains over the last couple of days."

"So, the rain prevents you from working?"

"Sometimes when we have water running off our logging roads, we like to keep the heavy truck traffic off of them. It keeps silt from entering ditch lines and eventually ending up in streams. Also, if we take our equipment out and yard logs to the landing, the heavy machines could damage the ground. We pride ourselves in protecting the environment. Of course, the Department of Natural Resources enforces strict rules and regulations, so we do our best to stay on their good side."

"Sounds impressive. With all the negative publicity on logging, it's nice to hear the loggers' perspective. You're more environmentally concerned than the press portrays."

"That's just the problem." Jay shrugged. "The general public really doesn't understand how hard loggers work to protect the lands."

Jay was a good guy all the way around. "You'd be a great spokesperson for the industry."

He chuckled. "Not my style. So, are you an exotic dancer?"

"Yes."

"There's nothing wrong with that. Ruby danced before we met."

"She got out of it then?"

"Yeah, it was a while back. Maybe that's where you two have seen each other before."

"I don't think so." She couldn't tell him she'd met Ruby with Alex. "So, how do you like the line of work you're in?"

"It's a living, but my goal is to become a real estate investor. That's what my dad does now. After I bought out his business, he went into real estate and has done very well for himself."

"That sounds like a great idea. You can't go wrong with real estate."

Jay smiled. "It seems that way."

Monet needed to get her thoughts in order. "May I use your restroom?"

"Sure, down the hall"—Jay gestured—"second door on the left."

Once inside the bathroom, Monet flicked on the light and closed the door. She took a deep breath to calm her nerves. She realized if she didn't leave soon, she'd be in a whirlwind of trouble. Even so, she added lip gloss. She told herself she would go back out, finish her soda, and leave.

She emerged from the restroom and rejoined Jay, feeling all tingly inside, and she wasn't even drinking alcohol. Damn. Just being with him … She had to get it together.

She emptied her can of Orange Crush and finally said, "I should get going. Thanks for the company and soda."

"You're welcome. I'll tell Ruby you stopped by."

Fear clamored in her brain. "No."

Jay looked at her oddly.

"I mean, don't bother. I'll call her."

"Okay." Jay shook his head.

Sensing Jay was lost, Monet forced herself to explain. "Ruby and I aren't exactly friends. I came by to settle our differences."

He arched a brow. "Differences?"

"Yeah. It turns out, she may know a friend of mine. It's a long story."

Jay didn't push. As they walked outside, a fresh, summer breeze tickled Monet's cheek. She looked up to see a cedar bough ruffle in the distance, and she heard a woodpecker peck away on a nearby tree.

Then Monet and Jay exchanged a glance.

She watched a trace of sadness cross his face and longed to reach out and touch him, tell him she'd be here for him even if Ruby wasn't.

Silence settled between them.

"I really should go," she said softly.

"I suppose you're right."

She could see disappointment in his eyes. Then he reached into his pocket and withdrew his wallet.

"Here's my card. If you, or anyone you know, ever needs any work of this kind, call me."

Their hands brushed lightly. Her whole body quivered from the contact.

"I might just buy that dream property someday and need your services." She scanned the white business card with green trees and mountains printed in the background. "Environmentally sound. Nice. Hmm," she said with interest. "Now, thanks to you, I know what that means."

He smiled, looked away, then stuffed his hands in his slack pockets. "Enjoy the rest of your day."

"I'll try." Although she managed to return his smile, part of her longed to stay with him forever.

He was warm, sensitive, caring—but married.

Chapter Nine

When Monet got back from Jay's, her heart was still racing. She retreated to her bedroom to change. Dixie Cup followed her, immediately jumping up on the bed. She changed into a pair of lightweight sweats and a cropped T-shirt, sat down on the bed, and drew her knees up. She leaned back against the headboard and scratched Dixie Cup's ears beside her. What was she going to do? She was seeing Alex, God's gift to women, but she wanted Jay, someone she couldn't have. It really made no sense.

The phone rang.

Monet was startled by the sound. She moved Dixie Cup aside, leaned over, and answered, "Hello."

"Monet, hey."

It was Cameo's elated voice. "Hey, what's up?" she asked, instantly cheered.

"Let's do a girls' night, and I don't mean out," Cameo

was quick to explain. "I mean, how about I bring over some peanut M&Ms and we talk some trash."

"You know, that sounds perfect."

Monet hung up, then hurried to the kitchen to check the fridge for something to drink. She opened it to find some cans of Sprite. She thought of Jay's and how there were at least five different kinds of soda. She felt heat climb into her face. Just the thought of their hands touching sent ripples of delight through her body. She closed her eyes and found a breath. Stop, she told herself.

She went to the living room to put her Alicia Keys' CD on at a low volume, then she found herself at the window. For a moment, she studied the lights reflecting off the smooth water.

Twenty minutes later, Cameo stepped through the doorway, clutching a big, yellow bag to her chest. "Hey, you."

"Hey, you," Monet returned.

When the two of them settled in at the kitchen table, Monet said, "This'll be fun."

"I agree." Cameo slid the bag of M&Ms across the table.

Monet poured herself a handful and asked, "Where's Tyrese tonight?"

"Out with the guys, probably checking out a strip club or something. So, how'd your day go?"

"I went over to Jay and Ruby's earlier"—Monet slid the M&Ms back and tossed some into her mouth—"hoping to see Ruby."

Cameo picked up the M&M bag. "I was going to stop you right there until you said, Ruby."

"I wanted to tell her I'm going to continue seeing Alex whether she likes it or not."

Around a mouthful of candy, Cameo said, "Right on. And?"

"Jay was home instead of Ruby." Monet chewed and swallowed.

Cameo sighed. "Well, now …"

"It was weird," Monet remembered as she got up, wandered to the fridge, and grabbed two cans of Sprite. She set one can in front of Cameo and settled back in just as Dixie Cup jumped up and claimed the chair next to her.

"Okay." Cameo gestured with her Sprite. "You need to forget Jay."

"I know." Monet put her can to her mouth, tipped her head back, and let the fizz burn her throat. Her thoughts jumped from Jay to Ruby. Very slowly, she said, "I need to know something."

Cameo sipped her soda. "What's that?"

"Do you know Ruby?" She had to ask.

Cameo got to her feet and crossed the room. "We're not exactly friends."

"She worked at Fantasy's, didn't she?"

Cameo nodded. "Yes."

"Then why didn't you tell me that the first night at the store?"

Cameo made her way to the living room window. "I suppose I should start at the beginning. Wow, okay." She let out a heavy breath. "Ruby got to be really close with Gus, if you know what I mean."

"When was this?" Monet asked.

"It all happened over four years ago. It ended up in a big mess to where a lot of the girls quit over it because, get this, anything Ruby wanted, she got."

"Like what."

"She got to pick her hours and got away with dirty dancing and jacking customers off, things like that. I heard she was charging triple and letting the customers ... well, you know, feel her up and who knows what else. Not to mention, if she didn't show up for work, she didn't have to call. She'd just go blow Gus in his office or something. I mean, most of us would get canned for that behavior." Cameo shook her head. "Not Ruby. She got to do almost anything, and then one night after closing, I joined her and Gus after hours ... in a threesome. Man, were we bombed!"

"You shouldn't have felt like you had to hide this from me. We're exotic dancers, baby. We're different. Hey, you know Tamara and Chrissie who are always together?"

"Yeah." Cameo came back and settled in at the table.

"You know how many times they've asked me to join them in a threesome? Just because I'm not into it doesn't mean it's bad, not to mention, I can't even count the number of times they've asked me to get high with them in the bathroom.

Since I always say no, they've given up. But I don't look down on them, and I don't look down on you because you did something you don't normally do. Besides, you said you were bombed. Come on, now." Monet chuckled.

Around a smile, Cameo said, "Let me put it this way. I'm surprised I can remember anything at all."

"Tell me about it." Monet sipped her Sprite. "What you remember."

"You serious?"

Monet grabbed a handful of M&Ms. "Sure."

"We hit it on the pool table. I think he watched us do each other, and then he did us each in turn, but I can't really remember details. Thank God," Cameo added, "because I really am not into that, and especially, with … well, you understand."

"That's why we're so close, Cameo. We're different, yet alike, and have a lot more in common than some of the other dancers out there who depend on drugs and alcohol to do what we do."

"So, we're all good?" Cameo snagged a couple of M&Ms from the bag.

"Of course," Monet assured her. "It's in the past. Let it go. I'm just lucky it was the time that I'd taken off and was teaching aerobics. Pretty amazing, when you think about it, that I never saw her there."

Cameo finished the M&Ms she'd taken a minute ago and said, "She only lasted six months, then quit. The other girls were onto her. And to be honest with you, I couldn't stand the sight of her after what happened. I still can't. Anyway, I was happy when she left. When I saw her at the store, I was like, shit. I didn't want to tell anyone about this because I was pretty ashamed, and I especially didn't want to tell you. I'm actually quite surprised she kept it to herself."

"You know you can always tell me anything." Monet paused. "The thing is, I had to tell Jay something earlier, about why I came to see Ruby. God, now I feel really bad for him, even though this all happened before they were married." She tipped her head back and finished her Sprite. "What I told him was that I came by for us to settle our differences. And it turns out, Ruby may know a friend of mine, but I didn't get into it. I couldn't say I was there to tell Ruby I refuse to stop seeing Alex because of her."

"Why did you stay?"

"That's an awfully good question." Monet got up and took the cans of soda to the sink, remembering Jay's easy smile, his gentleness, his caring personality, not to mention how sensitive her skin had been at his touch. Just the accidental brush of their hands had sent her heart into overdrive … and the deep timbre of his voice, the fresh smell of him.

"Just be smart," Cameo said, getting up from the table.

Monet pushed the memories of Jay away and crossed to the CD player in the living room to switch it off and set the radio to tuner. R. Kelly's "Bump n' Grind" drifted from the speakers.

As they sank down onto the couch with Dixie Cup in between them, Cameo said, "Tell me about your apartment hunting and when you think you'll need help packing."

Monet was grateful for the subject change. "Possibly tomorrow. I'm meeting with two potential roommates in Capitol Hill, so hopefully, one of them will work out and I'll be out of here pretty quickly."

"Good for you. I hope so." Cameo rubbed Dixie Cup's back. "If it wasn't for Tyrese, you and I would be living together."

"I know, and that's a nice thought, but I don't expect you to give it up, as long as you're happy."

"He keeps me very happy." Cameo wiggled her brows and grinned.

"I bet."

"So, when are you going to see Alex next?"

"I'll have to talk to him and find out."

"Well, keep me posted."

"I will," Monet said. "When Jay told me Ruby wasn't home, I should have left. I don't know how to answer your question about why I stayed."

Cameo reached over and patted Monet on the back. "It'll all work out and be okay, you'll see," she said and left shortly after.

Monet had no idea how long she'd been asleep when the phone woke her. She fumbled for it on the nightstand.

"Hello," she said, realizing it was just after midnight.

"Sorry"—Jay hesitated—"if I woke you."

The sound of his voice instantly snapped her awake. She shot up in bed. "It's okay."

"Alex gave me your number."

"Oh." Monet clutched the receiver between her ear and shoulder and pulled the sheet up around her.

"Look, Ruby hasn't come home yet. That's why I called. She doesn't have many friends, and I thought after what you told me yesterday, maybe you'd know where she might be."

Flustered, but aching to be truthful, Monet said, "God, I wish I did. I talked to my friend who knows her, though. It turns out they worked at Fantasy's together, but they weren't exactly friends."

Jay cleared his throat. "Why does that not surprise me?"

"I'm sorry, Jay. I really wish I could help you. I don't know where she is." Liar.

"I'll let you go then."

"Jay, wait." Her heart sped up but her brain stalled.

"What?"

"I hope she gets home soon," was all she could think to say.

"Me, too. Sorry if I disturbed you."

"That could never happen," slipped out.

After a short pause, Jay said, "You're sweet. Well, okay, then. Good night."

"Good night, Jay," she said and hung up.

Was Ruby with Alex this late? Anger and impatience at Alex's behavior urged Monet to call him and find out, no matter what the hour. If he was with Ruby, then she was through with him, too.

She punched in his number. Three rings later, he answered in a throaty drawl, "Yeah."

"Alex, it's Monet. I know it's late, but I need to know if Ruby's there."

"What the ... are you kidding? Hell, no," he said with a hard edge. "You think I'm that stupid?"

She breathed a sigh of relief. "No, but thanks to you, Jay called looking for Ruby. I just had to know she wasn't there."

"Why don't you come over, though." His voice softened. "I could use some company."

"It's tempting, but I have to get some sleep. I have too much to do tomorrow."

"Okay. Just remember what you're missing out on."

"How could I forget?" She smiled. Alex might make her forget about Jay ... at least for a little while.

"Who knows where the bitch is."

"I'll talk to you tomorrow after work, if it's okay to call late."

"It's never too late for me, cutie. I can go all night." She could hear his smile.

"I don't doubt it," she said, remembering the way he quenched her body's drunken need for sex.

Chapter Ten

Monet tried to keep her mind clear of Jay as she cruised across Ballard Bridge toward work. She'd just found a roommate to move in with in an apartment in Capitol Hill, and with Cameo's help had spent the rest of the day preparing for her move tomorrow.

She should feel elated, relieved. It was a step in the right direction. She'd even pushed herself on her Lifecycle, doing four sets of twenty-four-minute, level eight hill work, taking advantage before the move.

But ... she couldn't quite shake Jay from her mind. She should focus on sex with Alex. That's what she needed.

She pulled into Fantasy's parking lot, and when she whirled through the door, she spotted Ruby, lounging over the bar, chatting with the bartender. What was going on? Her day had just been shot to hell. It could only mean trouble.

Monet quickly changed, emerged out on the floor, and forced herself to ignore Ruby.

A young, dark-haired man sitting at a table next to the stage waved her over.

Without hesitation, Monet made her way there, let out a breath, and slipped in beside him.

"Hello, I'm Dave. Would you like something to drink?"

"I'm Monet, and yes, I'd love it. How about a dance to the next song?" she asked.

"Sure."

When Marvin Gaye's "Sexual Healing" started, Monet got to her feet. First, she nudged Dave's knees apart, then knelt down in the space between his feet. She pressed her breasts together with her black, lace-gloved hands, slowly making her way back up his body, brushing it with hers. She felt his hands creep up her thighs. Carefully, she slid them away, continuing to rub herself on him. She nuzzled his neck and inhaled the scent of his exotic cologne. His hands crept back up her thighs, grazing the tops of her thigh-highs. Gently, she moved them away again. She blew warm air into his ear before turning around to lightly grind his lap.

Her stomach tightened when she saw Ruby and Gus in a discussion at the bar. Was she trying to get her fired? When it came to Ruby, nothing surprised her anymore.

Monet continued dancing and turned back around to face Dave when the song ended.

Dave whispered in her ear, "Keep going."

"Just tell me when to stop," she returned.

After four more dances, he suggested she take a break.

She slid in beside him and adjusted her thigh-highs before a waitress stopped to take their drink order.

After she left, Dave said, "It's obvious you enjoy what you do."

"It's a unique experience." She turned and caught his smile, reminding her of the actor Chris O'Donnell.

"Are you currently involved with someone?"

"Yes," she was quick to respond. She never dated customers from work, for pleasure or money.

"Your table dances are hot."

"Thank you."

"How about a couple more after your drink arrives?"

"I'd like that." Her eyes wandered back to Ruby. She wished she'd leave. She hated distractions at work.

After their drinks came, Monet danced a couple more songs for Dave before excusing herself to freshen up.

She walked right past Ruby toward the restroom, as if baiting her. Out of the corner of her eye, she saw Ruby get up. Monet took a deep breath, preparing for battle.

Before the restroom door had a chance to swing shut, Ruby bolted in, reached out, and grabbed Monet's forearm, nails digging into flesh. She swung Monet around to face her with her eyes ablaze.

"Why are you here?" Ruby barked with impatience.

Monet blinked twice, as if she were a blur. "Excuse me?"

she said and broke free. "Does Jay know you're back here where your job was apparently getting guys off?"

"What?" Ruby's voice seethed with rage. She stepped right into Monet, their faces just inches away. "You don't know anything about Jay."

"He has manners, unlike you, that's for sure. But even the most tolerant man can only handle so much."

"You're messing with the wrong person," Ruby shot back.

"I'm not scared of you, Ruby," Monet said as her hands trembled.

Ruby produced a sickly, sweet grin. "You should be. So why are you here?"

"What does it look like? Some people have to work hard for their money, not steal."

"How dare you!" Ruby heaved with exertion. "You don't know anything about me."

"Want to bet? I know it all, Ruby. You can't get anything without using sex. I sort of feel sorry for you."

"Well, I don't feel anything for you … and … you'll never work here again."

"I'm working now, speaking of which, I gotta go."

Ruby grabbed her arm again. "Look, I'll make your life so miserable, you'll be sorry you ever met Alex. And if you even talk to my husband, you'll wish you hadn't been born. Is that clear?"

"Don't threaten me, Ruby. As I've told you before, I'm not into married men," she said as she pulled her arm free.

"You ..." Ruby's eyes glittered furiously. "Just so you know, Gus and I go back a ways. I can make things happen."

Monet arched a brow. "Believe me, I've heard."

"I'll get you fired so fast—"

"I don't think," Monet said, cutting her off, "I have to worry about getting fired. If I wanted to work for an escort service, I'd look in the yellow pages. It's obvious that's what you should have done."

Through clenched teeth, Ruby said, "You'd never make it as an escort." Then she turned on her heel and charged out the door. A blast of air blew in, along with the start of Madonna's "Vogue."

After work, inside her car, Monet was so fed up with Ruby, she could hardly think. She fired it up and punched in Alex's number on her cell phone.

"Yeah," came the hoarse reply.

"Alex, I'm sorry for calling so late."

"Don't be. What's up?"

"How about some company?"

"I'd love some."

"I'm on my way from work right now."

"Cool."

Monet heard a lighter's click, then a deep inhale. "See you in a bit," she said and flipped her phone shut.

So, at his door, she released a cleansing breath and reached for the bell just as he opened it.

Instantly, the scent of Drakkar, fresh soap, and wintergreen greeted her. She swallowed hard while taking in the faded, black jeans and diamond stud earring in his left ear. He wore nothing else.

"Alex," she managed.

A strand of black hair fell across his forehead. He hadn't shaved. She couldn't keep her eyes from wandering below his belly where dark hairs swirled, lower and lower. She glanced away quickly.

"Come in."

Her pulse skipped. The invitation swung her gaze to his. His eyes never left hers as he moved aside to let her in.

She stepped through the doorway and realized she'd never seen him without a shirt on. Wow.

Breathless, she followed him into a small kitchen. He got out two Coronas from the fridge.

She noticed the way his muscles flexed as he held the beer.

He handed her one, grabbed a bottle opener, and popped the tops.

"Thanks," she said.

Alex took her hand and crossed to the living room.

They sank down onto a brown, vinyl couch. He inched closer toward her. Their thighs brushed.

In a clingy dress and bare legs, the touch sent a shiver through her. She took a drink of beer and turned toward Alex.

"How was your day?" she asked.

He set his bottle down on the coffee table. "Fine, yours?"

She sensed they'd be going at it any second. "I found a

roommate with an apartment in Capitol Hill, and I'm all packed and ready to move, if you can believe that."

"Do you need any help?" His gaze coasted over her body.

She took another sip of Corona. "No, but thanks. I hire people for that. It's easier."

"That's cool then. How was work?" He picked up his bottle and took a long drink.

Her eyes followed the slight movement of muscles in his throat. "Ruby showed up there tonight."

"You're kidding?"

"I wish I was."

Alex slammed his bottle down. "What the hell do you think she was doing there?"

Monet nodded. "Who knows what goes on in her head." She didn't feel like going into lengthy detail about Ruby's situation at Fantasy's.

"I'll tell you what goes on in her head." His voice sliced into her thoughts. "Nothing, except how to fuck up other people's lives."

Monet reached for her beer. "I agree. She won't leave me alone."

Alex sighed. "I know how you feel." As he ran a hand along her thigh, he said, "Let's forget about her."

He took the beer from her hand and set it down beside his.

Monet could see the desire in his eyes.

"She's a waste of time," he said as he tugged the thin straps of her dress down her shoulders. "This isn't."

Monet tingled from the sensation.

And then he covered her mouth with his, sliding his tongue between her lips and inside her mouth, slow and deep.

She ran her tongue across his teeth, toward the back of his throat, aching to feel him deep inside of her.

He pinned her back against the sofa. Their mouths devoured each other. She tightened her arms around his neck, wanting all of him, feeling his arousal against her thigh, his tongue inside her mouth.

"Let's go to my room." His voice was thick and low against her face. "I wanna show you my best asset."

"I know all about it," she whispered, reaching for his crotch, kissing his stubble-covered jaw. She felt him through his jeans. He was thick and hard.

He took her hand and guided it inside his snug underwear. She curled her fingers around his erection, straining and moist at the tip. She wanted to just eat him up. Slowly, she rubbed the pearl of moisture all around his length, then brought her finger to her mouth to taste him.

A low groan escaped him before a loud pounding on the door bolted them to their feet.

"Fuck," Alex barked.

Alarm and a heavy sense of disappointment went through Monet. "Speak of the devil," she said.

"If I don't answer it, she'll never go away," Alex grumbled. "She knows you're here."

Monet nodded. "My car," she said and watched Alex cross to the door.

When he flung it open, Ruby immediately stormed past him. "Just what in the hell is she doing here?"

"It's two o'clock in the morning, Ruby. Guess." Alex grabbed her by the shoulders.

"We were just about to do what you should do with your husband more often." Monet's patience was wearing thin.

Ruby struggled to break free from Alex's hold. "For your information," she blurted at Monet, "my husband gets plenty."

In disgust, Monet looked away.

"You want to stay and watch?" Alex's eyes were blazing. "Maybe you could learn something."

Ruby's voice seethed with rage. "You're a sick bastard."

"Then leave, before I tell Jay what a lying, cheating bitch you are."

Ruby flinched.

"I agree," Monet said. "It wouldn't exactly be a lie."

"How dare you." Ruby lunged toward her.

Alex planted himself in front of Monet. "You have no right to threaten her. It stops now. Get out of my house."

"Do you think Jay would ever believe you?" Ruby challenged him. "I'll just deny everything and tell him that you made the move on me. And believe me, you'll never drive another log truck in this state."

Alex raised a hand, as if to strike Ruby, but instead ran it through his hair. "Get out."

Ruby shook a finger at Monet. "I meant what I said. I'm not through with you," she snarled before turning on her heel.

Weariness crept through Monet.

"Bitch!" Alex cursed as he slammed the door shut behind Ruby.

Monet started toward Alex, still at the door. She wiped a strand of hair from her face and sighed. "Thank you."

When she reached out to touch his shoulder, their eyes met.

Alex drew her against him in a hug. "Don't mention it." He pulled back to look at her. "I could use a drink. How about you?"

Monet smiled. "I guess I could finish my beer."

He slipped an arm around her waist and steered her back to the couch. After settling in, Alex picked up his bottle and drained it.

Monet took a sip of her beer. "I think the mood was ruined."

"Not if I have anything to say about it." He ran his tongue over his lips.

Monet's body responded, but thinking about Ruby bothered her. "I don't think tonight is—" She shook her head.

"Well, then, you could say Ruby got what she wanted." He rose from the couch and disappeared into the kitchen. Seconds later, he emerged with another beer.

Monet rose to her feet. She stroked his unshaven jaw, loving the sexy feel. "Alex, I'm sorry."

"Would you like to stay all night? I'm sure we could get back in the mood." He caressed her cheek with his fingertips.

Her breath caught at his touch. "I should get going." Reluctantly, she retrieved her purse.

Alex blocked her from moving and lowered his head until his mouth was inches from hers. "You sure I can't change your mind?"

She couldn't take her eyes off his full, moist lips. "You think Ruby will leave us alone?"

"Yep."

"I hope you're right."

He stepped out of her way and walked her to the door.

Once there, he turned her into him.

His bare torso grazed the thin fabric of her dress. She felt his erection against her and swallowed to wet her throat. "I'll call you tomorrow, okay?"

In answer, he leaned down and opened her lips with his tongue, slowly circling her teeth.

A tiny moan slipped from her mouth. She slid her tongue inside his mouth, unable to get close enough.

"If we don't stop, I'm going to take you right here," he whispered roughly against her throat.

"I know." She breathed in deeply and smoothed a hand down the front of her flimsy dress. "So, for now, I'm going." Then she brushed his lips with hers and left.

A touch of regret hit her as she stepped outside. Ruby's intrusion clouded what could have been another night to remember.

Chapter Eleven

Catching Monet at Alex's had been all she'd needed to come up with a plan during the night, and Cameo had obviously spilled their secret. What next? Her life was falling apart. She'd attempt to get Monet fired. It had to work.

So, the following evening, Ruby let out the clutch and sent her 'vette flying. The sooner she made it to Fantasy's, the better.

Upon arrival, she whipped into a parking space. As she slid from her car in a skimpy, black dress that showed her assets to perfection, she had a feeling that things would go her way. Giving the world's best hummers made life just a little bit easier. With a sway of her hips, she made her way to the door. She drew it open just as two businessmen in suits were leaving.

One nudged the other, and said, "Hey, I'd like to see that at Lucky Lady's."

Ruby threw them a wink, confident she left them drooling after her. At Lucky Lady's, they took it all off. God, she was hot.

As she slipped inside Fantasy's, Tupac's "How Do U Want It" boomed from the jukebox, along with a cloud of tobacco-laden air. She headed for the bar, wrinkling her nose at the cigarette fumes. Once there, she slid onto a stool beside her former boss. She leaned over provocatively to give him a view of plentiful cleavage and whispered over the music, "How about we have a little talk."

Gus finished his soda, nodded at the bartender, and got to his feet.

Ruby smiled. So far so good.

She followed him to the back of the club and up a few stairs to a door marked, PRIVATE. They entered his cramped office. Her anticipation mounted. At a quick glance, Ruby saw papers strewn on a desk. The walls were lined with sexy photos of women posing in next to nothing. Their faces sported the "Come Fuck Me" look. She rolled her eyes and gave her wild hair a toss. Not even sultry models compared to her.

Gus gestured for her to sit down. She chose a well-padded, metal chair and watched him grab the back of a swivel chair in front of his desk, pull it out, and lower himself into it. Then he lit a cigarette, shook out the match, and took a long drag.

"What's on your mind?" he asked around a puff of smoke.

Ruby's heart tripled in beats. "Well," she began, as her

stomach churned, "I think there's something you need to know."

He sat back, cigarette between index finger and thumb, and studied her through squinted eyes. "What's that?"

"I didn't want to have to tell you this," she lied, "but it seems as if Monet is breaking the rules."

"Oh?" His eyes rounded at her through thin-framed glasses.

Ruby licked her lips, nodding twice. "She's been pulling tricks from the club. That's bad enough, right? But my husband, Jay, is involved." Her eyes widened for emphasis. "I mean, my husband ... who would have thought. Oh," she said, pretending to cry.

"Well." He chuckled. "Sounds like a personal problem. It's all hearsay. I can't legally do a thing. If I fired her for that, she could sue me. I'm not touching that one."

His response infuriated her. "So, you're not going to do anything about it?"

"Ruby, I'm sorry, but there's nothing I can do."

She blinked hard, unable to comprehend.

"It's personal. I'm staying out of it."

A chill raced up Ruby's spine. Monet would definitely pay for this. Ruby couldn't grasp that her plan wasn't going to work. This didn't happen to her. Should she have him drop his pants and get down on her knees? No! She was too angry. "Fine." Ruby rose with elegance. "I guess we're finished then."

He turned to his ringing phone on the desk. "I guess we are," he said and crushed his cigarette out in a tin ashtray.

She stormed out of his office, raced down the stairs, and retraced her steps to the door.

Once in her car, she pounded the steering wheel with her fists. She wasn't through with Monet yet.

* * *

Monet finished on stage, anxious at Ruby's return, but was surprised when she'd watched her practically fly back out the door.

When she saw Cameo sitting alone at a table for dancers on break, she headed over to join her. "Hey," she said, settling into a chair.

"Hey, you. How goes the hustle?"

"It's been a pretty good night so far, up until … what do you think Ruby's up to?"

Cameo shrugged. "Beats me. I was wondering that myself."

"I'll bet she's lying to Gus."

"Oh, that I could see."

"She left in an awful hurry, though," Monet said.

"Yeah, maybe something didn't go her way."

Monet arched a brow. "You think?"

"Maybe her oral skills aren't as good as they used to be."

"Hmm … that could be a problem for her."

"Yeah," Cameo agreed, "but not for Ashley over there."

"What?" Monet whispered loudly over Aerosmith's "Sweet Emotion."

Cameo nodded at a long-legged brunette, practically on top of her customer. "I heard all about her services."

"So that's why she never gets turned down for a table dance." Monet shook her head in realization.

"Yeah." Cameo kept her voice low. "I think most of them know they can pretty much count on anything and everything afterward … and very affordable, I hear."

"Who told you?"

"Princess. I guess they used to be roommates, but Princess told me she wasn't into running a brothel."

"That would get old."

"So, while we're on the subject of sex, are you going to see Alex tonight?"

"I plan to."

"If Ruby shows up again, don't let it stop you from doing him. Got it?"

Monet smiled. "Got it. What do you have going after work?"

"I think I'll go home and toss the magazines down on the floor, then have Tyrese nail me on the coffee table. Sex over glass. Sounds hot, huh?"

"Very."

Four and a half hours later, outside, digging for her keys at the bottom of her purse, a familiar voice sliced through the air.

"Monet," Shane called. "I really need to talk to you."

She nearly dropped her purse. Slowly, she turned toward

him. Pale circles ringed his eyes. A black, wrinkled T-shirt clung to him. His black, baggy pants drug the ground. "What now?" she asked with impatience.

"I don't want to be without you. Monet, there's no one out there like you."

"Shane, you just tell me what you think I want to hear." She shook her head. "Why are you doing this?" And why was she standing there, listening to him?

"Doing what?"

"Not willing to face the truth." She unlocked her car and slipped inside.

Shane knocked on the driver's window. "Please, Monet, just give me another chance."

She buzzed her window down. "I'm sorry, Shane. Your chances ran out a long time ago," she said. Then she put the window up and watched him give her the finger.

As he stepped away from the car, she started it and backed out of the parking lot. She was so over him.

No matter what, she wouldn't let Ruby or Shane ruin the rest of her evening. Besides, she should be celebrating. She'd gotten all moved into her new place today.

What felt like hours later, she pulled into Alex's driveway. Light spilled from the windows.

At his door, before ringing the bell, she breathed in deeply.

Just as she reached up to press the button, Alex pulled the door open.

"Hey, cutie, I'm glad you're here."

Monet took in his white T-shirt, thread-bare Levi's, and beer dangling from his hand. "I hope I'm not interrupting anything."

"No way," he said on a chuckle and moved aside to let her in.

She smoothed her chiffon skirt over her thighs, stepped inside, and followed him into the living room. Setting her purse on the coffee table, she caught a commercial on TV showing a man's face freshly shaved and a woman at his side, running her hand over his face as if to prove the shaver's success.

Alex picked up the remote, muted the television, and put the stereo on. The words to "Sweet Child O' Mine" surrounded them.

Monet swallowed as she watched him close the distance between them.

Their gazes locked. Sexual hunger sizzled between them. Her body tightened and heated in response.

Reflections from the TV flickered across the walls in the otherwise darkened room.

She studied Alex, standing in front of her. Dark stubble shadowed his face and drew attention to the sensual lines of his mouth.

He set his beer down. "Work go good tonight?"

"Yeah, all except Ruby showed up again and disappeared with the boss for a while."

"I bet she blew him."

Monet laughed.

"Do you plan on dancing there for a while?"

"Sure, and also teaching aerobics again for extra income. I also need to sell my Lexus and get something cheaper, but the thought hurts."

"I'd buy it, but I'm just a poor log truck driver. I can sure drive, though." He hitched an eyebrow suggestively, slipping his hand beneath her skirt and up her thigh.

Warm sensations spiraled through her. On a choppy breath she said, "Nothing's going to stop me from having you tonight."

"How long has it been since you came?"

"Since with you," she whispered hoarsely against his lips.

He swept her mouth with his tongue before pulling her into him—hard.

His mouth clamped down on hers. He parted her lips with his tongue, and they kissed ravenously, like at a sensual feast.

Monet drank in the sensation. Her tongue collided with his. She tasted wintergreen, Corona … Alex. She slid her hands underneath his shirt and felt the hard plains of his back. His erection pressed against her stomach, making her dizzy with need.

"Alex," she said, kissing his cheek. "I want you inside me, now."

At her request, he scooped her up.

She wrapped her legs around his waist as he carried her down the hall and into his bedroom. Light spilled in through the blinds to give the room an intimate feel. Cologne mingled with the faint scent of Corona, cigarette smoke, and arousal, while the beat of music drifted in from the hallway.

The bed had been left unmade. The sheets were rumpled and white, like the T-shirt she was about to rip off of him.

She couldn't wait to feel every inch of him, again, buried so deep inside her she cried out in pain. Moisture intensified between her legs, causing her muscles to clench instinctively in anticipation.

He stopped beside the bed and worked her skirt down her hips. It pooled on the floor next to her lacy camisole.

She finally freed him of his T-shirt, pulled at the snaps on his Levi's, and slid a hand beneath the waistband, closing her fingers around his arousal. He was rock hard. The tip was round and smooth. She found a bead of moisture and brought it to her mouth, tasting, wanting more.

He made a groaning sound before hooking his thumbs into his belt loops and shoving his jeans down just over his hips. Before stepping out of them, he pulled a condom from a back pocket and slipped it on with practiced efficiency.

He tumbled her back across the white-covered mattress, falling across her, pinning her arms above her head with one hand. He took his other hand and slipped two fingers up and into the folds of her wetness, stretching her.

She made a small, helpless sound, drowning in the sensation.

Then, very carefully, he slid her legs up and over his shoulders.

She winced with momentary pain before he said, "Fuck me, you're flexible," and drove in deep.

She gave a sharp cry. "Alex. Oh, God!"

He gave her a swift thrust and then withdrew, almost completely, before sinking into her and plunging deeper.

She arched her neck. Her head thrashed on the pillow. She called his name, over and over.

He captured her mouth with his, quieting her screams as his thrusts grew deeper, filling her beyond need.

His hands found hers to lace their fingers together, and then he buried his face in her hair while continuing to hammer into her.

She felt him go so far up, she cried out in pain. "Alex," she shouted as pleasure speared through her.

His breathing came in hard pants. "Come with me," he groaned, continuing to drive into her—hard—again and again.

"Alex … oh God, Alex, yes. Oh yes!" She was so wet, she felt ready to overflow. She squeezed him tight. Her muscles pulsed and constricted around him. The walls of her body milked him.

And then … the sensation slid through her in rolling waves.

Alex was breathing hard, his hair clinging to his face with sweat.

Moments later, he rolled onto his side and propped himself on an elbow to look down at her. His dark eyes glittered, sending a shiver through her.

"That was awesome." He trailed a finger down her throat and touched the tips of her breasts.

Her nipples hardened instantly at his contact. "You're telling me."

"How about a cold beer? I could sure use one."

"Why not?" She lounged in the warm afterglow, unconcerned about driving home.

"I'll be right back." Alex winked.

"May I use your restroom?"

"Help yourself." He gestured toward the hallway. "First door on the right."

"Thanks."

Alex threw on his jeans and disappeared from the bedroom.

Monet pulled on her skirt and top and headed down the hall. Inside the restroom, she sorted through her thoughts. Was she in love with Alex? Whatever it was, the sex was way over the top. If they kept seeing each other, maybe it would become totally serious. No need to worry about the future. Just enjoy the moment.

Then, when she least expected it, thoughts of Jay moved through her mind. He was the kind of man a woman could easily fall in love with—attractive, caring, and honest. There was just something about him that she couldn't explain.

She splashed cold water on her face to wash away her ridiculousness.

When she found the coziness of Alex's bed again, she slid out of her clothes and realized it was just what she needed to keep her mind out of trouble.

A few seconds later, Alex appeared and handed her a bottle of Corona Extra. "It's nice and cold."

She took the bottle. "Thanks," she said after a sip, and sat back against the headboard.

Alex stripped off his jeans and climbed in beside her. "Hey." He clicked his bottle to hers.

"Hey," she said, pulling the sheet up around her. He was sexy. There was no doubt about it. His hard body caused her eyes to linger. "That was incredible." She nuzzled up against his chest.

He grinned, his teeth gleaming white in the shadow-lined room. "So, stay with me tonight."

She took another swallow from her bottle. "I'd like to get a few hours' sleep my first night at my new place."

"Monet, we don't have to answer to anyone."

"You know, you're right."

"I'll set the alarm. Six sound okay?"

"Well, sure, why not."

"If we're lucky, we can catch a couple hours of sleep. You won't regret it."

"I believe you. Besides, I don't think I should be drinking if I'm planning on driving home, right?"

He smiled. "Right."

"So, how about we find a good movie to watch?"

"Sure," Alex said as he grabbed the remote off the nightstand beside him.

He flicked on the television. Kevin Costner and Madeleine Stowe filled the screen in what appeared to be a cabin. They looked carefree and in love.

This might be good, Monet thought. She rested her hip against Alex's thigh.

He draped his arm around her shoulder, pulling her closer into him. "I've seen this. The part coming up is pretty intense."

She focused on the TV, sitting on a woodgrain dresser across from the bed. "I don't think I've seen it."

"Watch," he said.

Suddenly, a dog barked, then men stormed into the cabin, shot the dog, and beat up Kevin Costner.

A chill went down Monet's spine.

Alex's arm tightened around her shoulder.

She nestled in closer to him, unable to take her eyes from the screen.

Some men made Kevin watch while an older man held Madeleine and said, "Faithless whore" and slapped her, all while Kevin is getting beat up, more. Madeleine screams, "No!" The man says, "Pick him up. I want you to see what happens to whores." The same man says some more obscenities to Madeleine and slashes her face with a knife.

Monet's stomach turned. "That's horrible." She drew closer yet to Alex. "Does it get better? How does it turn out?"

"You want to see it?"

"I'd rather you just tell me."

"Okay, then we can concentrate on each other."

"Sounds good." Monet smiled in relief.

Alex clicked off the TV and explained the rest of the movie to Monet. "Madeleine's husband, the man who slashed her face, put her in a whorehouse where they forced drugs on her. Kevin searched for her, and at the end, found her very sick in a convent and she died in his arms."

"Wow." Monet shook her head, as if absorbing it all, something that wasn't easily forgotten.

As darkness closed around them, except for the light spilling in through the blinds, Monet couldn't seem to shake thoughts of the movie, bringing her to the conclusion that if you played with fire, eventually you got burned.

Chapter Twelve

As Jay dropped his daily report and truck trip tickets on Ruby's desk after another long day of hauling logs, an image of Monet's bare leg glimmering against her silky skirt stirred him. Not for the first time, he shoved the sultry memory to a far corner of his mind.

Then he saw last month's bank statement and did a double take. The ending balance couldn't be right. It seemed too low. He knew how much he grossed in a month. Could this be a bank mistake? He looked again, his gaze blurred by rising anger. Could Ruby be helping herself to the company's money? And if so, how long had this been going on?

A feeling of betrayal washed over him. He should have left the bookkeeping to his accountant, but Ruby had insisted on handling it. She said she wanted to help, so his accountant had shown her how to do the simpler tasks, and she'd been taking bookkeeping classes at night.

Jay had given her everything she wanted, hoping to make her happy. His heart felt trampled by Ruby's betrayal. This wasn't how a marriage should work.

Outraged, he threw the papers back down on her desk, a few gliding to the floor. He'd get a hold of her and get to the bottom of this.

He whirled around to head out and caught her standing in the open doorway, her perfect body encased in a tight, strapless dress, her face awash with surprise.

"Jay, I … I didn't know you were home yet," she stuttered. "I was just going to do some work. I won't be long." She gave her hair a toss.

"In that?" Jay said, gesturing to her cleavage spilling out of the dress. "Comfortable working clothes, huh, Ruby?"

She huffed. "I feel better when I look good."

"Yeah, right," Jay said, running a hand through his hair. "Whatever you say."

"You know I look good. Don't deny it."

Ruby's arrogance fueled his temper. He grabbed the statement off the desk and shoved it in her face. "How can this bank statement be right? Even with our high operating costs, we're still thousands of dollars short." In two steps, he closed the distance between them, fighting the urge to shake the truth out of her.

"It must just be a mistake," she said with a shrug of her shoulders.

"Don't play me for a fool," he said through clenched teeth. "Are you skimming money?" If she was, this marriage was over.

"No, of course not. Don't be silly." She chuckled. "Do you think I'd do that? I was just getting last week's deposits ready for the bank so I could do the payroll and—"

"Try and take a few thousand more for yourself?" He cut her off. "Add it to your paycheck, thinking I'd never know the difference? You lying ..." He reeled in a number of obscenities.

"No, Jay, I promise." Ruby looked helplessly toward the desk. "It's not like that. There must have been an oversight or a bookkeeping mistake. I'm sure it's nothing that can't be fixed." Her voice trembled. "Please, just give me a chance."

"You already took that chance and blew it." Tension angled his shoulders. "I'll have the accountant take over, and don't think for a second that you can get away with anything. I expect you to have it all cleaned up by tomorrow, or you'll be going over divorce papers. I mean it, Ruby." He stormed past her, into the house, and straight to the bedroom.

"Damn her," he cursed under his breath. "What did she think she was doing?"

Jay took a quick shower, hoping to wash away some anger and confusion. What to do? In the midst of all this, he found himself thinking of Monet. This unsettled him. What was it about her? The mysterious, complex wall surrounding her tempted him to tear it down. He sensed that she yearned for love and passion. He suspected that Alex would move on when he tired of her and that their relationship was casual, not serious.

Why in the hell was he even thinking thoughts that could only lead to trouble?

Jay pulled himself together and entered the kitchen to find Ruby sitting at the table with a glass of wine. His gaze didn't linger on the plump curve of her breasts. The sight of her only brought the bank statement to mind. Why would she steal from him?

Ruby crossed her arms, giving her breasts an unneeded boost. "What can I fix you? Anything you want."

As she got to her feet, Jay prayed she kept her distance. "I don't need you to fix me anything. I'll just grab a beer from the fridge." He pulled his gaze away from her. The silk of Ruby's dress clung to her creamy thighs. Unfazed, he just wanted to be alone, especially after a day like today when one of the log loaders blew a hydraulic hose and screwed him out of a load, bringing him home early. If he could come home to someone he could trust, he'd feel differently.

Ruby planted herself in front of the fridge before he could open it. With a mixture of exhaustion and sadness, he asked, "What do you think you're doing?"

"Oh, come on, Jay. I can make you feel lots better. Give me a chance."

He shook his head. "Get out of my way."

"Please," she pleaded. "Let me show you how much I love you."

"It's a little late for that."

"I'm sure you don't mean that." She gazed up at him through her lashes.

Forcing her out of his way, Jay opened the fridge. "It won't work this time, Ruby," he said as he grabbed a beer.

She blinked rapidly. "You never turn me down."

After opening his beer, he took a sip. It felt smooth going down. Maybe it would ease the tension that kinked his back and shoulders. Seized by frustration, his mind fought for the perfect solution but came up short.

Ruby nuzzled up against him, rubbing her cheek against his. "All I can think about is how much I want you."

"Not now, Ruby." He stepped away, running both hands through his damp hair. "If you needed extra money for something, we could have talked about it. Did you really take it for yourself?"

In a high-screeched voice, she wailed, "No. How many times do I have to tell you?"

His heart wanted to believe her, but somehow his mind knew better. He had a hunch it wasn't a bank mistake. "I've heard enough," he said and left the room.

Beer in hand, he headed toward the office. Jay knew he was being followed. The heels of Ruby's pumps snapped against the tile floor.

Once inside the office, he slammed the door before she could enter.

"Fine," she snarled from the other side of the door.

Jay slid into the leather office chair and thought back on his marriage. He'd been in love with Ruby when he'd married her. Now he wondered. He grabbed his beer, as if for moral support, and took a long, steady drink while scouring over some of the paperwork in front of him. Not usually his job, Ruby had forced it on him.

Two hours later, after figuring out what the payroll would add up to for this pay period, he slipped from the office and headed back into the house, hopefully to get some sleep.

Sleep was impossible, so he mentally mapped a plan of action. First, he would make Ruby return every dollar taken, then he'd have his accountant take over his bookkeeping. And as for his marriage, he'd try damn hard to save it.

When Jay felt Ruby slip into bed beside him, he glanced at the clock. He'd only been in bed for an hour. He longed for the buzz of the alarm so he could go to work and be in the woods, close to nature, taking in the scent of trees and the remote stillness of the air, a dream compared to the problem at home.

At five o'clock in the morning, Jay turned his truck onto the gravel road that led to their current jobsite. He crawled for the next ten miles to the landing. About halfway there, Alex called on the CB radio.

"Hey, boss, you go any slower and we won't be able to get our two loads today. I'm right on your ass."

"I'll pull over in a wide spot and let you pass. You can load first today."

"All right," Alex said.

Jay waved as Alex rolled by, then he followed him up to the landing, backing into a turnaround to wait for Alex to get loaded.

Jay got out of his truck and watched Alex's truck being loaded with hemlock logs from a pile neatly sorted beside the machine. He heard his other log loader with Gary at the controls, swinging trees into the landing site.

He thought about his work to push Ruby farther from his mind. Jay watched a feller buncher fall the trees while a processor mechanically limbed, measured, and sawed them off to the proper lengths. His was a totally mechanized logging system without chain saws, and with all the rules and regulations governing timber harvesting these days, it proved to be an environmentally friendly method.

After Alex pulled out, Jay backed in for the same process.

"See you in a while, boss," Alex said on the CB.

"Yeah, okay," he told Alex. He sat in his truck and filled out a trip ticket to PLS, a log-sorting yard in Everett where the load would be hauled. He glanced at the onboard scales in his truck. "Thanks, Mike. That's a load." Eighty-eight thousand pounds was the gross weight he could legally haul.

Jay pulled ahead, stepped out of his truck, and stamped the

logs with a branding hammer. Then he tossed his wrappers over the load and put binders on to secure it.

After the leisurely pace on gravel, he met blacktop and headed toward the freeway, which provided a straight shot to Everett. Somehow, he couldn't seem to shake Ruby from his thoughts. He'd believed in her, trusted her, and she'd taken advantage of him.

Jay turned into the log-sorting yard and passed by the trailer loader as Alex was loading his trailer onto the back of his truck.

Alex held the remote control in one hand as he gave Jay a wave with the other.

Jay nodded back and pulled into the unload area. A log stacker drove up and clamped on to his load to secure it, then he grabbed his binders and wrappers to remove them. The log stacker lifted off the load, and he moved ahead to load his trailer.

Still at the trailer loader, cleaning bark off his trailer, Alex asked, "Do you need any extra trucks tomorrow?"

"Possibly." At times, Jay used up to six hired log trucks.

"I heard some drivers talking on the CB, and a few of them were looking for a place to haul. I guess it's slow on their job."

"You'll have to let them know later after we see what the crew has accomplished."

"Ten-four."

Alex, as truck boss, was great. He lined up extra trucks

when they were needed, especially now when Jay's focus was somewhere else.

Jay headed out of the yard behind Alex, letting the flow of CB chatter wash over him. Alex, as usual, couldn't keep his mouth shut.

"Hey, boss, seems like you could use a little break. If you want to take some time off, there's plenty of available trucks to fill in for you. Maybe take the wife someplace nice."

At the thought of Ruby, Jay fought his rising temper. Did Alex suspect he was having personal problems? "I'll give it some thought," he said.

By the end of the day, Jay came up with a decision. No time off, other than to move equipment. He needed work right now to keep his sanity intact.

Back home, after a shower, he was ready to relax. He grabbed a beer from the fridge and settled at the kitchen table to wait for Ruby.

"Drowning your troubles?"

Ruby's voice set his nerves on edge.

He angled around in his chair. She stood there in a clingy, thin-strapped dress with a slit in front that showed bare leg. No shiver of awareness shot down his spine. No red-hot flame burned with need in his loins. He felt nothing as he looked at her made-up face. Her lids were shadowed in greens and blues. Black mascara coated her lashes. Her lips were painted a deep, shiny red.

Ruby stepped closer to him, closing the distance between them. He got a whiff of her warm, oriental-flowered fragrance.

She snatched the beer bottle from Jay's hand, took a sloppy drink, and handed it back to him. "I asked if you were drowning your troubles."

"No, I was enjoying a beer." He set it on the counter, as if she'd tainted it.

"Yeah, right."

"Look who's talking?" His patience with her was wearing thin.

"I'll pretend you didn't say that because now we're even. Let's enjoy a drink together. I'll pour myself some wine, and we can go out in the living room and talk." Ruby inched closer until their bodies touched.

Jay flinched from the contact. "That's where I'll be."

"You know," Ruby said coolly, "I'm suddenly not feeling social. I'll drink my wine in the kitchen. That way, I'm close to a refill. I don't care what you do. It's obvious you're not in the mood to talk to me."

Jay slipped from the kitchen and wondered how they were going to work things out. He knew one thing—he wasn't falling for her sexual innuendoes, and he also wasn't in the mood to talk to her. That's one thing she hadn't lied about.

Chapter Thirteen

At the knock on the door, Monet crossed from the kitchen to answer it.

"Hi, Mom," she said, and moved aside to let her mother in. "You found it okay."

Her mother stepped inside. "Yeah, great directions, and I love the area. I've always liked Capitol Hill. It's funky, different. It makes me feel as if I fit in."

Monet was about to ask her about moving to the area when she thought better of it. "It's nice to see you. You look good."

Her mother busied her hands, arranging her brown, silk pants and matching blouse. "Well, thanks. You do, too," she said, fingering a strand of gold chains around her neck. She looked elegant, nicely attired. Her shoulder-length, sandy-colored hair read beauty salon styled.

What had happened? Monet thought, feeling frumpy in

comparison in low-rise jeans, designer T-shirt, and wild hair pulled up into a messy topknot with trailing tendrils. "Like some coffee? I just made it," she said around the rich aroma of Irish Crème scenting the air.

"Sure." Her mother bent down to greet Dixie Cup at her feet. "How's he adjusting?"

"Good, actually. Better than I thought."

"Now what all did you say you had planned today?" her mother asked.

"I'm going to see about a job teaching aerobics, and from there, hopefully make a deal on a car. Then I'm meeting Cameo at a favorite steak house of ours before work at four thirty."

"Wow. Sounds like you'll be busy. I won't take too much of your time."

Monet sensed that her mother felt uneasy. "Don't worry, Mom, you're fine. I have time for you."

Lucy checked her watch. "I suppose."

"Go ahead and have a seat on the couch. I'll be right there," Monet said as she started for the kitchen to fetch coffee.

Her mother's voice stopped her. "Thanks for letting me stop by and see your new place."

"I'm glad you wanted to."

"The colors remind me of something I used to get for you at Eastertime."

M&M-like candies jogged her memory. Monet glanced

at the dining room's dusty shade of pink, the living room's pale green, and caught a glimpse of the yellow kitchen's light-blue, tile countertops.

"What's that?" Monet asked, even though she knew the answer.

"Remember Reese's Pieces Pastel Eggs?"

"How could I forget?" she said and disappeared from her mother's view and into the kitchen. She leaned back against the wall, wondering if she was ready for this … ready to remember all of the nice, little things her mother had done for her and forget the rest. She willed herself to keep it together for her mother's sake as well as her own, found a deep, calming breath, and poured them some coffee.

She returned to the living room with two steaming mugs, handed her mother one, and settled in on the couch a few feet away from her. "You look happy, Mom. This guy must be working out for you. What's his name?"

"Ryan." Lucy smiled and looked down at her hand, clenching the cup. "He's the best thing that's happened to me in a long time."

"That's great." Curiosity aroused, she had to wonder where her greedy, selfish mother was. Sitting beside her was who she remembered on the rare nights when they shared a meal or played a board game. "So, what did you want to talk with me about?"

A troubled look crossed Lucy's brow. "I need some money

to get clothes for the trip. I'll pay you back when I get my paycheck in a week."

"Oh? I thought maybe today would be different," Monet said, edging toward impatience. "Apparently, I was wrong." The money was between them again, the greed that bound them together. "I'm sorry. I don't know what to say."

Lucy sipped her coffee. "Monet, it's not what you think. I know you're changing your life. Well, I am, too. When I get my next paycheck, I promise I'll pay you back. I mean it this time."

It was only money, and Monet didn't want to isolate herself from her mother. She was all she had. It wasn't worth risking this chance with her mother, and deep down, Monet sensed she'd changed.

"I'll do it one more time," Monet said, "but I want something in return." She watched her mother try to smile. "I want to know all about your job, I want to know your plans for the future … and I want to know about Dad."

Lucy paused, hesitant. "Where do I start?"

"Wherever you'd like."

Lucy drew in a deep breath. "The convenience store cashier job is just temporary until I can do what I really want."

"Which is what?" Monet sipped her cooled coffee.

"Do you remember back when you were, oh, say about fifteen, and I told you I'd love to have my own bakery someday?"

Monet's mind did a quick scan. Nothing came up. "No," she said softly.

"Well, I've had this dream about opening my own bakery and making everything myself."

"Mom, that's so neat," Monet said with enthusiasm.

"I think so, too. You know, it's never too late to change your life, and I got to thinking that if Ryan and I work out, maybe he could help me get started."

"You're right, Mom, it's never too late. Look at me. I haven't done much with my life, either. I mean, I'm just starting to change it. I'd love to have my own interior design business someday, have a family of my own, but … I want to hear more about you."

"I think I'm happy right now. It's easy to tell because I haven't been in a long time."

A flood of emotion swamped Monet. She cradled her coffee mug in her hands. "I'm sorry, Mom."

"It's not your fault."

Monet suddenly felt as though she'd failed her. Giving her money couldn't replace loneliness. She got up, went to the window, and stared out at the sunlit street of Tenth Avenue. "If only we'd spent more time together over the years. And if you weren't happy, we could have figured something out."

"Monet, I never gave you a chance to talk. I never listened. All I thought about was myself and paying my rent. Don't blame yourself, blame me."

"I don't have to blame anyone." Monet angled around

and wandered back to the couch. She longed to reach out and lay a hand over her mother's. "Tell me about Dad," she said instead.

"We were young." Lucy tipped her cup to her lips. "Your dad was very independent and didn't want to be tied down. I felt like ..." She stumbled over the words as her eyes misted.

Monet's chest tightened with sympathy. "Go on."

"I didn't want to feel anything. The pain of your father leaving was huge, so I started drinking more and more to forget about him, someone I truly loved and wanted to share a lifetime with. It hurt like nothing else, but the drinking only made things worse. I knew I'd be a stronger person if I could just let him go, but somehow"—she looked away, thoughtful—"it always haunts me, and I regret not trying harder ... for you."

Tears stung Monet's eyes. "It's not your fault," she said, meaning it.

"I regret not being there for you. I was lonely, angry, and pissed off at the world. None of that was your fault, but I couldn't change. When I got pregnant, it scared your father away, and I got to thinking, what if ... what if I'd gotten rid of you? Would he and I still be together? And then I hate myself for thinking such a thing."

Monet stared at her mother, blinking slowly. Her feelings ran over each other. "Don't."

"If you're wondering why I'm different, it's because I've stayed off the booze for a few days."

"Good for you," Monet said with encouragement.

"It's tough, but overall, I feel better."

"I'm proud of you."

"There's something else. It's not just about giving up the bottle for a few days. God knows that's nothing, anyway. And it's not just about finding someone I feel is special." She drew in a deep breath. "I've been seeing a psychiatrist, taking medication to help me deal with ... well, everything. I'm figuring things out, one step at a time. And if it's okay with you, I'd like to see you more often, like this, but not just for you to pay my rent or loan me money. I want to share a cup of coffee, or a meal, or go shopping and talk about the men in our lives. And speaking of that, you'll have to tell me all about how you and that truck driver are doing when I get back from Victoria." She flicked a glance at her watch. "I'd better let you get ready for your day."

Monet couldn't look away. Her mother had confided in her. She grasped the pleasant feeling and held on. "Well, Mom, it sounds as if you'd better keep right on doing what you're doing. And of course, I'd like to see you more often. Just remember this—you're worth it. And you'd better hold on to Ryan. He could probably help you in more ways than you know."

"I think you're right."

Monet smiled. "This has been nice."

"I agree. We will do it more often."

"I'd like that." Monet got up to get her purse. She drew

her checkbook out, wrote her mother out a check, and slid it into her hand.

"Monet, I really appreciate this. I promise—"

She cut her mother's words short. "I believe you."

Her mother rose to leave. "Well, good luck with the aerobics teaching job and making a deal on a car."

"You know"—Monet couldn't help sharing—"a part of me wants to just keep everything the same ... just dance and only dance, keep my Lexus ... and that's part of the reason I think I stayed with Shane. I'm scared of change, Mom."

Her mother smiled knowingly. "Me, too. It was easier on me not to deal with reality, not face responsibilities, to never change or do anything with my life, but now I see a light at the end of the tunnel. You will, too."

After her mother left, the thought of building a relationship with her warmed Monet. It sounded as though, because of Ryan, her mother was willing to accept help in order to begin healing from her painful past.

After a successful visit to the health club and car dealer, Monet walked into the steak house later that afternoon. She spoke to the hostess, who led her to Cameo, sitting at a table in a corner.

"Hey." Cameo acknowledged her. "Were you able to pick up some work at the health club?"

Monet slipped in across from her. "I'll be teaching four aerobics classes a week. They were actually short on aerobics instructors and personal trainers."

"That's great. I should get my personal trainer certification. We could work there together," Cameo said.

"You could have it in six months through American Council on Exercise's home study program."

"Yeah, but I'm afraid I'd hate having to study when all I have to do now is look good and not have to think."

On a laugh, Monet said, "Just something to keep in mind."

Cameo shook her head. "Hey, what are you driving? I'm dying to know. You know how materialistic 'we' exotic dancers are."

"I did it," Monet said without enthusiasm. "I actually traded down. Can you believe it?"

"For what?"

"A used Acura Integra."

"How on earth did you manage that?"

"The dealer who had the Acura took my Lexus in on consignment and will sell it for me, then treat it like a trade so I won't have to pay sales tax. I paid my Lexus off with a credit card, and when it sells, I'll pay that off."

"I can tell it wasn't easy on you."

Monet sighed. "It wasn't, but hey, enough of that. Besides, if I have my own interior design business someday, I can easily replace it."

"There you go," Cameo said when the waitress appeared at their table.

After they each ordered 7UP and the salad bar, Cameo slid from her seat. "Let's go dish up."

"I'm right behind you," Monet said.

Minutes later, they returned to the table with a variety of vegetables, shredded cheese, plenty of olives, and French dressing. Their sodas had arrived while they were gone.

Before digging in, Cameo clinked her glass against Monet's. "Here's to you making some changes and moving in the right direction."

"I hope so."

Cameo leaned toward her. "Okay, let's talk about sex. I want to hear about Alex and last night."

Monet smiled. "He's so good."

"Elaborate." Cameo plopped a cherry tomato into her mouth.

Voice lowered, Monet said, "He put my legs over his shoulders … and you can imagine the rest."

"That's deep," Cameo said as a waiter hurried by. "Does he do the in-and-out thing? You know, how some guys slide all the way out, and then back in, sinking deeper every time?"

"Oh God, yes, does he ever. Alex is like a drug … the sex, I mean. It helps me forget."

"Forget what?"

"Jay."

"Well, keep taking him."

Over the next half hour, their conversation drifted to the usual stuff at work and Cameo's day at Pike Place Market with Tyrese.

In between talking and eating, Monet took in the

restaurant's burgundy-and-brown color scheme, as well as an old-time sawmill picture with some workers posing on a deck of logs laying in disarray and scattered like spilled matchsticks.

This reminded her of Jay ... how time became meaningless when she was near him, how just the subtle contact of his skin against hers sparked an inferno of desire. Her throat caught. She put the differences in her feelings for Alex and Jay into completely different categories.

The waitress returned, set two glasses of 7UP down on the table, and picked up the empties.

"So, how did it go with your mom?" Cameo asked when they'd finished with their salads.

Monet spoke of her mother's visit at her apartment earlier.

"I think it's the neatest thing, you and your mom finally making a connection."

"It's a nice feeling." Monet sipped her 7UP. "She's like a completely different person, now that she's quit drinking and is seeing a psychiatrist. And I know that Ryan has been a big help in all of this, not to mention, he's given her hope in men again."

"What did she say about your dad?"

"That he was very independent and didn't want to be tied down, so he just disappeared."

"How do you feel about that?"

Monet blew out a breath. "Angry that he avoided his responsibility, but maybe I'll be able to let it go as my mom and I build our relationship. Maybe then I won't feel like I need him so much, and I'll also be able to forgive what he did—just forget and move on. I don't like placing blame on people."

"But he's your father. You have a right to blame him."

"I resent what he did, but I'll never know who he is. I have to be able to accept that and go on with my life."

"And I have a feeling you'll do just fine." Cameo reached across the table and closed a hand over Monet's.

Later that night after work, Monet headed to Alex's. He wanted her. She wanted him. And he satiated her need for sex.

The second she stepped through his door, he claimed her mouth with his, slipping his tongue between her parted lips. Her tongue slid sinuously against his as he plunged his deeper into her mouth. The kiss, hot and wet, drove Monet wild.

A moan drifted up from her throat. She tangled her hands into his hair and pulled, growing dizzy as he pressed his hardness into her stomach. She arched against him. He grabbed a hold of her hair and jerked her head back.

Monet gasped. "Alex."

Seconds later, their clothes pooled at their feet.

"I'm going to make you ride me so hard it hurts," he said roughly against her face, "while I'm buried in this." He slipped a finger deep into her wet heat.

Her delicate muscles clenched around him. She was hot and moist, her body screaming in mad desire.

When he inserted two fingers, she said in a silken whisper, "Alex, don't stop."

He pressed his fingers deeper, probing, stretching her tiny, hot core, inch by inch, and then he slid them out and let her soak up her own juices. She sucked on his fingers ravenously, like a porn star giving a blow job.

As he pulled her down to the floor with him, right there in the entryway, her cravings burned wild with the urge to consume him—all of him—and then she straddled him and threw her mane of hair behind her, much like her bounce on stage in her floor show.

He grabbed her tiny waist, and not gently, lifted her slightly up and then plowed into her.

"Ride me fast, hard, deep. I know that's how you want it," he groaned. He lifted her up again and, showing no mercy, slammed her down and onto him.

"Alex," she cried out as her tightness adjusted to his size. She tossed her head all around in wild abandon and began to move on him, faster.

He held her hard with his hands, driving her deeper, thrusting her down on him, harder. Her body pulsed and throbbed with need as she soaked him up and worked her hips, faster, harder, taking more of him as he continued to drive her into him, deeper each time, stretching her to the hilt.

When she didn't think she could take any more, he lifted her and inched out of her. Her breath caught, and then he set her down on him, slowly, to slide in and out, in and out, again and again, his hands guiding her waist, his hips matching her rhythm. Gradually, he started moving her faster again until her body swallowed every bit of him.

"Alex, please," she begged, feeling a mixture of pleasure and pain. He strained her, stretched her, filled her to bursting before inching out one last time and then slamming her down onto him until they both erupted into a liquid fire of shattering release.

She savored every last tingling sensation in her body before collapsing against his chest.

When both of their bodies relaxed, Alex said into her hair, "That was hot."

"I can't argue," she said and brushed a kiss across his shoulder.

"I could use a beer. How about you?"

Slowly, she slid off of him. "Water sounds better."

"You got it." He rose to his feet and pulled on his boxers. "I'll be right back," he said and disappeared.

Her thoughts trailed Alex. What did she really want from him? She grabbed her clothes and quickly dressed. The sex was magnificent, although she wasn't sure this would last. She realized she needed something more—much more intimacy—and sadly, she didn't feel she and Alex shared that.

When Alex reappeared, he handed her a glass of water. "It's nice and cold."

"Thanks," she said and took a sip.

They retreated to the couch. Alex picked up the remote from the coffee table and channel surfed. He stopped on the speed channel, lit a cigarette, and nearly polished off his Corona in one long pull.

After a little bit of conversation, Monet finished her water and left.

As she headed home, Monet thought more about her mother and her relationship with a man who made her happy. And Jay, and the dead end she saw there, which led her to believe that if she couldn't get him from her mind, she must not be serious about Alex. She wouldn't keep leading him on. It wasn't fair.

Sleep eluded Monet. She plumped her pillow with a fist, tossing and turning, unable to get comfortable. The sheets mingled with her legs as she lay on her back.

Somehow, she must have dozed off. When she glanced at her alarm clock, it was after ten in the morning. Before climbing from bed, she called Alex.

"Alex," she said when he answered, "we need to talk."

"You're wild. I like that about you. It's really cool."

This was going to be harder than she thought.

"Oh, yeah, guess what? Ruby stopped by after you left last night, and after being with you, I couldn't even stand the sight of her."

"She was out late," Monet said.

"That's Ruby. She does as she pleases. I told her to fuck

off. Look, I'm glad you called. How about going to a big birthday bash this weekend at Jay's?"

Monet swallowed. "Whose is it?"

"Gary, a coworker. I want to flaunt you in front of Ruby. Maybe she'll get the message if I bring you over again and she'll leave us alone. She can threaten all she wants, but she's full of it. She's a liar."

"I'd love to go," Monet said, surprising herself.

"Cool. I'll talk to you later in the week."

Monet hung up, unable to believe she was going to see Jay again. Her heart blossomed like a flower. Now she really had to get in perfect shape for this weekend. She wanted to look better than she ever had. And what was she thinking? This was crazy.

The phone rang, drawing her attention. Maybe it was Alex.

"Hello," she answered.

"Bitch, stop seeing him or you'll regret it."

Monet's mood crashed.

The dial tone buzzed in her ear.

How had Ruby gotten this number?

In a rush of rage, Monet stabbed at the sequence of numbers she'd memorized.

Three rings later, Jay answered, "Hello."

The voice caressed her through the phone line. *Why wasn't he at work?* She gently put the receiver in its cradle before another second ticked away.

Sitting up in bed, Monet drew her knees up and cradled

them with her arms. Longing raced through her, along with regret. She should have told Jay what his wife had just done, but she really didn't want to add to his problems.

Chapter Fourteen

All afternoon, Monet lost herself in the upbeat music practicing for her aerobics classes, excited to see Jay again.

So, by the time she got to work that night, she couldn't wait to tell Cameo.

"Alex invited me to a birthday party this weekend at Jay and Ruby's," she told her while they primped before heading out to hustle some table dances. "Should I go?"

"What do you mean should you go? Of course." Cameo's eyes met Monet's in the mirror.

"Even though it's all about sex?"

"Heck, yeah. That's how they all start out. Besides, that's the best kind. Enjoy the ride while it lasts. After the party, give him a hummer driving home. They like that. Then he'll give it to you really good later. Hey, speaking of that, how went last night?"

"Hmm ... he's a nice ride."

"Like an Escalade on twenty-two-inch rims?"

Monet nodded. "Twenty-fours."

"Whoa. Hey, you never know. It could turn into something. Give it time. Quit analyzing. Go. You'll have a great time. I think the more Ruby sees you with him, the better. Maybe she'll eventually get a clue."

"I hope so, but why am I excited about seeing Jay?"

"Because you can't have him."

"We always want what we can't have. Somehow, it makes it more appealing."

"Well, you're going, aren't you?" Cameo pried. "If not, I'll dump Tyrese and go with Alex myself."

"Yeah, right. Don't worry, I'll go, but let's meet at the donut shop later after work."

"You got it."

"It'll be good for Ruby to see Alex and me together."

"In which position?"

"The one last night," Monet joked. "Ruby needs to remember she's married."

"I agree. Alex isn't seeing her anymore, is he?"

"I assume not, but she still threatens me."

"That's Ruby. Never giving up on something she'll never have."

"According to Alex, you're right."

"Come on, let's go make some money," Cameo said, closing her clutch.

Monet smiled. Their job offered instant gratification.

At two thirty in the morning, Monet ordered coffee, a bran muffin, and chose a secluded, bright-orange booth in the back of the donut shop. A pudgy, teenage boy sat at the bar, wolfing down maple bars. It would be so easy to do. She took a bite of her muffin, a sip of her coffee, and glanced at the photos of frosted donuts adorning the walls.

Cameo arrived and ordered before joining Monet. Her hair tumbled around her shoulders in wild disarray. Figure-hugging, white pants, matching heels, and a bright-green halter drew the attention of the teenager. "Hey, what's going on?" she asked, scooting in across from Monet, a white sack and cup in her hands.

"Hey." Monet sipped her coffee. "I know you'll think I'm crazy, but I don't think I should see Alex anymore. After the party, I mean."

Cameo frowned. "Okay, you know what? What's up with that?"

Monet finished her muffin and leaned back against the hard booth. "I don't want to waste his time."

"Sex is never a waste of time," Cameo said as she bit into her Bavarian cream donut.

Monet straightened. "I know but, it's just—"

"Jay," Cameo completed. "Okay, yeah, whatever, but what's wrong with just having sex with Alex? Hey, if you can have an orgasm every time, why stop? Besides, you're not looking to get serious anyway, are you?"

"I didn't think so, until I met Jay." Monet let out a long, slow breath. "It's complicated." She leaned across the table and lowered her voice. "The sex with Alex is fucking awesome, but … I want more than that."

"Wow, you said fucking. You never talk like that. Alex must be getting to you."

"No, Jay is."

Cameo rolled her eyes. "Oh, please, here we go."

"Just listen. I want that emotional bond, that connection. Someone I can share blueberry scones with at a coffee bar down on the waterfront, quiet nights reading novels as the sun sets, and order a flaming dessert after a romantic dinner at the Space Needle." What was happening to her?

"Are you getting all serious and romantic on me?" Cameo arched a brow. "Come on, Monet, we're still young. For now, just enjoy Alex."

"Believe me I have, but—"

"Okay, here's how I see it. For one, you worry too much. Just go with the flow. I do think it's great that you're making changes in your life, but please, enjoy men while you can, before you do get married and tied down with kids."

She didn't seem to want anyone else but Jay, and that worried her because she couldn't have him. "As always, you're right."

"Just think really hard before you let Alex get away. Be smart. Don't do something you'll regret."

Monet sipped the last of her coffee, watching Cameo devour chocolate, deep-fried dough, and Bavarian cream. "I won't."

"You'll be fine then." Cameo crumpled up her napkin. "And don't get into any cat fights with Ruby over her husband."

"Right."

Time ticked away as Monet greeted people filing in for her aerobics class. In between greetings, she took in the aerobics room. It was surrounded on three sides by full-length mirrors across the walls, hardwood floors, and a plush stereo system equipped with a microphoneheadset for the instructor. She caught a glance of herself in the mirror. Her hard work lately showed. Her flat abs and toned appearance in a blue bra top and matching running shorts gave her that extra boost of confidence.

She chatted with a few familiar students. Before getting started, she did a quick sweep of the class. Various colors adorned different shapes. Out of around twenty people, five of them were male and the rest female.

"Hello, I'm Monet. I'm replacing Becky. I worked here about a year ago. Some people I recognize." She smiled specifically at them. "Everyone ready?" Microphone headset in place, she turned around to start the music.

"Okay, here we go." She counted eight beats in her head

to C+C's, "Gonna Make You Sweat." As the song blended into the next, she continued counting. "Okay, two more."

Well into the class, people sweated, straining, gleaming. She enjoyed helping people work to better themselves. After being back, she realized just how much she'd missed it.

When the Saturday of the party finally came, Monet was ready. She was going to see Jay again. Excitement raced through her. She'd chosen a long, black, clingy dress and styled her hair and makeup with extra care.

While she spritzed on her favorite floral fragrance, a knock came at the door.

She breathed in deeply and in strappy heels crossed to answer it.

For just a moment, she imagined doing a private dance for Jay, the sensual kind she did for her customers but longed to do for someone special ... brushing up against them, blowing in their ear, grinding on them.

She opened the door and saw Alex. His diamond earring sparkled against his skin. He wore black dress slacks and matching, designer shirt, a seductive smile in place.

"Wow." She stared. "You're decked."

He took in her body. "You look awesome."

She smiled. "Thank you. Want to come in for a minute?"

"Sure, then we should get going."

Monet stepped aside to let Alex in.

He scanned the townhouse. "Nice place."

"I'd love to have it all to myself, but saving instead of spending makes it tough."

"Is your roommate cool?"

"Yeah, she's great."

"Then enjoy both."

After a quick tour, they headed out and were on their way.

"This should be pretty cool," Alex said, lighting a cigarette. "It's all a big surprise for Gary."

"Sounds like it'll be fun."

"So, are you ready to make Ruby jealous?" he asked, exhaling out the partly open window.

A tremor of nerves rattled through her. "I guess so."

"Good." He flashed a sexy grin.

She wondered how the evening would turn out, torn between the anticipation of seeing Jay again and the dread of seeing Ruby. "So, how's work going?"

"Busy. Jay's got work lined up all summer." Alex leaned over, brushing her bare leg with his hand. "I can't wait 'til later."

"Me, either." She forced a smile. She'd talk to him seriously after the party. Why ruin the evening yet?

Some thirty-five minutes later, Alex parked behind mostly 4x4s and SUVs. Monet's anticipation mounted. They were here.

Before stepping out, Alex took one of her hands and guided it to his crotch. "Just wanted to remind you of what you can look forward to," he said, wiggling his brows.

She felt him through his slacks. He was rock-hard. "Nice," she said before pulling her hand away.

Alex adjusted himself and checked his appearance in the rearview mirror. He ran a hand through his hair, snatched up a sack in the back, and hopped out. Then he helped Monet out.

As they walked to the door, he draped an arm around her waist and pulled her into him. "Let's make the best of it. Then later, we can do each other 'til we can't move," he muttered in her ear.

Before she could answer, Alex stopped, turned into her, and covered her mouth with his.

She kissed him back, unable to draw away.

He broke the kiss, slid his lips over her cheek, and whispered, "I'm still hard."

She swallowed. Why she couldn't just enjoy an awesome sexual relationship with no strings and no commitment, she couldn't quite figure out.

After Alex rang the bell, it wasn't a moment later when she saw the reason.

"Hey, Alex, Monet, come on in," Jay said with a smile.

Jay's voice sparked excitement inside her. She tried to turn off the switch. She shouldn't be having these feelings for a married man, especially when she was out with someone else.

When they stepped inside, Jay's masculine scent pulled her in. She couldn't take her eyes off him, even though dozens of people mingled about in the background. Thick, dark hair was combed back off his forehead. He wore a light-green, linen shirt and tan pants. He looked stunning.

"It's nice to see you again, Monet."

His voice caressed her skin like a lover's touch.

"Nice to see you, too, Jay." Monet angled toward Alex to break eye contact.

"So, where's Gary?" Alex asked.

"He'll be here any minute." Jay's eyes slid to Monet.

"Cool," Alex said. "Hey Mike, how much wood you got sorted for Monday morning?"

"There's a couple of loads ready to go."

Alex slipped away from Monet to talk with Mike.

As she found herself alone with Jay, Monet fiddled with her hands, battling nervousness.

"You look nice." Jay's gaze lingered on her.

She caught her breath. "So do you," she managed, longing to touch his smooth-shaved face.

"Jay," Ruby called out. Her eyes widened when she saw Monet. She whirled to a halt in gold, five-inch, ankle-strap heels. "Oh, there you are." She cut Monet a smile, speaking to Jay.

"Hello, Ruby. You look great as always," Monet said. Ruby's shimmery, gold dress showed more than it covered. No wonder Jay was married to her. With a woman like this, who needed fantasies?

Without a word, Ruby steered her husband into the kitchen.

Alone now, Monet wished she hadn't come. In a weak moment, she hadn't been able to turn down the chance to see Jay.

"Monet," Alex said.

Momentarily, she felt better.

"Come on, let's get you a drink." He grabbed Monet's hand and crossed to the kitchen. He took two Coronas from the fridge, popped the tops, and handed her one.

"Thanks." Monet turned at familiar laughter filling her ears. It was Ruby, giggling at something someone had said, her body all over Jay's. Jealousy crept in. Monet doused it with a chug of Corona.

Even with twenty people crammed into the kitchen, Monet noticed Ruby glaring at her. She slipped an arm around Alex's waist and pulled him closer into her. *Take that*, she thought with a glare back at Ruby.

She and Alex made their way outside to a patio, sinking into well-cushioned lounge chairs surrounding a large, food-filled table. Alex introduced her to a few other couples who sat at the table with them.

"Hey," Alex said as he leaned back, causing the two front legs of his chair to come off the ground. "There are three things that aren't worth shit until they get hard." He took a swig of his beer and tossed Monet a wink. "Ice and cement are the first two, and I've never had a problem with the third," he finished on a laugh.

Monet and the others joined in on the laughter. She had to agree. Alex certainly didn't have a problem in that area.

"Okay, here's another one," he said.

As Ruby and Jay joined them, Monet's heartbeat tripled.

"How do you make your sex sizzle on vacation?" He drilled Ruby with a look. "Leave your wife at home."

Everyone fell into laughter.

Monet glanced at Ruby. Anger rolled off her like steam. Jay's chuckle diminished fast. Monet couldn't stop grinning. Ruby shot Jay a glare.

"Anyone for another drink?" she asked bitterly.

Nobody replied.

Ruby hustled back inside.

As Monet listened to the flow of conversation, she took in the elaborate blend of shrubs and small trees.

When Gary and his wife arrived, the party was well underway.

Suddenly, Monet found herself alone in the kitchen with Jay. She scrambled to come up with something to say. "This all looks incredible," she said, her attention on him. As soon as it came out, she hoped Jay would think she meant the food.

Fresh, colorful fruit mixtures adorned the counter. Elegant vegetable trays were filled with fancy garnishes, meats, cheeses, breads, and an assortment of crackers. Hot food, including BBQ wings, roast beef, and ham, as well as a dessert tray, consisting of various fruit tarts, mini-éclairs, and cream puffs, completed the vast menu.

Her mouth watered, but it wasn't just the food.

She looked into Jay's eyes. Time stilled.

Monet swallowed hard. "Great party."

"Thanks. It was catered."

She imagined her fingers running through his slicked-back hair. "All the food looks so good." Need made her cheeks heat. This was so wrong yet felt so right.

"Have some."

His deep voice sent electrical currents through her. "I think I will." Being this close to him fogged up her mind.

He handed her a plate, lightly brushing her hand with his.

The touch seemed surreal, as if she were in the midst of a dream.

"So, how're things going with you?" he asked.

"Good, actually. Busy, though. I returned to teaching aerobics classes, too."

"How's that working out?" He dished up red grapes, honeydew, and slices of Havarti cheese with Ritz crackers.

"Pretty well." Monet picked up cantaloupe and watermelon wedges with tongs and set them on her plate. Her hand nearly brushed Jay's side. Awareness shot through her. "It forces me to stay in shape."

"That's great."

"Hopefully, I can keep it up."

"How're you and Alex getting along?"

"Just fine."

"Can I fix you a mixed drink?" His blue eyes held hers.

Lost in the depth of his gaze, she whispered, "Sure."

Monet followed Jay to the garage, unable to keep her eyes off his broad shoulders, small waist, and great butt through tan slacks.

In the garage, she noticed a keg and oversize table full of various pints, fifths, and mixers.

A clearly buzzed young man raised his drink. "This is great out here. Nice variety. Just wouldn't want to spill on the wife's Corvette."

"Yeah, why do you think I moved my pickup to the shop for the night?" He turned to Monet and asked, "What would you like?"

She shivered. "I'll have whatever you're having." Her heart beat too quickly. At this rate, she wouldn't make it through the night without acting like a fool.

* * *

Jay mixed Crown Royal and Sprite into two cups. "Hope it's all right." His fingers graced her hand as he handed her the drink, his eyes never leaving hers. Delight tumbled through him. He found her intriguing. Seeing her bare legs in the black, silk dress and strappy heels led his thoughts to slowly undressing her.

"I'm sure it will be."

Her soft voice caressed his ears. He gulped his drink, letting the fiery liquid slide down his throat. "Sure it's not too strong?" he asked Monet.

"No, it's great."

Jay's attention wandered to Ruby. She strutted into the garage, stealing everyone's attention. His wife was sexy. He couldn't deny that. Cleavage poured out of a body-hugging dress, leaving very little to the imagination. He almost wished he'd told her to wear something different. Right now, he felt like his wife was on display. However, being a hypocrite wasn't his style. She'd dressed like this when she'd met him. He certainly hadn't had a problem with it then.

"Well, here's where the party's at." Ruby stopped and planted a hand on her hip.

The garage fell silent.

"Monet," she said with distaste, "Alex is still outside."

"Thanks, I'll join him. I was just getting a drink. By the way, your husband makes a fabulous one, but I'll take Alex another Corona. It's his favorite." Monet smiled and left.

Ruby flashed Monet a warning look. "Nobody better be messing with my car," she said to everyone else. With a twitch of her hips, she crossed to her red Corvette.

Jay drew in a deep breath. "Nobody's even close." He watched Ruby fix herself a straight Yukon Jack. She usually drank wine. She'd be on her lips before long, and he didn't look forward to that.

"Hey, I think Gary's really enjoying himself. We did a fabulous job, didn't we, Jay?" She sidled up to him and wrapped herself around him like a present.

"Yeah," he managed, and pried himself from Ruby to

empty his cup. "Where's Gary?" he asked her. "I suppose we should cut the cake pretty soon."

Ruby swallowed up any distance between them and threw an arm around him. "I think he's in the living room."

"Why don't you go get him?" he inquired in a polite tone.

Ruby eyed him quizzically. "Trying to get rid of me?"

Jay dropped a kiss on her cheek. "Of course not."

She was his wife—at least for now.

* * *

Ruby wanted to kill Monet. What was she doing out here with Jay, anyway? Hadn't the bitch heard a word she'd said? She'd threatened Monet until she was tired of it herself. Shit!

When Jay told her Alex was bringing Monet, she'd checked it with Alex. He'd told her to get screwed, but not by him. When Ruby found Monet out in the garage with Jay, she'd nearly choked on outrage. Monet was pushing her to her limit … a limit that scared even Ruby.

Ruby needed a new plan of attack.

Chapter Fifteen

"Great party," Alex told Jay. "I think Gary was actually surprised." He slipped an arm around Monet as they made their way to the door.

Jay pulled the door open for them. "I think you're right."

"You leaving?" Ruby intercepted them, her eyes sliding from Alex to Monet, then back to Alex.

Alex stopped at the door, Monet at his side. "Yeah, I guess we'll call it a night."

"Thank you so much for everything." Monet's eyes danced to Jay's. "It really was a wonderful party." She couldn't seem to pull them away.

"Glad you could come," Jay returned, his voice husky.

"Yeah." She smiled. "Me, too."

"Yes," Ruby said sweetly. "Nice to see you again, Monet."

Monet and Jay exchanged a brief smile. Her smile faded when she saw the challenge in Ruby's eyes.

"We'll see you two later." Jay wrapped an arm around Ruby's waist, pulling her close.

"Hey Jay," someone called.

He held up a finger. "Excuse me."

"It's okay, Jay," Alex said. "We're leaving. Thanks again."

After Jay disappeared, Monet possessively slid a hand across Alex's stomach.

Ruby's face worked furiously. "We'll be seeing each other again."

Monet felt the weight of her stare. "Possibly."

Once outside, Alex turned to Monet as they made their way to his Bronco. "She was pretty fired up."

"More like drunk. By the way, nice stomach," Monet complimented him.

Alex winked. "That's what they all say."

Monet grinned and shook her head. Alex was too self-centered for her, and the previous men in her life weren't. The more she was around him, the more he just didn't seem like a long-term kind of guy. When she'd met Alex, what had she expected? A diversion, a fling, a great lover? Well, he'd definitely been all of those, plus funny, sexy as hell, and in need of a little help. So, what was her problem? And why end a good, no-strings kind of relationship? Because the more she saw Jay, the more she felt like she wanted more, not to mention, just *him*.

Her thoughts snapped back as Alex's hand traced the muscles of her thigh up to her waist to help her into the leather bucket seat of his ride.

"By the way, nice backside," he said.

She smiled. "I think I'm starting to feel the effect of the aerobics classes already."

Alex squeezed her butt through the thin material of her dress. "Definitely buns of steel."

"I don't know about that." She tightened her arms around her midsection after getting situated. She knew what he planned tonight.

They rode in momentary silence.

"I hope you're ready for some real fun," he said, sliding Monet a dangerous smile.

The look was scorching hot. Her anxiety level rose. "Oh, a game of chess?" she said, in an attempt at humor.

Chuckling, he said, "Cutie, the only game we've played is let's see who can come first. You couldn't get enough of me the other night, remember?"

"Hmm ... I remember."

"In fact, I can barely keep my hands off you. You look gorgeous tonight."

"Thank you."

When she glanced around, she noticed they were already at Alex's. Her emotions churned.

Already out on his side, Alex opened her door, pulled

her into him, and slid her down the front of him and right into his erection.

"See how much I want you?" he said, then he grabbed her hand and guided her to his door. She wondered how she'd get through the night without pissing him off.

"Alex," she said, before they entered. He smelled of citrus and sensual woods. "I have to get up early."

"There's always time for a beer."

"Okay, but then would you take me home?"

"We'll see what happens." He traced her cheek with soft lips.

Monet closed her eyes, reveling in the feel of his warm lips against her skin. How could she just leave?

Alex fished a key from a front jean pocket, opened the door, and ushered them inside.

"I'll get us both a beer," he said.

She had to start talking. Regret suddenly welled. She knew she shouldn't have gone with him tonight. "Alex, I—"

"Want you. I know," he finished for her. "Make yourself comfortable." He gestured toward the couch.

"Sure," Monet said, making her way to the living room.

He returned in a flash, handing her an open bottle. "Drink up." He clinked his bottle against hers and said, "To us. I really like you, Monet."

Panic seized her. "To us," she returned. She tipped the bottle to her mouth and drank fast.

Alex took her free hand and pulled her down on the couch with him.

Monet set herself free and sat up. "Look, Alex. I have to be honest with you," she said, setting her beer down.

He took a slow sip of Corona, then his eyes zoomed in on her. "Yeah?"

She still found him incredibly sexy. "I can't."

"Can't what?"

"Pretend this is all I want."

"Me, either, so let's get started," he whispered in her ear.

Guilt spiraled in her chest. "Not tonight, Alex."

He slammed his bottle down on the coffee table. "You back with dickhead?"

She frowned. "No."

"You sure?" He blinked.

The thought of Shane made her reach for her beer. "I'm very sure. Besides, if I was, what would I be doing out with you?"

"You tell me." He raked a hand through his hair. "Then what's the problem?" he demanded, taking a swig of beer. "I'm not used to this."

She drew in a breath. "You're kind of stuck on yourself, aren't you?"

"I'd rather be stuck in you."

She laughed and swallowed some beer to wet her throat. "Alex, we don't even really talk. All we do is—"

"Have sex." He cut her off. "And what the hell's wrong with that? You enjoy it. I enjoy it. So, what's the problem?"

"Just listen. I need an emotional connection. I want more than just good sex. I don't know." She sighed. "I guess I should sort out my feelings."

"What do you expect … for me to say 'I love you' after we've fucked twice?"

"Three times."

"Whatever." He shook his head. "No problem, though. I'll just bang someone else while you deal with the female feeling thing, or whatever the hell you need to do. Come to think of it, Ruby's not so bad."

She waited a beat. "You serious?"

"Does it look like I'm joking?" His eyes were dead serious. "I'll take you home, if that's what you want."

"Alex, please," Monet pleaded.

"I thought you didn't want me to fuck you tonight."

"What?" she said, confused.

"Don't worry about it. There's plenty more where that came from." Bottle in hand, he gestured at her crotch.

With effort, she buried a flash of anger and rose from the couch. "Thanks for taking me tonight. I mean it."

"It shows." He jumped up, took the bottles, and disappeared.

She retrieved her purse and followed him out to his SUV.

They rode in silence the entire way. He'd turned into a stranger. What did she really expect? His looks got him what he wanted from women. Actually, he and Ruby were perfect for each other. She'd hoped to be friends. Scratch that idea.

He pulled to a stop in front of her apartment building, left the motor running, and cranked up the rock station on the radio.

Monet turned to him. "I don't want it to end like this."

"Then what do you want?" he asked, avoiding her gaze.

She hauled in a breath. "It's not that simple."

He slid her a sideways glance. "Then get out."

"I'm sorry." She closed her eyes, as if shutting out his harsh words. "Look, it's not you, Alex, it's me. Just don't hate me," she said before reaching for the door handle to let herself out.

She heard tires squealing and watched his taillights disappear into the night. It about summed up her relationships with men. Maybe she was meant to be alone.

She let herself into the dark apartment, feeling for the light switch, and flicked it on. Dixie Cup bounded into the lit kitchen, curling his tail around her calf.

"At least I can keep you around. You understand, don't you?"

Dixie Cup meowed his agreement.

After Monet prepared for bed, she found herself in the kitchen, helping herself to Rocky Road ice cream. As she dug in, her thoughts mulled over the events of the evening.

Would Alex ever speak to her again? She scooped up a spoonful of chocolate, marshmallow, and roasted almond as if it held the answer. Somehow, she had a feeling he was through with her.

Monet swallowed the smooth ice cream and thought about Jay, remembering the party and … that mysterious, inner pain in his dark eyes when he'd looked at her … the way their hands brushed … the way he listened when she talked. Just the highly charged sexual chemistry between them was enough to numb her mind. Her body skyrocketed every time she was near him. She was in deep.

She devoured half the container of ice cream before slipping into bed. She'd ended it with Alex because of Jay. What had she done?

* * *

Jay punched in his home phone number.

"Hey," he said when Ruby answered. "Just calling to say I'll be home earlier than usual. The processor broke down, and we only got one load today, but I'll be down at the shop for a while, fixing an air leak in one of my trailer hoses. I'm just leaving the trailer loader at PLS now, so I should be home in about forty-five minutes."

"How about dinner at five? You think you'll be done in the shop by then?"

"Hopefully. That should give me plenty of time. See you in a while."

"Yeah, see you soon."

As he headed out of the log-sorting yard in Everett, Jay thought hard about his marriage. Was he still in love with

Ruby? Of course he loved her. Sure, he didn't feel the same as when they first met. He was in love with her then ... now he loved her, even after the bookkeeping fiasco.

An hour later, back home, the privacy of his own shop gave him peace. Right now, he couldn't accept the fact that his marriage was slipping away. After finishing up, he made his way to the house. He wondered if he and Ruby were willing to put in the amount of work their marriage needed.

He entered the house through the garage after dropping off some paperwork in the office. The pleasant scent of tomato sauce with basil and oregano greeted him. He breathed it in appreciatively while washing up. On his way to the bedroom for a shower, he stopped midstride.

"I know you still want me. Why are you acting this way? After all the great sex we've had, how could you not want me?" Ruby's voice, a hushed low, whispered into the phone.

Disbelief stole through him. Rage rattled every bone in his body. How long had this been going on? He'd somehow sensed something was up. He'd had a feeling, and that was why he was so quick to distrust her. Sadness squeezed his heart. His marriage was over.

As he stood, unmoving, thoughts of Monet slipped into his mind, and how just being near her at the party caused his heart to pound and his loins to ache. She may have touched something inside of him that Ruby never had. Were Monet and Alex serious? If so, he couldn't interfere. He shook his head, as if changing channels to Ruby, and through his haze of anger, entered the kitchen.

Ruby stood at the stove in one of her slinky, black dresses, stirring something in a big pot. "Jay." She whirled around to face him, licking red sauce from a finger. "I didn't even hear you come in."

"Really." He grabbed an imported beer from the fridge, her innocent act fueling his anger.

In quick strides, he crossed to the kitchen table, pulled out a chair, and forced himself to sit. Then he set his beer down, and elbows on the table, let his head fall into his hands, threading unsteady fingers through his damp hair.

"Something wrong?" Ruby scrambled to the table and set two plates down. "Jay, what's going on?"

With effort, he reigned in his temper. "Why don't you tell me?"

"Tell you what?" She blinked twice.

Jay shot to his feet.

"Jay, what's got into you?" Fear lined Ruby's voice.

He finally snapped. "I'll tell you what's got into me! How could you be unfaithful?" He watched her expression collapse. "Well, let me tell you something. Whoever it is you are screwing is smart. I have to give him credit for not wanting you anymore. I heard you on the phone, Ruby."

Ruby froze, then through trembling lips, said, "Jay, it's nothing, really. I mean, it's just … I … uh … was talking with a friend. We were joking around a little, that's all. You and

I haven't been ourselves lately, so I've just been confiding in someone else, not screwing them, for God's sake."

Jay's eyes held hers. "Don't lie to me, Ruby. Just admit you've been fucking someone else." Perspiration formed between his shoulder blades. "Who? I have a right to know who my wife is spreading her legs for."

"How dare you accuse me of something like that!" Ruby shouted and turned her back on him. "I know what you think you heard, but you're jumping to conclusions."

Surprising himself, Jay laughed. He suddenly grabbed her arm and forced her around to face him.

"Ouch, you're hurting me!"

Jay loosened his grip. "Who's hurting who here? Now, are you going to tell me what's going on, or am I going to have to find out for myself? Ruby, I won't stay in a marriage like this."

"It's nothing. And besides, it's nobody you know, anyway. We laugh and joke around. Come on, Jay, I knew you were in the shop. What, do you think I'm stupid?"

"Yes." Anger heated his face. He clamped down on the surge of emotions running rampant through him. "Until you stop lying, this discussion is over."

Ruby only stared at him.

He had to get out of here. He left the house and started for the shop, his feelings colliding with different thoughts. His dad had helped him build a profitable company, and he wouldn't let Ruby take it from him. He wouldn't sell out just to give her the share she had coming. Maybe he should stay married. No. There was no way he could live like that. He didn't want a marriage if it wasn't worth keeping. He wanted one person, and one person only—Monet. A flicker of awareness sparked through him. The deep, sensual sensation of being near her didn't just feel like desire or lust. It felt more like a connection, an extraordinary bond, a brand-new feeling just waiting to be explored.

He felt tightness in his lower body that had nothing to do with anger.

Ruby left him with one choice. Divorce.

Tidying things up in the shop and looking over his truck, he found himself unable to concentrate on anything. Who could he turn to? He didn't want to say anything to his parents until he knew more. Alex came to mind. Not only was he his truck boss, he was a friend. He'd give him a call.

He picked up the phone and made the call.

"Hello," Alex answered after a few rings, breathing hard.

"Hey, Alex. Did I catch you at a bad time?"

"No, not at all. I was just outside and heard the phone, so I rushed to answer it. What's up?"

"Oh." Jay sighed. "I just wanted to talk to you about something." He waited a beat. "Something personal."

"What's on your mind?"

"When I got home this afternoon, I overheard Ruby on the phone. I think she's been screwing around, but I don't want this getting back to anyone else."

* * *

Shock seized him. Alex stiffened. Guilt pressed in from both sides like a vise, squeezing tighter and tighter. "That sucks," he managed. What else could he say? Oh, by the way, that was me she was talking to. I've been trying to break it off with her, but she clings to me like bounce clings to clothes in the fucking dryer. "Did you confront her about it?" he asked, raking a hand through his hair.

"Yeah," Jay said with exhaustion, "but I think she's lying."

Alex wouldn't push. Maybe Jay knew it was him she'd been talking to and was waiting for Alex to admit it. "Did she say much else?" Shame, remorse, and regret surged through him. He would give anything to erase what he'd done with Ruby.

"No, and then I headed out to the shop."

Alex sighed with relief. "What are you going to do?" He'd never suspect him, would he? A chill raced down Alex's spine. No, otherwise he wouldn't have confided in him. As of right now, he was through with Ruby.

Quietly, Jay said, "I really can't trust her anymore."

Could you ever? Alex shook a cigarette from his pack, lit up, and crossed to the kitchen for a cold beer. He grabbed a Corona from the fridge, opened it, and took a swig while searching his brain for the right thing to say. "God, Jay, I feel for you, man. I really hope you work it out … I don't know … what I mean is, I don't want you to get screwed, so hopefully, you'll work it out."

"That's another thing. I'm not so sure I want to work it out with her."

How could anyone want to stay married to Ruby? "Spend a little time away from her and clear your head." She was just a good fuck, and that's why he was in the predicament he was in now.

"I am."

"Good." Still rattled, Alex hesitated, then asked, "Same time tomorrow up on the landing?"

"Same time. See you then. Thanks, Alex."

"For what?" *Sleeping with your wife?* Alex needed another beer.

"For listening."

"Yeah."

A couple of beers later, Alex was still deep in guilt.

* * *

Ruby threw the unused plates into the sink, then grabbed her bottle of white zinfandel out of the fridge. Just what she needed to forget. Instead of bothering with a glass, she drank straight from the bottle. The crisp, fruity wine slid down her throat to pool in her belly. She guzzled as long as she could before running out of breath, searching for that calm, tingly feeling.

Angry at Jay for ditching her for his truck, Ruby shuffled to the table with her bottle, fell into a chair, and took another swig of wine. Damn him! The reality of Jay catching her unnerved her. Did he suspect Alex? She hoped not. The way Alex was treating her, she'd be lucky if he slept with her again. What was wrong with him, anyway? He enjoyed the sex as much as she did, but ever since he'd met Monet, he hadn't been the same. She had to do something about her. On the other hand, Ruby couldn't let Alex forget how good she was in bed.

A sudden plan slapped her in the face. When Alex brought the truck by the house this weekend to wash it, like he usually did, and if Jay was gone doing maintenance on the equipment up in the woods, she'd try to rekindle Alex's interest again. And when she was through with him, he'd be sorry he ever thought about ending their affair.

But right now, she was famished. She snatched a plate from the cupboard, piling it high with spaghetti. She took the plate and bottle of wine back to the table and ate alone. She didn't need Jay. If he wanted to divorce her, fine, as long as she got to keep her ZR1 Corvette, her three-carat, marquise-and-round diamond wedding ring, and enough money to live well—very well. She didn't need the house or any of his shitty business. Huge alimony payments every month would be okay by her.

She twisted her fork around some pasta drenched in homemade sauce and brought it to her mouth. It tasted good, flavorful, and full of Italian spices. She washed it down with gulps of wine until the bottle was empty.

That night, she climbed into bed—alone. When she woke with a deadly hangover the next morning, Jay was gone.

Getting up seemed too big a task. Somehow, she managed to crawl out of bed and slip into the bathroom. She gazed at herself in the mirror above the double sinks. Mascara smudges ringed her tired eyes. Her hair was matted and sticking up.

"God, I look like hell," she muttered into the mirror. She needed caffeine and food before attempting to change her appearance. She dragged the turquoise, silk robe from its hook on the wall, slipped into it, and padded barefoot to the kitchen.

She started the coffee percolating, then frantically searched for something to devour. She decided on scrambled eggs and ham.

At the breakfast nook, she wolfed down eggs loaded with cheese and two thick slices of maple-flavored ham while she dealt with her restless thoughts. What should she do next? She stared at a big cedar tree that held no answers.

When she'd married Jay, what had she expected? That he'd be so in love with her, he'd never want to work and they could vacation most of their lives? She knew from doing his books that he didn't have to drive his truck if he didn't want to. He could just supervise. Some people had it all, unlike her with no choice and only street smarts for survival. She despised them for it.

Things should have been different after they married. She'd expected to travel to exotic places and return only to check up on things at home. Boy, had she been wrong.

Reality returned by slow degrees. She suspected Jay's love had died. Could she blame him? She watched the sun shine through the morning haze reflecting off the cedar tree. A slight morning breeze ruffled the boughs. Her mouth twisted sadly. How could she ever leave here?

She settled back in her chair, contemplating. She exhaled slowly. Would she and Alex live happily ever after with Jay's money in some tropical paradise? Maybe not, and all because of Monet.

Ruby thought about what might matter most to Monet. Apparently, Alex. And her job. If Monet couldn't work at Fantasy's, how could she support herself? Even though exotic dance clubs were plentiful, Fantasy's was one of a kind. She should know. She'd worked there and had been more than ready to move on. It was too much of a club for weak women who didn't have the courage to strip. If Ruby hadn't met Jay, she would have worked at a real strip club where they take everything off, and she would have loved every minute of it. She'd been about to quit cocktailing at that Mexican restaurant anyway. Then Jay happened and financially swept her off her feet.

Ah-ha. That was it! She had to get Monet out of that place, and the only way to do it would be to destroy the building—if she couldn't destroy Monet. Besides, Gus had refused her. Wouldn't it be nice to put him in his place? Even though he wasn't the owner, he managed it and that was enough. She'd never met the owner of the club, but it didn't matter.

Suddenly pumped, Ruby tossed her dishes in the sink and crossed to the bedroom to get ready for the day ahead.

After a refreshing shower, she slipped on a short, form-fitting, slinky, white dress. No bra, no nylons, and a next-to-nothing thong should grab Alex's attention. She was glad Jay was doing maintenance on his equipment this weekend. A self-employed husband had its advantages, like today.

Her thoughts lingered on Jay. At least they were talking, even if he'd rejected her advances. At the thought, Ruby hurled Jay's clothes off the hamper and across the room. Nobody treated her like this, including Monet.

She caught a glimpse of herself in the full-length mirror and smiled. Her hair was wild and loose. Her green eyes were accented with gold and bronze, and her lips were coated in shiny red. The sprinkling of freckles across her nose and cheeks was dusted with a shimmery powder. And her body … well, it certainly couldn't get any better. She looked sexy, flamboyant, and very fuckable. She was ready for Alex, but was he ready for her?

Heart beating in anticipation, Ruby turned and headed to the kitchen for a glass of wine. With her favorite friend in hand, she went to the living room and sank onto the couch, swirling the wine in its glass. It went down smoothly and calmed her nerves.

Then she heard the truck. Quickly, she emptied her glass of wine and scurried back to the kitchen for another. She polished it off, standing at the refrigerator, then raced to the bedroom and grabbed high-heeled pumps. It usually took Alex four hours to wash the truck, but if she was lucky, she'd seduce him before he got started. She paused for a final glance at herself in the mirror and made her way outside, thinking Alex would not refuse her today.

She made her way toward Alex, her hips swaying. "Hey," Ruby called, watching him climb out of his truck. He'd parked it in the usual space, alongside the shop next to the hose hookup.

Alex gave a muffled snort. "Shit."

"Not a very warm hello. What's the problem?" Ruby asked, batting her lashes.

"You are. What are you doing out here dressed like that?" Alex asked and jumped back in the truck.

His disinterest inflamed her. "Quit being a dick. I don't like being ignored."

Alex stepped back out of the truck. "I don't want anything to do with you, Ruby."

She gave her hair a toss. "Hah."

"Besides, I'm busy. Stay out of my way." Alex whipped past her and drew a key out of his pocket.

Ruby planted herself in front of the walk-in door to the shop, blocking access. She folded her arms across her chest, her breathing heavy. With effort, she replaced the anger with a warm, seductive tone. "Jay caught me on the phone with you, but he doesn't know it's you. You can't deny that you still want me." She inched herself closer and threw her arms around his neck.

"I've never wanted you. I've just fucked you. Get it through your head," Alex warned. "Jay called me and told me about catching you on the phone with someone." He broke free of her and spun around to unlock the door.

Her men talking about her shook her to the core. Unable to stop Alex from entering the shop, fury misted Ruby's vision as she watched him gather supplies for washing the truck. She knew Jay and Alex were close, but were they close enough to talk about what she was up to? Close enough for Jay to talk about his marriage? Alex was his driver, not his shrink. Why would Jay tell Alex about catching her on the phone with someone?

Ruby stepped just inside the door to block Alex's exit. "You can wash the truck after I'm through with you." She refused to believe Alex didn't want her.

"Get out of my way." Alex shoved her with the arm that held the bucket of soap.

"I suggest you put that down." She gestured at the bucket. "I'll take you for a ride in that truck you'll never forget. And I don't mind if it's dirty," she added suggestively.

Alex heaved a sigh. "If you don't get out of my way, I'm going to push you out of my way."

"Exactly what I'm after," Ruby taunted. "I'm getting to you, huh?" she said, gesturing at his crotch. "Uncomfortable?"

Alex dropped the bucket he'd been holding. Then, with both hands, he grasped Ruby's shoulders and shoved her to the left.

She scrambled back to him. "Do me," she whispered in his ear, staring up at him from under made-up lashes. "I promise it won't take long." She knew how to make it happen quick. She had to prove to herself that Alex still wanted her body, if nothing else.

"Save it for your husband," Alex grumbled. He took the bucket and stormed outside toward the truck.

Ruby dashed after him, watching him put the bucket down and hop back in on the driver's side of the truck. *Perfect.* She'd trap him in there. Besides, it was her truck as far as she was concerned. He was just the one who drove it, and now she'd drive him.

She scrambled to the passenger side of the truck. Her choice of outfit didn't make it easy to step up and in, but she'd get it done. With considerable effort, she worked her dress up and over her hips and carefully went up the two steps on the fuel tank to the cab. She tightened her hands around the grab handles on the muffler for support, then she swung the door open and climbed inside.

Alex's eyes flashed with rage. "Get out of my truck!"

"No," she snapped. "I know you want me. Don't deny it."

Ruby's voice became softer, more seductive. She leaned into Alex, closing any distance between them.

Alex dropped his head.

Had her charms worked again? She believed so. Alex appeared defeated.

Heat stole through her body. The silence woke her senses. She pulled Alex into her and slowly closed her mouth over his.

"Make it fast," he muttered against her face.

"My specialty." Ruby patted the passenger seat. "I suggest you climb over here, big boy. It'd be impossible to do it in your seat. The steering wheel might get in the way."

She watched Alex maneuver himself to her seat. He quickly unsnapped his jeans. She half-stood to let him get situated, her dress still up over her hips.

Then she straddled him.

The next thing she knew, he was inside her so deep, she cried out, "Alex, please."

"Please what? Fuck you harder?"

She felt him clasp her hips tightly, his fingers digging into her flesh. He worked her up and down on him, fast, forcing her to take all of him. "Alex, my God," she mumbled into his hair. "Yes ... oh ... yes ..."

She stole his mouth again and they kissed in rhythm. She grinded on him, squeezing him inside her, fiercely.

He ended the kiss and made her ride him until she practically begged him to stop. "Oh, Alex!" she screamed.

Just when the pain turned to wild passion, she felt him climax. It all happened too fast. She remembered kissing him intensely, the painful but pleasurable feeling of him buried so deep inside her. Then it was over. She felt cheated.

"Come on, get off me. I've got work to do." He moved Ruby away and pulled his jeans back up.

"You mean that's it? That's all I get?" Ruby's voice choked with outrage. "So now you can just get back to your chore and forget about me? Don't I mean anything to you?"

"Ruby, you never meant anything to me, and I swear to God, this is the last time this is going to happen, so get used to it. If you pull this shit again, I'll tell Jay. I mean it. I don't care what happens anymore. I just want out. You got it? Now get out of this truck."

Burning with rage, Ruby stepped down from the truck so fast, she nearly lost her balance. Screw Alex, screw Jay, and screw Monet. She was so angry, she couldn't think.

Then realization dawned ... heated, inflamed, to the point of blazing fire. She would stop at nothing—including arson.

She pictured it in her mind. Fantasy's burned to the ground. Monet out of a job. Lovely.

Chapter Sixteen

Monet drew in a sharp breath as her eyes adjusted to the scene in the truck. Ruby would stop at nothing to hurt Jay, and it looked as though Alex was no different than Shane. She backed her car up carefully and headed out the driveway before she did something foolish. She had to get away from them—and fast.

As of this minute, she was through with Alex. Thinking of Jay's feelings, her grip tightened on the steering wheel. Her heart hurt for him. Monet didn't know how much longer she could keep this secret from Jay.

Back home, Monet quickly made coffee and called Cameo.

"You'll never guess what I just saw," Monet blurted.

"What?" Cameo prodded.

"Just come over."

"I'm on my way."

Monet ushered Cameo inside upon her arrival. "Coffee?" They headed to the kitchen table.

"Sure. Now tell me before I die of curiosity!" Cameo exclaimed.

Filling two mugs with the Irish Crème-flavored brew, Monet brought them to the table and slid in a chair across from Cameo.

"I went to see Ruby to tell her that Alex and I were possibly through, so leave me alone and stop threatening me. I saw Ruby, but not like I'd expected. She was with Alex in his truck, and they weren't exactly talking, if you know what I mean."

"Oh, that bad boy." Cameo clucked her tongue. "Can't he keep his dick in his pants? Were they ... you know ... or was she giving him a hummer? Ruby does have the perfect mouth for it."

Monet chuckled. "They were in the passenger seat. She was straddling him."

"Sounds like quite a ride. You ever tried that?"

"Not in a truck."

"I get the picture. So, what's up with Alex then?" Cameo shook her head. "I guess some guys can't keep their dicks in their pants."

Monet smiled despite the situation. "And when you're a guy, and it's Ruby, I guess it makes it that much harder."

"Literally."

Clutching the ceramic mug, Monet sipped her cooled

coffee. "Cameo," she said, turning serious, "I can't stop thinking about Jay. What do I do, and especially after this? By the way, in case you didn't guess, Alex and I are history."

"Gotcha, and maybe ditto for Jay and Ruby. Do you know what this means for you?"

Monet's heart beat in anticipation. "What?"

"What you just witnessed may be the best thing that ever happened to you. Get what I'm saying? Proof."

"Hmm," she said around a smile.

"I think maybe you should tell Jay. Shoot, I don't know." Cameo twirled a strand of hair around her finger. "What do you think?"

Monet looked away as if searching for a genie in a bottle.

"I know," Cameo said. "You don't want to be selfish, but it's about Jay this time, and it could work in your favor. I mean, when you think about it, the poor guy. Not only because his wife is unfaithful, but to top it off, she's screwing the guy who works for him?"

"It's like I want to tell him, but I don't know if I can hurt him. He'll be devastated."

"Better coming from you than hearing it through the grapevine. I'd say now's your big chance."

Monet nodded. "I just don't know if it's the right thing to do."

"Okay, well think about it. Now, tell me all about the party." Cameo sat back and folded her arms across her chest.

Monet began the sweet remembrance. "Just the way our

eyes met and held sent tingles up my spine. I can hardly explain it. Being near him … I suppose everything about Jay stirs something inside of me." Dixie Cup hopped up and into Monet's lap, purring contentedly as she rubbed him underneath his neck.

"What else?" Cameo leaned across the table, her hands propped underneath her chin.

"It's easy to tell he really listens when I talk to him. You know how sometimes when you're talking to people and you think they're listening, and they really aren't? It's like they don't even hear a word you've said."

Cameo nodded in agreement. "Totally."

"And when he fixed me a drink, his fingers grazed mine and I felt like I was on fire."

Cameo whistled. "Wow, you know what? Since his wife is banging his truck driver, and you're not banging the truck driver anymore, I say now's the time to bang him. Go for it, but don't forget to be smart and watch your back."

"How could I not after all that's happened with Ruby?"

Cameo winked. "You know I have a way with words. What I mean is, take it slow with Jay … be honest with him, open up to him, and go from there."

It all sounded so easy.

After Cameo left, Monet coaxed herself into calling Jay. No sense in putting it off. She retrieved his business card from her purse, punched in the number, and hung up just as quickly. What would she say if Ruby answered? Hello,

Ruby, this is Monet. Is your husband around? I'd like to talk to him about your affair with Alex. Forget that.

Or what if Jay answered? She couldn't do it. She wasn't ready yet.

* * *

Later that evening, Ruby tried again. "I said I'm sorry, Jay," she begged. "I fixed it. Just give me another chance with the bookkeeping. I promise it'll never happen again." *Right*, she thought smugly. She'd tell Jay whatever she had to.

Jay shoved a hand through his hair. "How can you expect me to trust you? I need time."

Time? Screw that! She wasn't going to sit around waiting for anything. As it was, she had to rethink her future plans after putting all the money back. "Don't you believe me? I said I fixed it." She braced herself against the counter, clutching tightly to the edges with both hands behind her. "Everything adds up now. Aren't you happy? It was a mistake, Jay, but you want to believe the worst ... that I stole from you."

"Ruby, right now, I don't know what to think, or feel, for that matter. What I really don't know is who you were talking with on the phone that night. Try telling the truth."

"How can you be so cold?" Ruby wheeled around and fled from the kitchen.

She started toward the sliding door in the living room and, once there, slid it open and stepped outside into the clear night air. Frogs chirped nearby. Dogs barked in the distance. She felt enveloped, closed off, nearly suffocated, and it wasn't from being out here. Inside of her, the different emotions tore her up. She felt like a caged tiger, and she wanted to scream. Maybe the stillness of the night would calm her.

Jay wasn't going to give her another chance to take care of his books, and he may not give her another chance at their marriage. Didn't he believe her story when he'd caught her on the phone? The bastard. She'd tried being extra nice since then, and she had to admit he hadn't responded.

Still outside, she fell into a chair. Her thoughts took a turn toward action. First things first. Torch Fantasy's and get away with it. The thought of getting caught and going to jail chilled her. She'd be very careful.

"Ruby," Jay called, stepping onto the patio.

Surprise, surprise. A breeze ruffled his thick, dark hair. A jolt of sadness hit her. She'd destroyed their marriage. What had she been thinking? "Yeah," she answered through the haze in her brain.

"I'm going to bed. Just wanted to say good night." He ran a hand through his hair.

"Good night." She glanced up at the sky so she wouldn't have to see his handsome face. A cloud skittered away, revealing a full moon. It was the perfect night. The moon cast a silver-like light everywhere, creating an eerie feeling within her. She shuddered.

"If I don't come to bed soon," she added, "it's because I need to think." Ruby felt an urge to reach out and touch him, and ask him to tell her everything would be okay. Maybe that's what had attracted her to Jay besides his money … that caring attitude he had that even she could see. "Sorry." She felt her face heat. "I'm real emotional now. What time are you leaving for work, six o'clock?"

"Something like that." Jay stood with his hand at the door latch.

"I might take a drive. Who knows when I'll be back." Ruby sighed. "You get some sleep."

Concern crossed Jay's face. "Just don't do anything stupid," he warned and went back inside.

His tone unsettled her. Did he know? No. There was no way he could. She'd need some wine or perhaps something stronger to go through with this.

There was a lot at stake here. Basically, her life was on the line. She was throwing herself out on a limb, and for what? To put someone whom she despised out of a job? When she thought about it, it sounded completely insane, ludicrous, but she'd also get back at Gus for not firing Monet. When people treated her disrespectfully, they had to pay.

She rose and went inside before fear changed her mind.

After a couple nerve-settling glasses of white zinfandel, she planned the next step.

As she tiptoed into the bedroom, she noticed Jay's steady breathing. Good. He was asleep. In the bathroom, she washed up, leaving no trace of makeup on her face. She stifled a hysterical laugh as she studied herself in the mirror. At least she didn't look as boring as Monet. To do what she was about to do, she wanted to be unrecognizable.

She glanced at her watch on the bathroom counter. She had five hours before torch time. Five hours would seem like a hundred. She drew a steady breath. In an hour or two, after very careful planning and going over her strategy, again and again, she'd leave home to kill the rest of the time at a convenience store, downing coffee to keep her alert. She simply couldn't afford one tiny mistake.

Just after midnight, she left the house and made her way to the shop, her feet crunching on gravel. Inside, she grabbed the gas can, one of several two-and-a-half-gallon, square, plastic, red ones Jay had stored in a corner of the shop for the lawn mower and welder.

With the full gas can, she returned to the garage. The can felt as if it weighed at least twenty pounds. She opened the back compartment of her car and set it down on the newspaper. One couldn't be too careful. She'd dressed down in black jeans, matching tennis shoes, and T-shirt.

Once in Ballard, she pulled into a 7-Eleven and went inside to purchase coffee and two Hershey's candy bars. This should keep her up. Then she drove down Market Street and headed toward the water, seeking a peaceful view to calm her nerves.

Before breaking into the coffee and candy, she swallowed the fear lodged in her throat. It was too late to turn back now. She wouldn't go all soft and emotional. She'd made her choice and she intended to stick to it, no matter the outcome.

At quarter after three in the morning, she drove to Fantasy's from the Ballard locks. Second thoughts raced through her. This was a big mistake. She'd never get away with it. Why couldn't she just be happy with Jay? She realized she'd probably never be happy. Besides, Jay didn't want her anymore.

Ruby held the gas can away from her body. She didn't need to smell like it and give anything away. She tipped it and hurriedly splashed it on the side of the building, then stood back, struck a match, and flicked it against the gas-soaked siding. She grabbed the gas can, her adrenaline spinning wildly out of control.

At her car, she tossed the empty gas can onto the passenger side floorboard and sped away, catching sight of the roaring flames in her rearview mirror. Thank God she couldn't hear the hiss and crackle of the fire. Seeing it was enough. With a last scan, she saw the flames leap at the building, brightening the night. Her heart beat a rapid drum in her chest and her body quaked with fear. She was so shaken up, she barely remembered driving home.

But she made it.

First, she put the empty gas can back in the shop, locked it behind her, and drove the couple hundred feet to the house.

She parked her Corvette in the garage and quietly crept into the laundry room off the garage. She breathed a sigh of relief. Feeling dizzy, she hardly remembered the events of the evening.

When her thoughts focused, she wondered if Fantasy's had burned to the ground like she'd intended, or if the fire department got there and put it out. She'd find out tomorrow.

Right now, she knew she needed sleep. A part of her was exhausted, another part exhilarated. Sleep might not come easy.

Silently, she made her way to the bedroom. Jay would be getting up soon to move equipment. She was grateful she'd gotten back before he got up. In the bathroom, she undressed and stuffed her clothes far down to the bottom of the hamper.

Without a trace of clothing, she slipped into bed beside Jay. He never even stirred.

As she put her head to the pillow, fear crawled up her spine. Somehow, she had a bad feeling about this. Things would never be the same.

* * *

Was that smoke he smelled?

It was suddenly everywhere, enveloping him, suffocating him. Without another thought, he called 9-1-1 and then dashed out of the building, only to see it up in flames.

He'd been in the back room with the safe open, counting money and putting valuables in it for the night. He rushed back in to close up the safe. It was fireproof. He wanted to save all he could, but now … his heart told him that it may be too late. He may have made a huge mistake that would cost him his life. He wasn't so sure he'd make it out of there alive. He swallowed and tried to breathe, but thick smoke coated his lungs, closed off his airways, and blinded him.

He lost his way and then blacked out.

Chapter Seventeen

The phone interrupted her aerobics practice.

She jogged to pick it up. "Hello," she said, her breathing labored.

In a voice filled with alarm, her mother said, "Monet."

Her heart pounded. "Mom." She clutched the phone tighter. "What is it?"

"It's your father."

"What?" Shock numbed her. "What's happened?"

"He's in the paper this morning. Oh, Monet." Lucy paused. "I don't know how to say this."

A chill spread through Monet. *He's dead*, she thought. How was she supposed to feel sad when she didn't even know him? Her throat tightened, making it impossible to speak.

"His picture's in the paper this morning. The only way I recognized him … well, let's just say I know that face even after thirty-one years. But … he changed his name."

"Mom, please, what happened?" Monet pleaded.

"Monet, the club where you work ... he was the owner. It burned down. The paper said it was arson. Your dad was in it and made it out before it was too late."

"What?" Monet's hand felt clammy as she mopped perspiration from a brow. "Somebody burned down Fantasy's? How? Why? Who?"

"I don't know, but I think we should go to the hospital together," her mother said, whisper soft.

"Oh my God!" Her voice cracked. *Her father.* This was so bizarre that she could hardly believe it. An eeriness crept up her spine. What would happen now? She needed time to absorb this.

"Monet, are you there?"

Her mother's voice broke into her thoughts. She would finally meet her father after all these years, but she'd seen him often enough at Fantasy's. The world was small. The father she'd never known, never been able to talk to, and never shed a tear over had been in her life for the past thirteen years and she hadn't even known it. Stunned, she said in a delicate voice, "Mom, I'm here."

"I said, I think we should go to the hospital and see him."

Monet pulled in a breath. She wanted so much to know this man, but she was afraid. She knew she should go, if only to lay her past to rest. "I think you're right."

"I'll pick you up. What time?"

"Give me an hour."

As mother and daughter—a family—together they could unravel the past. She couldn't turn down this golden opportunity to ask him why he deserted them.

She immediately called Cameo.

"Yeah," Cameo answered.

"This is going to blow your mind."

"Jay and Ruby are getting divorced?"

Monet didn't let the thought of Jay linger. "No. Fantasy's burned down last night. The owner, Dan ... he's my father."

Silence stretched.

Monet felt her heartbeat tick in time with the rosewood clock on the wall. "Cameo."

"Oh, my God. What happened?"

Monet repeated her mother's news.

"I ... I can't believe it. I can't believe it burned down. Somebody did this intentionally. Oh God. And Monet, your father? You ... I don't ... I can't ... I can hardly speak."

Monet felt the same way. "What are we going to do?"

"God, I don't know. The thing is, what are you going to do?"

"My mom's picking me up. We're going to go see him. I just couldn't *not* do it."

"I'm proud of you."

Monet batted at the tears welling.

"I think I'll go see Fantasy's, see what it looks like. This is weird."

"I know," Monet whispered.

"Hey, while you're visiting your dad, I'll check into job opportunities at other clubs."

"I'm done." Monet felt emotionally drained. She knew she couldn't dance anymore. It didn't matter where. "I've already started changing my life. Besides, I think someone is trying to tell me something ... to keep moving away from the past, and don't look back."

"Good girl."

When her mom arrived, Monet went out to greet her. A gentle breeze stirred her hair. She'd left it down, chosen a cardigan with front tie and matching, pink camisole trimmed in lace, a linen skirt that swirled to her knees, and white, loop, wedge sandals. With just a trace of makeup, she'd gone for presentable, stylish, not too overdone.

She climbed into her mother's silver, ten-year-old Honda Civic. "You look nice, Mom."

"Thanks, so do you."

Her mother wore an off-white, floral print skirt and matching sweater tank. "How do you feel about all this, Mom?" Monet asked as they headed down Broadway.

Lucy tightened her hold on the steering wheel and drew in a sharp breath. "It's hard." She shook her head. "I don't really know yet."

Monet reached over, put a hand on her shoulder, and squeezed lightly. "Me, too."

"It's the past, Monet. We have to face it, especially if

we're going to enjoy the future. I talked with Ryan on the phone and told him everything. He says we're very brave."

Monet's eyes misted. "I'm so glad you met someone who makes you happy, Mom. I can see it all over your face."

Lucy gave her a sideways glance. "Really?"

"Really."

"How's that truck driver?"

"Alex?" Monet said, even though Jay came to mind. "Uh ... we're taking a break."

"As long as you're happy."

Anticipation mounted the closer they got to the hospital. Monet felt perspiration form between her shoulder blades. "Mom, we're almost there. You've got to help me. What do I say to him?"

"Just be yourself."

"Where do I start?"

"Start by—" Lucy started to cry.

"Mom, I know. I feel it, too." Monet sniffled. "I've felt angry. How could he treat his own family this way—his daughter and the woman who loved him—and never try to contact us?" She shook her head at the sadness.

"I've never forgotten." Lucy wiped a tear from her cheek. "I've never been able to let it go."

"But you know something," Monet said softly, "I didn't come today to throw guilt in his face. I came for resolution ... to be able to get on with my life in a positive way without the feelings of doubt that have always held me back."

Lucy patted Monet's arm. "I'm proud of you."

After they arrived, Lucy parked in a visitors' spot in the parking garage. The tension in the small space of the car slowly started to fade. After a much-needed embrace, and words of encouragement, Monet and her mother finally whisked through the hospital's automatic doors at the west entrance.

Monet kept reminding herself to take deep breaths.

They went straight to the information desk. A woman directed them to room 223, where Dan shared a room on the regular ward.

Heading to the elevators, Monet took in the bustling atmosphere of the young and energetic staff. She noticed that Harborview had a vitality, a craziness to it. The doctors couldn't be more than in their early thirties. Most of the staff appeared to be in their mid-twenties. The air around her swirled with enthusiasm.

Standing in the busy hallway outside her father's room, monitors beeped and let out a brief, high-pitched sound. Lights flashed on computer screens. High-tech equipment gleamed.

A man in an official-looking uniform exited Dan's room.

Monet paused at the door, steeling herself for his reaction. An image of him at the club on those rare occasions sprang to mind. Brown, wavy hair sprinkled with gray and lines at his eyes showed his age. Her dad was apparently lucky to be alive.

Somehow, she'd hoped that he'd be sleeping. They wouldn't want to wake him, so they could just come back later. The sight that hit her surprised her.

He lay in bed in a hospital gown, hooked up to an IV. Open, quarter-inch tubes sat in his nose, went around the back of his head, over his ears, and under his chin and were attached to a portable tank. One of his fingers was enclosed in a finger clip. A nurse checked his blood pressure, then leaned over and took his pulse. When she was finished, she lowered his wrist gently and moved toward the door.

Still just outside his door, Monet peeked into the room at his roommate, who reminded her of someone you might find at Pioneer Square, never seen without a bottle of booze hidden in a brown sack. His arm was bandaged and he appeared to be sleeping.

"How's Dan doing?" Monet asked the nurse exiting his room.

She hesitated, as if not wanting to freely disclose information.

Monet cleared her throat. "I'm Dan's daughter, and this is my mom." Her mother stood at her side.

The nurse smiled in acknowledgement. "He's coughing a lot but should recover easily, considering what he's been through."

"When was he brought in?" Lucy inquired.

"He was admitted early this morning and rushed straight to emergency where he got immediate treatment. A couple hours later, he was moved here." She glanced at Dan. "He's short-winded, coughing up a lot of black phlegm, and blowing it out of his nose. But other than that, he's doing just fine."

Monet shuddered.

In a reassuring tone, the nurse continued. "That's normal for a patient being treated for smoke inhalation. We're going to keep him here to watch closely for pneumonia and to make sure he's getting enough oxygen. We're monitoring his respiratory system. A respiratory therapist comes in every eight hours. He'll be on oxygen for about a day and then will probably be taken off of it tomorrow for a while before he's released so we can make sure everything is okay before we let him go."

Inquisitive, Monet asked, "What's that clipped to his finger?"

"It's an oximeter. It measures the percentage of oxygen in his bloodstream. The clip has a sensor on it. It should read above ninety-two. Ninety-eight to one hundred is normal," she explained, continuing her progress report. "Overall, he's doing well. He's up, around, and walking, and should be ready for discharge sometime tomorrow."

Lucy asked, "What does that process involve?"

"Actually, a resident on unit will write up the discharge orders and he'll be discharged back home and to his regular doctor since there are no private physicians here. Attending resident MDs only."

A shiver went down Monet's spine. She had no idea where her father lived, let alone who his regular doctor was. It was a bit creepy having this nurse talk to them like they were a normal family.

"Was that a police officer who just left?" Monet asked.

"He's an arson investigator from a squad. Also, a fireman, deputized as a police officer," the nurse informed them.

After the nurse disappeared, Monet and Lucy hesitantly entered the room. Dan lay in the bed, wide-eyed, staring as if unable to believe the scene in front of him.

"Zack," her mother whispered softly, not an ounce of anger in her tone.

His real name. A chill washed over Monet. He'd hurt her mother so badly, yet Lucy faced him with such a self-reserved calm, Monet saw her mother differently, stronger. He was in the hospital on oxygen, not exactly the place to come unglued and rehash the past, thirty-one years later. It was an opportunity, though, and Monet would take it.

She knew her mother had changed, in part because of a man who made her happy. She thought of Jay and blinked his image away. There was no accusing, underlying grudge or blame in her mother's expression. Lucy was so settled and in such control that it baffled Monet.

"I … Lucy, what are you doing here? After what I did to you?" He broke into a coughing fit, fighting back an obvious wave of emotion. "It's been so many years. How? Why?"

Then his eyes landed on her, and Monet knew it. He

recognized her from Fantasy's. His face registered shock, disbelief.

He shook his head slowly from side to side on the pillow. "You can't be—"

"Your daughter," Monet finished for him, feeling all the muscles in her body tighten up.

"Oh my God," he said in bewilderment.

Monet hesitated, not knowing exactly what to do. Should she walk closer to him? Adrenaline pounded in her ears. Her heart knocked against her rib cage.

"What do I say?" He looked down at his clasped hands.

Monet felt an emotional tug. "First, we want to know how you're doing."

Lucy nodded.

He let out a hacking round of coughs and then explained to them how it all happened.

"I was about to put some things in the safe when I smelled smoke. Frantic, I called 9-1-1, then rushed out of the building to see it up in flames. At the time, I didn't spot anyone. My focus was on the fire, swallowing up the building—fast. I prayed the fire didn't start on other buildings adjacent to mine. I rushed back in to close the safe. My memory from there is blacked out. Obviously, an aid car made it there quickly and rushed me here."

Monet shook her head. "That is so horrible. What an awful thing to experience. I don't see how anyone could intentionally do something like that."

"The paper said they're still looking for leads, but so far, they haven't come up with any," her mother said.

"There are a lot of people out there who hate the kind of business I run." Dan paused for a coughing attack. "So, I guess they have to take that into consideration. I really don't know what I'm going to do now."

Monet went to him, handing him a cup of water from a portable table by his bed. The unfamiliar nearness felt almost natural, but she still shivered. "I wasn't going to work there much longer anyway." She smiled sadly for him.

Dan took the cup from her hands and very carefully lifted it to take a drink. "Thank you." His voice was strained.

"Tell him what you'd like to do now," her mother coaxed.

"I'd like to go to school to become an interior designer." This didn't feel real, telling her father, the owner of Fantasy's, about her dreams.

In that moment, she saw a gleam of tears fill the corners of his eyes. Her heart clutched.

"For my daughter, I think that's better than being an exotic dancer."

She smiled into his watering eyes, lined with age, stress, and too many summers in the sun. He'd called her his daughter. Even so, where had all her anger toward him for the last thirty-one years gone? It couldn't just vanish, could it?

The hushed silence lengthened.

Monet crossed her arms around herself. Inexplicably, she felt a chill. She didn't want to disappear into that realm of reality. Ruby floated to mind. She had seen how vicious hate, greed, and fear had controlled Ruby. She had a feeling, by Ruby's actions, that deep inside she was a frightened mess.

Rousing her from her thoughts, her mother said, "Tell your daughter you're sorry for taking the easy way out. I could have done the same thing, but I didn't want to live with the guilt of knowing that I'd gotten rid of an unborn child. But"—she sniffed—"God knows, I was a terrible mother."

"Mom, don't." Monet stepped over to her and embraced her. "It's not your fault. It's not his fault." She motioned toward her father, who looked paralyzed by the scene before his eyes.

He glanced away as he said, "I'm the one to blame. I'm so sorry. But at the same time, I know that's never going to be enough for what I did to both of you. I abandoned you when you needed me most. I didn't want anything to do with a family, not then. I was too immature, and I was always running away from things. For you to forgive me would be almost impossible." He turned his head on the pillow, gazing out the window into the late morning, blue sky.

Monet was so overwhelmed that she didn't know what to say.

"Dan," she said, not surprised at all to find that her voice was weak and shaky. She wasn't prepared to call him Dad. It was too soon.

He turned, focusing his eyes on her.

Her eyes clung to his, fighting a sudden urge to cry. "It's never too late."

He smiled sheepishly, then to both of them, he said, "I've thought about you over the years, what I did." He paused, looking uncertain about whether to go on.

Monet felt, rather than saw, her mother's features soften beside her.

She looked straight into her father's eyes and held them. "I've thought about you a lot and wondered where you might be, what you might be doing, and then … I worked at your club." Monet shook her head, still having a hard time swallowing that truth.

He closed his eyes briefly. "I never would have …"

"That's not the important thing, is it?" Lucy interrupted.

"It is to me. All of it is. I feel like I owe you so much … answers. I regret right now what I did thirty-one years ago when I walked out on you." His gaze rested on Lucy.

Misty-eyed, Monet said to her father, "The hurt that you never wanted me broke something inside me. I can't continue that way. It's not easy, but holding on to resentment is too hard. I need to let these feelings go, build something to take their place, something that will last."

Around a cough, her father said, "I'm so sorry, Monet. You're more beautiful than I had imagined. I lost more than I thought, but I was too weak to contact your mother. I was afraid she'd reject me. Besides, I figured it was too late. You're a grown woman now, and I believed your mom would build a better life without me." He looked right at Lucy. Slowly, he turned his watery, hazel eyes on her. "But if you'll let me, I'd like to get to know you … and in time …" He left the statement unfinished.

Monet let out a cleansing breath. A weight had been lifted from her heart. Right now, from this moment on, the past was really the past. Her dad wanted to know her, and when he explained that he ran from responsibility, the failure was his, not hers. She could move on. She felt free to care deeply about somebody besides herself—Jay.

Lucy stepped toward the bed to stand beside Monet. "Now we can start over."

Dan nodded "yes" slowly, his eyes drooping.

"We promise we'll come back tomorrow and see you," Monet whispered.

Her mother took her hand in hers, squeezed tightly, and together they left the room.

Once outside in the fresh, summer air, Monet turned to her mother and said, "How about picking me up at the same time tomorrow?"

Lucy smiled into her eyes. "Sure."

Not long after her mother dropped her back at home, Monet called Cameo and filled her in on the hospital visit.

"Your dad sounds amazing," Cameo said, "and it seems like your mom has really changed."

"I know. I can hardly believe it," Monet said, still trying to absorb it all.

"So, what happens next with Jay?"

"I don't know. I should tell him about Ruby and Alex, but I—"

"Can," Cameo finished. "And the sooner the better."

"I'll see what I can do," Monet said, not liking the thought of hurting him.

"Wait, I just thought of something."

Monet's pulse raced. "What?"

"What if he doesn't divorce Ruby?"

Dread skittered down Monet's spine. "It could happen that way."

"I mean, I'm just throwing this out."

The thought of it chilled Monet. How could something that felt so right turn out to be wrong? "What would I do then?"

"You'd move on."

"I'd have to."

"Okay, or what about this. Let's just say he and Ruby worked it out and stayed married, but he wanted to have an affair with you."

"I don't even want to go there."

"Go there for a minute. What would you do?" Cameo asked.

"I'd be tempted, but I couldn't do it."

"You sure? Not even just one time to get back at Ruby?"

"Two wrongs don't make a right," explained Monet.

"It's just . . . you never know what he might do. You really don't know him that well."

"I just want to."

"I know, and I'm just saying all this because it's something you should face."

"What would you do?" Monet asked.

"I'd do exactly what you're going to do. Tell him you saw Ruby and Alex. I know it won't be easy, but if you care about him, it's all you can do. I don't think the saying 'What he doesn't know won't hurt him' applies here. Jay seems like a smart guy. He'd figure it out soon enough."

"You're right." Monet managed a smile.

"And worry about what happens after that later."

"It's a start."

"You'll do great," Cameo said.

"Thanks for the boost of confidence. I'll need it."

Monet hung up, weary with doubt, worried that she and Jay were just a fantasy, not a reality.

What had she been thinking? Why had she just assumed that she and Jay would wind up together?

Because that's what she hoped for.

Chapter Eighteen

Monet held Jay's business card in her hand. It looked like she felt—worn out and frayed around the edges. Before another second ticked away, she took a deep breath, prayed Ruby wasn't home, and punched in the number.

"Hello," Jay answered.

Her heartbeat quickened. "Hi, Jay. It's Monet."

"Monet," he said with enthusiasm and surprise.

"Am I interrupting anything?" she asked, feeling her palms sweat.

"Not at all. How are you? I heard what happened to Fantasy's. That's awful."

"I'm okay." She'd go into it later. "It was really … I … uh … it was quite a shock. But look, there's something I'd like to share with you." Her throat closed off. She paused. "Would you like to meet for coffee somewhere and talk?"

"Sure, I'd like that. I'm just finishing up some paperwork, and then I can leave."

Relief swept through her. He hadn't mentioned Ruby. That could either mean she wasn't there, or something had gone wrong between them already. "How about somewhere around Lake City between my place and yours?"

"Sounds fine."

She felt anticipation mount. "There's a Denny's right there on Lake City Way. Would that be okay?"

"Sure, what time?"

Monet glanced at her watch. "How about four thirty?"

"Great. See you there."

"Okay, see you soon."

Monet hung up, unable to contain a smile, but it disappeared as the reality of their meeting surfaced.

Freshening up in her bathroom, she touched up her makeup, spritzed on some floral fragrance, called it good, and headed out.

After Monet walked through the door at Denny's, she was seated at a booth toward the back. She checked her watch. She was fifteen minutes early. Scanning the restaurant, she found empty tables here and there. Apparently, the dinner crowd hadn't yet arrived.

She ordered coffee, added cream and sugar, and rehearsed in her mind how she was going to do this. She clutched the white mug tightly, feeling anxious. Was this the right thing to do? If so, why was she having second thoughts? There was no easy way to do what she felt she needed to do. She couldn't back out now.

As she sipped her coffee, her ears picked up on a conversation from two young women at a booth across from her. They chattered about customers, and how their wandering hands always seemed to break the rules.

"When they do that, I just charge them double," one of them said, audible enough for half the restaurant to hear.

Small world, Monet thought. A couple of exotic dancers out having a bite to eat before work.

"Did you hear what happened to Fantasy's?" one of them asked the other.

Monet's heart stopped.

"Holy crap! Can you believe it? Someone must have been seriously pissed. What'd we use to call it … the starter strip club? Most girls only work there a year or two, and then they leave to work at a real strip club."

"Hey, if I can't show all my assets, what's the point?"

Monet swallowed some coffee. She'd stayed at Fantasy's instead of moving on. Why? Because it wasn't all about the status and the ability to be able to take it all off on a stage as she became more experienced, and to say she made good money. It wasn't because she was insecure or lacked self-confidence. No, it was the short-term career path she'd chosen to make life easier financially. Besides, she'd become comfortable at Fantasy's. *Now it was gone.* Except … her short-term career path had turned into thirteen years.

Restless, her gaze swept other occupants. A mixture of elderly and middle-aged couples with kids now filled tables and booths. This made her think of Jay. Did he want a family? She'd always wanted one. She wondered why he and Ruby didn't have kids. Ruby just didn't seem the motherly type.

Then her eyes flew to the door.

It was him.

Jay was talking with the hostess, and when he spotted Monet, he met her eyes with a smile.

Monet swallowed to wet her throat.

He made his way to the table in black trousers and a teal, crew-neck T-shirt. He looked even better than she'd remembered. Her stomach tightened. A residual current weakened her determination to tell him the truth.

"Monet," Jay said, skimming her approvingly, "you been waiting long?"

Her heart beat rapidly. "Not at all."

"Good." He slid in across from her.

His presence comforted her.

"Did you order?" he asked as a waitress headed toward them.

"Just coffee."

"Well then, I guess I'll have the same." His eyes caressed hers.

His look was electric, holding enough power to generate a blackout.

After ordering coffee, he said, "It's great to see you."

"You, too." A mysterious chemistry shivered through her.

"Tell me, what happened with Fantasy's?" Jay settled himself into the booth. "I could hardly believe it when I read the paper this morning."

"It was like … it didn't register at first," Monet said, watching the waitress top off their coffee. She cradled her warm cup in her palms and looked at a point on the wall to calm her emotions. "Apparently, it was arson. It happened early in the morning after the club was closed. So, whoever did this wasn't exactly into hurting anyone. For some reason, they just wanted to destroy the club."

Jay nodded, not saying anything, as he openly studied her face. Then he asked, "Would you like a bite to eat?"

"Oh, no thanks, I'm fine." She set her cup down and leaned against the back of the booth with a smile. Being with Jay was easy—too easy.

"What are your plans now?" He sipped his coffee while watching her over the rim of the cup.

He looked at her as if he cared about her future, his interest evident in his blue eyes. Her pulse pounded. She could hardly drag her eyes from his, so deep and clear, she swore she could see directly into his soul. "I've been giving it a lot of thought."

"Are you going to dance at another club?"

"You know, I'd really decided to get out of dancing, and basically, for now, teach aerobics." She lifted her cup to her lips and sipped cooled coffee. "And hopefully, in the fall, I'd like to start going to school for a degree in interior design."

He took a slow, deep breath and met her eyes. "That's great."

"As long as it works out," she said, looking up at the waitress.

Pen and pad in hand, the ponytailed brunette took Jay's order for a chocolate shake.

He asked Monet, "You sure you don't want anything?"

"Oh." She smiled. "Why not? There's always room for dessert. Do you still have that Reese's chocolate peanut butter pie?"

"Certainly."

"I'll have a slice of that, whenever you have a chance. No hurry," Monet reassured her.

"Interesting," Jay said.

"What?"

"My favorite candy bar is a Reese's Peanut Butter Cup."

"You've got good taste," Monet replied, unable to stop staring at him. His hair was so dark, it looked black. She imagined running her hands through it, dripping wet after a shower, kissing his smooth face, his gorgeous lips, and then …

"I've loved Reese's since I was a kid. I remember when I would ride with my dad in his truck, and we'd stop at this little store every day. Guess what he'd buy me?"

"A Reese's." Sharing an interest with Jay, even if it was only food, heightened the intimacy between them. It brightened an emotional day. She'd nearly forgotten her reason for coming here today. She took a drink of coffee, then moved her cup aside.

"I have to tell you something really strange."

"What's that?"

Monet swallowed hard. "I found out that the owner of Fantasy's is my father."

Jay's blue eyes widened. "You just found all this out today?"

She nodded. "My mother picked me up earlier and we went to see him."

In a hushed whisper, Jay said, "You never knew this?"

Realization dawned. She'd told Alex about her father, not Jay. "I never met my father until today."

In a low, strained voice she explained her upbringing.

Jay pushed a hand through his hair and listened as if so absorbed, he could feel her heartache and exactly what she was feeling, as if he experienced her pain with her.

This was the connection she longed for. And then, a prickle of unease went through her. Tell him.

Before she could, the waitress, like Lucky Charms, magically appeared with something magically delicious.

"Thank you," Monet told the waitress, grateful for the interruption. As she took the first bite, the mixture of rich chocolate, peanut butter, whipped cream, and Reese's candy chunks melted on her tongue. Talk about sinful. Only having Jay for dessert would be better.

Jay stirred his thick-looking shake. "That looks good." He gestured at her pie.

"Would you like to try some?" Monet asked.

"No thanks." He smiled into her eyes. "You enjoy."

Her face grew warm. She set her fork down. Monet imagined tasting him—everywhere—taking the whipped cream from her plate and licking it off his …

And then she remembered why they were here. Tightness closed her throat. "There's something I need to tell you about Ruby and …"

He raised a brow. "Oh?" A look of tension settled on his face.

Monet felt air being pulled from her lungs as she leaned across the table, and in a lowered voice, she said, "I came by your house earlier. I saw Ruby … with …" She searched Jay's face for shock, anger, but instead saw a look of confirmation. He knew.

"I caught her on the phone with someone," he said.

Silence absorbed their thoughts.

Monet's mind spun. Talk about heartless. Were Ruby and Alex trying to get caught? Finally, she forced the words. "It was Alex I saw her with."

Jay went still, then took a deep breath and let out a long, weary sigh. "Alex," he said with disgust.

A chill skidded across her spine. *Alex.* The same name she'd called out in ecstasy. Monet suddenly felt sick and pushed her pie plate away. She wanted to offer Jay comfort—anything to dull the pain and shock he must be feeling.

Jay slumped back against the booth and looked to be in ruins, like an old building that might crumble to the ground.

Monet's heart ached for him. Could she put him back together?

"Alex," he repeated. "I called him to confide in him." Jay shook his head as if he were lost.

Speechless, all Monet could do was feel for him.

Jay looked down at his hands, at his wedding ring on his left finger. "When it comes to Ruby, I have to honestly say not much surprises me. She's been acting so distant lately, like she's not even my wife. It's as though …" He scanned the ceiling as if searching for the perfect answer to his marital issues. "I'm sorry." He drew in a ragged breath. "This is not your problem."

Monet's emotions twisted in her gut. "I came here today because I wanted to … because I wanted to be here for you. You can tell me anything," she whispered, softly and vulnerably, "and I'll listen."

Silence settled between them, broken only by the sound of voices and clanging dishes.

Their eyes met and held.

"You're special," he said.

Her pulse skyrocketed. "So are you."

After a beat, Jay said, "Ruby's actions don't totally shock me, although Alex's do. It's crazy, huh?" He chuckled, without humor. "Who can you trust? I let Ruby manipulate me. I can't believe I didn't know this was going on."

"Sometimes we can't see the things that are the most obvious."

"How do you always know what to say?"

"I don't." She heard the tenderness in his voice and saw the emotion in his eyes. Her heart caught. Jay didn't deserve this. She could never do this to him. How could Ruby? Nausea pooled in her stomach. "I'm so sorry, Jay. I couldn't keep what I know from you. I mean, I couldn't keep it inside of me without going crazy. Alex and I were never serious, and after this, I can't tell you how much I regret ever getting involved with him. He's no better than Ruby."

On a devastated sigh, Jay said, "Ruby even screwed up the bookkeeping. Obviously, her classes were a lie, too. She tried to steal money from my business." He sliced a hand through the air in dismissal. "Sorry, I'm rambling."

"I don't mind. I'm listening." Monet leaned across the table.

He shook his head. "I don't trust her now," he said, his eyes reflecting pain. "I'm not so sure I ever did. That's the funny part. And you know, it's like I already knew something was wrong, but I just couldn't face it. I figured maybe if I let it go, it would all just disappear and everything would be all right again. But it never was to begin with."

"It sounds like you wanted to believe everything was okay. It was easier."

"But ... marriage without trust? What kind is that?"

"Not for me," Monet said.

Time stopped.

Abruptly, he leaned forward. "The kind that's not worth a damn thing."

"I agree."

"When we were first married, I was so infatuated with Ruby, nothing else mattered. I assumed, since she married me, that I could trust her, but she just needed someone to take care of her. I think I loved her." Sadness dampened his eyes. "Not anymore. She's a walking time bomb just waiting to go off. She's unquenchable, spoiled, selfish ... so unlike you."

Monet's emotions tripped over themselves. "You're nothing like Alex, either." This connection between them scared and excited her. It was totally new. She felt panic yet exhilaration.

"Maybe we have more in common than we know," Jay said simply.

A tingling sensation worked its way through Monet's whole body. "It's got to be hard to trust someone after that. Why I put up with Shane for two years, I'll never know." She took a deep breath, still rattled by Jay's comment. "Then I met Alex. He can be charming, but it was more than that. He had issues, and I wanted to help him solve them." She wouldn't say any more on the subject. Maybe later. And if anything developed between them, she'd share everything.

"Tell me," he encouraged, "what you put up with for two years."

He seemed to have shoved thoughts of Ruby aside. "With Shane? Oh boy," she whistled softly, "where do I start?"

* * *

Jay loved looking into the warm depths of her honey-colored eyes. It helped to get his mind off Alex ... and Ruby. "Start at the beginning." Anticipation rippled through him. He wanted to know everything about her.

"I met him where I used to dance, and then we lived together, on and off, for about two years. I prayed that his lies would eventually turn into the truth. They didn't. I'm just thankful it's over. The thought of marrying him and spending the rest of our lives together now gives me the chills." She crossed her arms, looked away, uncrossed them, then continued. "He used to talk about marriage. That would have been the worst mistake of my life. It never would have worked out."

"Sounds familiar, except you were smarter than me." Jay chuckled, despite his predicament. "You didn't get married."

"I wouldn't exactly call it smarter."

Jay wondered if he'd made the worst mistake of his life marrying Ruby ... except he'd met Monet. Hearing her voice ignited a growing ember of desire.

"What Ruby did to you," Monet continued, "I'm sure has nothing to do with you. I would guess it has to do with her. I honestly don't think that you lack anything."

Her words lightened his dark mood. He sat, silently admiring her integrity and realism.

"Besides, I've been going around in circles all my life. You'd think at thirty-one, a person would have it all figured out."

Jay watched emotion cloud her clear eyes. "Not necessarily. Thirty-one's young."

"It depends on who you're talking to."

"I suppose."

She is real easy to look at, he thought. The loveliness was generated from within, unlike Ruby. Should he start talking to an attorney about a divorce? The way he enjoyed Monet's company forced him to wonder if he and Ruby had ever been right for each other.

"You'll do what's best, I know," Monet said, as if reading his thoughts.

"We'll see." He clenched his teeth in fury. How long had it been going on? "I wonder," he said, twisting and pulling on his wedding ring as if to rid himself of Ruby, "how Alex could appear so normal at work and act like nothing was going on? The two people I trusted most were disloyal."

"They're the inadequate ones, not you," Monet assured him.

He smiled his appreciation of her kindness and realized, right now, with her helping to soothe his ache, this wasn't the time or the place to vent the rage building inside of him.

"You appear to have done very well for yourself," she said softly. "I'm sure you'll come out of this in one piece."

"I'm glad you think so."

"You're a smart businessman. It really shows. You should be proud of yourself. Ruby's greedy. She would never be satisfied no matter how much she had."

"You know, I think you're right." His anger and self-blame slowly subsided. She made him realize he'd done nothing wrong. This was about Ruby. Apparently, she wasn't happy in the marriage and needed something else. Maybe not even someone—just something.

The waitress stopped by for a courtesy check.

Jay noticed Monet had left her pie untouched since she'd told him about Ruby and Alex.

Alex. Anger rushed to the surface again. He felt his face heat up and emptied a full glass of water.

"Are you okay?" Monet's eyes held worry.

He nodded.

She looked away.

He sensed she knew he needed a minute to gather himself.

He'd fire Alex. Period. There was no way he'd continue to let him work for him now. He'd worry about replacing him later. The gossip that would spread about Alex and Ruby had anxiety and tension stiffening his shoulders. The back of his neck suddenly ached.

He reached for his shake and glanced at Monet, who'd picked up her fork again. Drinking through his straw, he watched as she took a bite of her pie. The way it went down her throat aroused him. He ran his tongue over his lips, totally unaware of where it led her thoughts.

Mesmerized, he watched the way her lips slid back over the fork after taking a bite. He wondered what they would feel like against his mouth. Inviting and soft. The thought awakened his sexual appetite. Ruby had turned it off. Her pitiable attempts to seduce him lately were useless. His arousal for Monet left him confused. It was so enticing … and wrong.

Yet, Ruby and Alex … A surge of rage uncoiled, almost overpowering his control.

Until her voice pulled him back.

"When I first met you, I"—Monet's eyes lingered on his—"I had a hard time not thinking about you."

His heart sped at NASCAR speed. "Me, too." He'd known then something wasn't right with his marriage. If it'd been right, Monet would have had no effect on him. He was raised with strong family values. His parents' successful marriage proved that. He'd looked for the same thing with Ruby. It never happened. Maybe with Monet? He needed closure with Ruby first. Except, his hunger for Monet just wouldn't go away.

Now, as she spread a shiny gloss on her lips that smelled like ripe strawberries and then gently slid a finger under her bottom lip to wipe away the excess, his body hardened. He wanted to lick the sweet-smelling stuff right off those luscious lips. He moved his gaze to her hair. The mixture of gold brought out the color in her eyes. Her long, flowing mane caused him to wonder how it would feel draped all around him as he filled her up.

Jay had some serious thinking to do, but for now, he wanted—needed—to savor Monet. Her pink, lacy top hugged her breasts when she moved. He ached to replace it with his lips, creating images in his mind of how she might quiver when he tasted her. He'd better say something, and fast.

He pulled himself from the visual, adjusting himself in the booth. "So, how's your mom holding up since your dad surfaced?"

Monet squared her shoulders and folded her hands on the table. "Actually, she's pretty amazing. Calm and sympathetic."

Jay inquired, "How about you?"

"I'm okay." She paused. "I'd like to forgive my dad, but"—she looked away—"I don't think it'll be easy. Yet, somehow I know it'll be worth it."

Her gentleness tugged at his heart. She made happiness seem attainable again, almost simple.

Monet smiled. "I'm glad we did this."

"Me, too. We'll have to do it again." But not until after he got his own life in order.

"I'd like that. I'll stay in touch." Monet patted her purse. "I've got your card."

Jay's face relaxed into a smile, remembering when he'd

slipped his card into her hand. Seconds ticked away in rhythm with his heart.

Monet rooted in her purse for a pen. Then she jotted a number down on an unused napkin and silently moved her hand across the table to slip the folded napkin into his.

Her touch triggered an instant response, leaving him speechless.

When she moved her hand away, Jay took out his wallet, slipped a few dollars onto the table, and swiped up the bill. "I know it's not much, but I'd like to buy."

"I don't expect—"

He waved a hand in the air to silence her.

"Thank you."

Then, unable to stop himself, he took her same hand in his and squeezed it, reluctant to let go.

As he walked with her to her car, not even the traffic whizzing by on Lake City Way affected him. With her, it seemed utterly quiet.

Then their eyes met as they stood facing each other.

"I made a mistake with Ruby," he said. "Just being with you feels different. Ruby and I never connected other than physically."

"I think the same about Alex … and feel the same about you."

"Ruby's appeal was blinding in the beginning, but now, I've finally opened my eyes to something real—you."

Monet smiled.

"I'll see you again," Jay said with absolute certainty.

As she drove away, he wrapped his thoughts around her. He admired her strength, her courage, the depth to her personality, not to mention, she seemed to shine from the inside out. He realized she may be the one he just might want to spend the rest of his life with.

Chapter Nineteen

Ruby's skin crawled as she remembered the article in this morning's paper. *"Believed to be arson. No leads yet as to who may have done this crime."* She'd rumpled the newspaper and taken it with her to dump at the grocery store after her spa treatment. She'd thought the pampering would ease her tension. No luck. She'd committed arson. Her nerves surprised her. It pleased her to know the building had been completely destroyed in the fire. Good job. Despite her fear, she gave herself a mental pat on the back.

She shifted into fifth gear, hoping Alex would quiet her rising fear. There was nothing like good sex to ease a high level of anxiety. Her Corvette purred like a lion as she raced the country roads to his house.

Her thoughts sped to Jay. He had come home from moving equipment, and then left, without a note or a call.

Screw him. When she'd returned home from the spa and grocery store, she'd expected to spend a nice evening with him. And if he was lucky, she'd planned to make fajitas for dinner, only as a start ...

So now, the sooner she could get to Alex's, the better. She had to know if his plans clashed with hers. Would he continue to see her, or had he been serious when he'd said it's the last time? The way he was acting lately ... well, screw him, too! She was prepared to fix him and fix him good. She knew what men wanted. What man, in his right mind, could turn down the best blow job of his life?

A sinful smile crept across her face. By the time she finished licking up the last drop, he'd be begging her to stay with him. Hah! That's what she wanted. Hey, maybe she should try that on Jay later, too? Even though he didn't know she had started the fire, he would probably leave her. She couldn't think about him now. It would distract her too much.

She shifted down, still edgy from the fire she'd started thirteen hours ago.

When she reached Alex's place, she pulled onto the concrete slab behind his garage door. As she rang the bell, her heart sped up, anticipating his reaction to her sudden appearance. They hadn't spoken since he'd told her to get off of him. She'd make him speak now.

She rang it again, worry dampening her palms. There was

a light on. She knew he was home. Impatient, she imagined a variety of unpleasant thoughts when the door swung open.

Surprise and disgust crossed his face. "What do you want?"

"It's about time." Ruby pushed past him. "What took you so long?"

In a weary voice, he said, "I was on the phone."

"With whom?"

"You sure you wanna know?"

Ruby's lips parted as understanding struck. "No." She nodded, feeling a hysterical urge to choke the life out of him.

"I told you I was through," Alex said. "Well, I meant it. I told Jay I'm going to work for my dad in Oregon. I'm moving to get away from you."

Relief washed through her. She knew she could change his mind. He could still work around here until they could move somewhere together. She put a hand to her heart. "Silly me." She chuckled. "I thought you told him about us. Phew."

"I did."

Shock paralyzed her. She fought to breathe. She'd lose everything—her husband, her lover—plus she could wind up in jail for the rest of her life if she was caught.

"You what? Goddamn you!" A bolt of anger sizzled through her.

"You heard me." He turned away.

"Don't walk away from me." She raced right up to him, pummeling his chest with her fists.

He pulled back and grabbed both of her wrists. "I don't think you want to do that," he warned.

"Come on, Alex. Why?" She cried.

"I never felt anything for you. You're a piece of ass, Ruby."

She started to lash out, but he caught her hand in midair. Through clenched teeth, he said, "I'm not playing. Get out."

"Is that all you can say?" She looked up at him through tear-stained lashes.

"You suck."

That thought gave her hope. She smiled slowly, running her tongue all the way across her full lips. "You mean that in a good way or bad, Alex? I know you know I can give one hell of a hummer. As a matter of fact, that's why I'm here."

"Get real. Besides"—he shrugged—"I've had better. I thought you knew I'd tell Jay. Apparently, you don't listen to shit. And you know what I think?"

She was breathing so hard that she could see her own chest rise and fall. She fought to keep still.

"I think you're nothing but a nymphomaniac who can't get enough of me. Sorry, I'm cutting you off." He grabbed a nearby lit cigarette, took a drag, and blew smoke right into Ruby's face.

Rage clouded her vision. She blinked away the haze. "You're an arrogant bastard!" Even though Alex acted like he didn't want her, Ruby knew better. How could he get so damn hard if he didn't? "I know you think I'm hot, and you know you want me. So, why deny it, huh? How can you suddenly act like you want nothing to do with me after all we've been through?"

"Been through?" He laughed.

His laughter fueled her anger. "This isn't a game."

"Oh?" Alex muttered. "What is it then?" He took a drag of his cigarette, turned his back on Ruby, and crossed to the living room. "I'd appreciate it if you'd leave. I have nothing to say to you." He crushed the cigarette out in a filled ashtray on the coffee table.

Ruby eyed the ashtray, littered with cigarette butts. How could she have ever wanted him? He smoked too much, drank too much, was a jerk, and she could sure think of more to add to the list. She followed him anyway and grabbed him by the shoulder, forcing him to look at her. "Alex," she pleaded. "You don't mean what you're saying."

"Really?" He chuckled. "Why would I say it if I didn't mean it?" He broke free from her.

"Because you want me." She stood right under him and fluttered her lashes. "Just say it."

"No, I don't. I don't care about you, and I never did. As I said before, you were nothing but a piece of ass to me. Get it? Nothing but ass!"

"You're a typical truck driver, or should I say log truck driver?"

"Whatever you wanna call it. Call me a doctor, a lawyer. I don't care. I really don't give a shit."

"In your dreams."

"Yeah, at least you're not in them."

"You make me sick."

"Then leave."

Fuming, Ruby straightened her shoulders, held her chin high, and turned on her heels. It was his loss.

Once outside, she fired up her car and left, burning rubber in the process.

In the beginning, they couldn't get enough of each other. Then why was he acting as if it meant nothing to him? *Because it didn't*, she thought. Anger and sadness collided inside of her.

She cranked the radio. Loud hip-hop boomed out of the speakers, the beat heaven to her ears. And then LL Cool J said, "The only thing left to do is climax." Shit! Didn't anybody think about anything else but sex? Apparently, Alex didn't with her anymore. Ever since he'd met Monet, everything had changed. She was the root of all of Ruby's problems. A wave of hate washed over her. Then, as if breaking on the sand, it disappeared. Monet couldn't mean much to Alex if he was leaving for Oregon. Good.

Ruby realized she'd been so overcome with fear about torching Fantasy's and getting away with it that she hadn't really thought about accomplishing her main objective—Monet out of a job. Gus, too.

As Ruby pulled into the garage, her thoughts tumbled like dominoes. Her pulse pounded. Did she want Jay to be home? Yes. She needed to confide in him. Apparently, he was all she had left. Alex didn't want her anymore. She could only hope Jay still did. He couldn't leave her now.

* * *

Jay watched Ruby enter the house, telling himself to stay focused, calm, controlled, and to handle this with the utmost care and precision. His whole life was about to change.

"Jay, I'm so glad you're home," Ruby said, a little too dramatically.

Her tone sickened him. "I bet." His words were laced with sarcasm. He stood with his back against the counter, a cold soda in his hand.

"What are you doing?"

"I was just going over some maps for the next job and, as usual, wondered where you were."

Ruby sighed. "I've just been out doing errands, shopping, things like that." She crossed the tile floor to stand beside Jay.

At her nearness, Jay couldn't help but visualize her and Alex. Nausea swirled around his stomach. He turned around to lean over the counter. Alex had called and said he was leaving because of personal problems. He hadn't exactly told him about he and Ruby, but they both knew. He wouldn't just say, "I slept with your wife," but he'd said enough. Jay had never been good at firing people. Alex had just saved him the task by quitting.

"Hey." Ruby put a hand on Jay's back. "Are you okay?"

Stay in control. He whirled around, knocked her hand off of him, and breathed in deeply. "How about we sit." He angled his can toward the table. "There are a couple things I'd like to go over with you."

She shrugged. "Sure."

Jay could practically see the wheels of her mind spinning.

"Better yet, why don't you talk while I make your favorite—fajitas."

He shook his head. "No, Ruby, that can wait. Come on, have a seat." He walked to the table, pulled a chair out for her, and settled into one.

"I think I'll have a glass of wine first. Can I get you something stronger? Maybe a beer?"

"No," he snapped. "I don't need a beer."

"Fine." She tossed a lock of hair behind a shoulder. "What's gotten into you?"

"Get your wine and you'll find out." He mentally rehearsed how he was going to go about this. He wouldn't tell her Monet had filled him in, but he could tell her about Alex and see if she offered any of the truth. The bookkeeping was another thing. Why did it feel like it took an act of God to get the truth out of her? Had it always been this way?

With frenzied haste, Ruby poured wine into a glass and sloshed it around. "Oops." She giggled. "I'll clean it up. Be there in a sec."

Jay's patience grew thin. Anxiety tightened his muscles. He just wanted to get this over with.

Ruby maneuvered to the table with her full glass of wine, after clearly stalling.

"Who have you been with?"

She took a big swallow from her glass. "What?" She stretched the word into two syllables.

"You heard me, Ruby. Don't you think that I would catch on sooner or later? You really don't think I'm that stupid, do you?" He finished off his orange soda and crushed the can one-handed.

"Oh my God." Her voice rose a pitch. She nodded, tipped her glass back, and nearly emptied it. "I can't believe you're sitting here accusing me of such nonsense."

He pushed to his feet so fast his chair skidded. "Then I'll stand." He slammed a hand down on the table—hard. It caused her glass to tip over, spilling what little wine was left on the Ralph Lauren woven placemat. He didn't care.

Ruby covered her face in her hands and began to cry.

"You think that's going to work?" She was unbelievable.

"I don't know anymore." She sobbed. Ruby slowly rose and stood inches from him. "Please," she begged, "I didn't do anything wrong."

She attempted to grab his shirt. He stepped back and out of her reach. "You don't think that sleeping with someone else is wrong?"

"But … I didn't, Jay. You have to believe me."

"No!" He swung around and away from her. "I don't. Why do you think Alex called me and quit, huh?"

"Alex? Screw him."

He whirled around so fast that her hair fluttered in the breeze. "Apparently, you have."

Ruby shook her head defiantly. "But … no, Jay, it's not like that. It's not what you think."

"You have no idea what I'm thinking because if you did, you'd tell me the truth."

She blinked in astonishment. "What do you mean?" Her voice held a trace of fear.

"I mean," Jay said, pushing a hand through his hair, "how do you expect me to stay in this marriage when I can't trust you?"

"You can trust me."

He laughed in spite of the seriousness of the situation. "No, Ruby, I can't. Unless—"

"Okay." She cut him off and sniffled. "Alex and I … listen, Alex was the one who started everything. You have to believe me," she added, a tear streaming down her face. "I wanted nothing to do with him, but he threatened me and said if I didn't sleep with him, he'd tell you all kinds of lies about me."

God she was a good actress. "It's not working, Ruby."

"He told me he'd tell you that I was … that I was seducing all the guys who worked for you, and that you'd never find out about us. And that he wanted a future with me."

Jay felt a rush of cold anger. "Uh-huh." He shook his head. "You expect me to believe that crap?" He looked at her in disgust.

She sniffed again. "Why not?"

Jay hesitated, trying to control his rising temper. "Because it's bullshit!"

"No, it's not," Ruby whined. "And about the bookkeeping ... I never stole from you. Did you ever stop to think that maybe it was the bank's fuck-up?" She spun away and left the room.

He knew better. Between his accountant and the bank, they'd figured it out. Ruby had put it back, but she'd never have the chance to steal from him again.

Jay made his way to the bedroom. He couldn't stay with Ruby tonight. Since he just had his equipment moved to a new jobsite, he had some time off before the next haul.

He found her on the bed, pillows propped up against the headboard. She was slouched against it, her arms crossed tight over her chest, her face awash with different colors of eye makeup smudged from crying.

"I'm going to get a motel tonight," was all he said as he began throwing things in a small suitcase.

"Why?"

"You know why."

He crossed to the bathroom, grabbed some essentials, and suddenly wondered where he was going. He had no idea. He'd figure it out on the way.

Minutes later, he turned out of his driveway and onto a winding backroad that took him past fields of horses. Dandelions, daisies, and salmonberry brush sprouting red flowers and berries nestled amongst maple, cottonwood, fir, and cedar trees lining borders and weedy lawns.

Once in downtown Maltby, he took the scenic route. An old-time service station, signs, windmills, and steam tractors surrounded a café.

At a red light, he saw the modern convenience store and gas station across the highway. A sign read, "Fried chicken, deli sandwiches, espresso, beer, and wine." His stomach rumbled, but there was no way he could eat now.

Chapter Twenty

Monet dressed in sapphire-colored pants, a white, shaped blouse, and pulled back her hair in a beaded clip. Time to visit her dad in the hospital.

As she checked her watch, she realized her mother would be here in twenty minutes. Her dad was going home today. It meant a lot for them both to be there and to maybe even see where he lived. She and her mother would discuss that part on the way.

She found herself in the kitchen doing last-minute cleanup before her mother arrived. Thinking of Jay's husky "I'll see you again" ignited all five senses. She wondered what it would feel like to run her fingers through the silky strands of all that dark hair. She imagined exploring each other in the shower with water sluicing off their gleaming bodies. Heat flickered inside of her. God … how she wanted him.

When her mother arrived, they didn't linger at the apartment. Monet locked up and they headed out.

"New outfit? That fuchsia is a great color on you," Monet said, once they were on their way.

Her mom brightened in a smile as she glanced down at her V-neck shirt and matching trousers. "Yes, it is. As a matter of fact, I went to the Nordstrom's Anniversary Sale last night. It's still going on, you know."

Monet smiled. "I know. I look forward to it every year."

"Oh, speaking of that, I have your money. With all that went on, I forgot to bring it yesterday."

"Mom, you don't have to explain. Hey, about Dad. Did you want to stay until he's discharged, or what did you have planned?"

Lucy hesitated. "Actually, I was just going to play it by ear. Ryan and I talked about it a lot last night, and he told me to do whatever I'm comfortable doing. He's so amazing."

"I've found someone whom I think is amazing, too."

"Someone other than the truck driver?"

A quick smile tugged at her mouth at the image of her and Jay that she'd conjured before her mother arrived. "His boss."

"But he's married."

"The truck driver was sleeping with his wife."

"I thought you were seeing him?"

"Not anymore. And ironically, when I met Jay, I felt something—something different that I'd never felt before. It has nothing to do with him being successful or having more than Alex, his driver. It has to do with the way I feel when I'm near him, and I'm hoping that something special happens between us. Jay and I have done nothing wrong. I could never do what his wife did to him."

Her mother's smile was soft and understanding. "Reminds me of a soap opera. I'm glad you're different from his wife and that you're not seeing his driver anymore."

"So am I."

When they arrived at the hospital and entered Dan's room, Monet was surprised to see him walking around without the oxygen.

"Hey, feeling better today?" she asked around a smile.

"Lots better. It's nice that you both came again. I didn't expect you to, you know." He shuffled around the room in slippers and a hospital gown.

He looked so frail.

It felt odd when she pictured him at Fantasy's. Monet remembered back … how many times had she seen him over the years? She supposed she could count them on one hand, and it had been briefly, in passing at the bar or from a distance when she was out on the floor. She'd really never paid much attention to him. She just knew he was the owner.

"So, are you going to be released today?" Lucy asked.

"Yeah." He coughed a little but recovered quickly. "I think, if I'm lucky, in a few hours or so." He made his way slowly to the bed.

Monet put a hand on the small of his back to guide him. It felt strange, spontaneous yet right.

He settled into the bed, raising the back to sit up.

Monet and her mother took a seat in the visitors' chairs.

"Would you like a ride home?" Monet asked, hands folded in her lap, "or have you made other arrangements?" It was still hard to know how to act, what to say, and what to feel.

Weariness crowded his features. "I don't expect either of you, after what I—"

"How are you feeling?" a nurse asked, cutting into their conversation.

Monet was grateful. She watched the bubbly, young redhead check his vitals. The color of her hair reminded Monet of Ruby. Would Jay divorce Ruby? What if he didn't?

"Will he be going home today?" Monet asked, to reposition her thoughts.

After taking his blood pressure, the nurse replied, "Yes. Sometime this afternoon, a resident will write his discharge orders and discharge him back home to his regular doctor."

"I see you're doing much better today." The nurse's enthusiastic tone comforted Monet. "Not so much of that awful phlegm with your cough."

He nodded. "I do feel better today."

"I'm glad to hear it. Call if you need anything."

Monet noticed an uneasiness to his voice. Yesterday, he'd been more out of it from the trauma. Today, reality set in.

After the nurse left, Lucy pushed to her feet and ambled toward him. "Do you have a way home?"

"Yes … I mean … no, not really, but," he said, hesitating, "I can get a ride. You don't have to take me home."

Monet went to stand by her mother. "We'd like to. It would be nice to see where you live. Don't worry, we're not planning to interfere with your life. We just want to be a part of it, if you want."

His eyes misted. Then, in a very quiet voice, he said to Monet, "I'd like to know about your life, too."

"Okay." She looked to her mom for guidance.

Her mom smiled encouragement and then intervened. "I never made it easy on her growing up. She took better care of me than I did of her."

"Mom," Monet whispered, her throat tightening. She carefully touched her shoulder.

Lucy nodded rather than spoke.

"We both took our time growing up." Monet squeezed her mother's hand. "And then, I started working at Fantasy's thirteen years ago. Basically, I've been there, on and off, ever since. In between, I teach aerobics. Not much to tell, really." She wiped at her damp brow, feeling stretched thin.

When she looked back over her life, she realized there was so much more she would have liked to accomplish in thirty-one years.

Then, in a voice laced with bitter memories and regret,

Dan said, "On your terms, I'd like to be a part of your life now, both of you."

Monet let it sink in. "We'd like that."

His eyes reflected pain as he looked at her mother. "You first."

While her mother spun the web of her past, Monet felt like her life had just begun. Here. Now. With her parents beside her as if they were putting the pieces of their lives back together.

When Lucy finished, Dan said, "So you never married. But I'm glad you finally found someone who makes you happy. I did at one time … too." His eyes were bright with unshed tears. "Right after I left you, I changed my name. I didn't want to be reminded of that person anymore—Zack. And then fifteen years ago, I met a woman who couldn't have children. It was a perfect match for me. I'd made up my mind after leaving you that there would never be any children for me." Raw emotion flitted through his hazel eyes. "We were so happy together, and then … she got cancer and was gone in a matter of months."

Monet's heart broke for her father, who had been through so much pain in his life, like her mom.

"That's when I bought Fantasy's. I didn't want to get involved with anyone or anything. Fantasy's was perfect for that. It was working for me, until—" He went into a fit of coughs.

Monet handed him a small paper cup from a portable table.

After a few sips, his coughing subsided.

He got up slowly and stood. "Come here." He held his arms out and drew her close.

Monet embraced him like she never wanted to let go. Her emotions fluttered on the edge of control. She stared at the ceiling, numb and trembling. She fought a losing battle of tears and felt her mother at her side, placing a reassuring hand on her shoulder.

"It's okay," her mother whispered as she clutched Monet's hand.

"I know," Monet said, and then when she looked at her father, something inside her healed. Bottled up years of feelings poured out new and fresh, like a celebration of bubbly champagne, and Monet let go.

Here she was, feeling the anticipation of love and hope to fill an empty place inside her heart.

While waiting for discharge orders, Monet asked with interest, "Where exactly do you live?"

A warm smile lit his thin face. "In a condo near the Ballard Locks with a view of the water."

"Must be nice," Monet said softly.

"Yeah, it is. It gets lonely at times, but now," he said with emotion-filled eyes, "you can come and visit me."

"I'd like that." Monet smiled, feeling a peacefulness settle around her. "Do you go to Ray's Boathouse much? I think it's a fabulous restaurant."

"Of course, but I usually eat in the upstairs café. It's more casual."

"I know," Monet said. "The wait for their dining room can be weeks long. What do you like to order?"

"I enjoy the deep-fried calamari in the tempura batter, and their fish doesn't come any fresher."

"I heard the view of the sound and the Olympics at sunset are incredible," Lucy added.

"We'll all have to go sometime." Monet turned and smiled at her mother, then looked at her dad and said, "You know, I appreciate the fact that you didn't make excuses or blame anyone else for your choice in the past. You were open and honest, and it had to take a lot of courage to be that way. I just want to say thank you."

Other than the steady breathing of Dan's roommate and the blip of the monitors, a short stretch of silence filled the hospital room.

Then, in a raspy but soft voice, her father said, "I want to see you again, your mom as a friend." He slipped Lucy a glance. Then his glassy eyes found Monet's. "And you as a daughter, but only on your terms."

Slats of light snuck in through the partly open curtains, bathing the room in vertical stripes.

Monet's heart turned over in her chest. "I feel as if I'm finally part of a family."

As the three of them left the hospital that warm, summer afternoon, Monet carried with her that sense of closure she'd longed for.

Chapter Twenty-One

"Where have you been?" Ruby's accusing voice hit Jay the second he stepped through the utility room door from the garage.

"At my attorney's. It's over, Ruby," he said, pushing past her.

He entered the kitchen, took a glass from a cupboard, and crossed to the fridge to get the pitcher of water.

"What?" She blinked in astonishment, grabbing his forearm. "You can't mean that."

He shook his arm free and poured himself a glass of water. "I'm sorry, Ruby, I do. You've cheated and lied. I just can't trust you. Either I move out temporarily until things are settled, or you do."

"I'm not moving out. This is as much my house as it is yours. Remember, we're still married."

"Not for much longer. You'll be served with papers."

"It was only one time with Alex. I didn't plan for it to happen," Ruby said in a whining tone.

"Ruby, I can see right through you. I know you're lying. Remember, I talked to Alex?"

"I can't stand you, and suddenly, I can't stand this house." She hurled her empty wine glass across the room, striking the tile floor and shattering into bits.

He closed his eyes to reclaim his calm. "Then you can leave." Perspiration dampened his brow.

"Fine, I will. I have a lot of men drooling over me anyway."

"Thanks for informing me. Now, would you like to talk like two adults and hear what's going to happen?"

"I could care less. Besides, I've got some packing to do. I'm taking my clothes, jewelry, and my car, and you can have the rest of the junk. I'll just expect the balance in cash." She pinned him with a dangerous look and fled the room.

Distress mounted, but he refused to be stung by her harsh tone. Jay didn't even want to argue. He'd let the professionals handle it. With an unsteady hand, he took his glass of water into the living room. He'd wanted to discuss this with Ruby. He hoped she'd sign the papers without making a big fuss. She could hardly afford not to. He had a hunch she would, as long as she got her settlement. He would keep the business and place the same and just pay her off. If there was one thing he knew about Ruby, when it came to dollar signs, her eyes lit up.

He set his water down on the coffee table, picked up the remote, and channel surfed. He stopped at a baseball game.

Suddenly, Ruby whirled into the living room, her face beet red, her eyes blazing. "Don't think I'm going to make this easy on you."

"I know. I'm not worried, Ruby." Jay pushed to his feet and stood to face her. "You can't hurt me anymore."

"I'm taking a few suitcases now. I'll be back later for the rest." She swiveled on her high heels, struggling to pick up a suitcase in the hallway.

Jay went to her rescue. "Here, let me help."

"I don't need your help," she cried.

"Let me help anyway." Jay's heart clutched. Three years of marriage didn't just wear off overnight.

In silence, he helped her take her stuff to the garage. She reached in her car and pressed the rear window release button. They set the suitcases inside.

"Where are you going? I'd like to know so I or my attorney can contact you."

"Where else? My lousy parents' house," she burst out. "I happened to have a shitty childhood, in case you forgot, unlike you, who grew up with everything your heart desired. Spoiled bastard," she muttered under her breath.

Jay almost felt sorry for her until he heard her last words. "Some people never let the past go," he said. "They're stubborn throughout life and hold a grudge with all their might until it destroys them and the people close to them. I tried my hardest to get through to you. Obviously, it wasn't enough. Try and take care of yourself, Ruby."

"What do you care?" she asked on a sob.

Jay watched her maneuver herself into the Corvette he'd given her on their first anniversary. His eyes burned. His throat ached. He had to let it go … and move on.

Then she pounded the automatic garage door opener above her head, fired up the sports car, and backed out.

She wasn't easy on the tires, or the driveway.

Jay shook his head and watched her go.

Chapter Twenty-Two

Monet wondered why she wasn't happier, making it through the first month of school. It was fall, her favorite time of year, and she was fascinated by the study of interior design.

She and Cameo saw each other on a regular basis. Cameo had even given up exotic dancing. She now worked at Thirteen Coins, an around-the-clock restaurant where grill cooks worked in the open, portions were large, the bread was good, and the service excellent. Monet had gone there with her father a few times to see Cameo and have a bite to eat. Then afterward, they'd gone back to his condo to play chess and drink vodka and cranberry juice out on his deck while the water sparkled in the distance. He told her he was thinking about opening a nightclub in the University District that specialized in reggae music, local rock, and blues. Monet thought it was a neat idea.

Monet and her mother had also kept in close contact. And just last week, Lucy met Monet and her father at Ray's Boathouse, like they'd discussed at the hospital. Lucy and Ryan were still together. Everything seemed to be working out.

So ... why wasn't she happy? Why did she feel like there was a void in her life? There was only one answer—Jay. She hadn't talked to him since they'd met at Denny's several months ago. They said they would stay in touch. It never happened. She didn't feel right intruding in his life. Had he forgiven Ruby? Had they reconciled and that's why he hadn't called? Were they still together?

Her heart clutched at the thought.

Monet tossed her keys and purse on the kitchen counter, opened the fridge, and grabbed a can of Orange Crush. That's what she'd had with *him* the first time they were alone. Jay's image appeared in her mind.

When the phone intruded on her musing, she sighed and thought, *Let the machine pick it up*.

"Monet, it's Jay," he said into the machine.

At the sound of his deep voice, she scrambled to the phone, emotions whirling in excitement, anticipation, and dread. Maybe he'd called to say a final good-bye.

She frantically punched the on-off button on her answering machine and said, "Jay, hi."

"How are you?"

"Good." She lied a little. "And you?" She heard his sharp intake of breath.

"Better now."

Perspiration beaded between her breasts. "Why is that?"

"My divorce is final. Look, I … uh … I'm sorry it's been so long. I just felt like I needed time to myself."

Joy surged through her. "You don't have to apologize for anything."

"It actually went okay. Ruby was easier to deal with than I expected."

"I'm happy for you."

"Thanks. I'm just glad it's over."

The silence was deafening.

Monet's heart knocked against her chest.

"Hey," he said, pausing. "I was wondering if you'd like to go somewhere with me?"

Her mind raced. "Where? When? I mean, I'd love it."

"Lincoln City on the Oregon Coast. Tonight. This weekend. I just got a wild hair and got to thinking, you know, where's my favorite place to go? Who would I like to share it with, and I thought of you."

Her world turned over. "I'd love to go with you," she said. "I've only been there once when a friend of mine in the eighth grade invited me for her birthday one year with her family. You know something I remember?"

"What?"

"When you're coming into town, there's a sign that says, *The Beach Is Just the Beginning*."

"I know."

She could hear the smile in his voice.

"I'll make the reservations right away."

"I can't wait."

After they hung up, Monet was so ecstatic, she didn't know where to begin. Jay was picking her up in a couple of hours.

Perfect. She didn't have to be in school until Monday morning or teach an aerobics class until Monday night. But first things first. She phoned her roommate and arranged for her to feed Dixie Cup. Then she took another shower and shaved her legs carefully to a silky-smooth finish.

After folding some clothes neatly into an overnight bag, she gathered necessities from the bathroom.

And then she buzzed Cameo.

"Guess what?" she said when Cameo answered.

"What?"

"Jay called."

"Oh my God!"

"Oh my God is right." Monet couldn't get her heart back to normal speed. "His divorce is final. He's taking me to the Oregon Coast this weekend."

"Yeah!" Cameo cheered. "Good for you. Wow, Monet, I'm so happy for you. I just knew it."

Monet heard her slap something and smiled.

"I just knew that you two would wind up together some day. Good things come to those who wait. You deserve this. You've been through so much lately."

Tears glossed Monet's vision. "Don't make me cry."

"Damn girl, you're the one who is going to make me cry. Now go have the time of your life."

The doorbell rang at four fifty-five. The sound awoke every muscle in Monet's body.

She opened the door after taking a deep breath that came out a whisper when she saw him standing there.

"Jay." He looked and smelled wonderful. The masculine scent of Armani, his freshness, and presence took her breath away.

"Monet." He met her eyes with a smile.

Her heart kicked up a notch. "It's great to see you."

"You, too."

After a quick tour of the apartment, she grabbed her purse and overnight bag and they headed to his gray Chevy pickup. He held the door open for her, closed it, walked around to his side, and climbed in.

Once they were on the road, Jay said, "I've thought about you so much. It's crazy."

Monet swallowed. He was gorgeous—so gorgeous she had to work at concentrating on what he said. "Me, too." She let her eyes drift over him. "I even thought about calling you, but I didn't want to interfere. I didn't know what you'd decided, and I figured it wasn't my business."

"You wouldn't have interfered, just distracted me." He shot her a smile.

She smiled back, leaned against the seat, and remembered to breathe.

They headed south on the interstate. After stopping for a quick dinner in Tacoma, they took another highway to Astoria, followed by another that brought them right into Lincoln City.

Taking his eyes off the road for a second, he skimmed her body.

A fire flashed through her. Desire weakened her senses.

"The sign," Jay said, reaching out to run a finger through her hair. "There it is—*The Beach Is Just the Beginning*."

Monet shivered. She felt content, excited. "This is too good to be true."

Jay pulled into the oceanfront resort. Several three-story buildings with brick on the front lined the beach. Cars were pulled up close to rooms on the bottom floors, only a sidewalk and landscaping in between. More vehicles lined the vast parking lot out in the middle. The place had the look and feel one could only get at the coast. Even in the growing darkness, it felt tucked away from everyday life. Jay had already filled her in on the surfside dining, lounge, and entertainment, as well as the indoor swimming and therapy pools.

Monet didn't need entertainment other than Jay.

After they checked into adjoining rooms, Monet was freshening up in hers when she heard a tap on the door.

She pulled it open and smiled.

"Just thought I'd make a quick run to the store," Jay said. "Would you like anything in particular?" His blue gaze coasted over her.

Her heart warmed. "I would love a wine cooler."

"You got it. Be back in a flash."

Perfect, Monet thought as she prepared herself for the most provocative dance of her life. After dressing, she stopped in front of the mirror. She looked classy, all sparkly. Her tanned skin was covered in Victoria's Secret shimmer body lotion. Her golden hair cascaded well below her shoulders in a passionate tumble. Her body—delicate, firm, and toned with curves to match—looked sexy, and her breasts would fill Jay's hands perfectly.

When he returned, Monet slipped into his oceanfront room with him.

They enjoyed a cooler while watching the massive waves breaking on the sand, lit up with a reflective feel in the ever-growing darkness.

And then ... she felt Jay come up behind her.

His voice feathered her ear. "I've waited so long for this."

A tremor ripped through her. She closed her eyes and leaned her head back against his. "Me, too."

"I've dreamed about you."

"Jay," she whispered, thin as lace.

His fingers wound their way down her neck and onto her shoulders. "What?" They continued to glide down her arm, stopping to circle her wrist.

"I can't think," she said as she whirled around and into him, "when you're touching me."

"Don't."

"I want to."

"Why?"

Monet's fingers reveled in the smoothness of his face. "I'm going to turn my fantasy into reality."

"What's that?" His voice was husky.

"Watch."

In ankle-strap high heels, she slowly slipped out of her skirt and top to reveal a white, lacy bra and sheer, white stockings hooked to a tiny garter belt.

She watched his eyes blaze, his lips part, his breathing become heavy.

She closed the distance between them, pressing her body tightly against him, loving the feel of his solid erection.

With her lips barely skimming his face, she whispered in his ear, "I promise you won't be disappointed."

"I'm ready," he muttered and laced his fingers through hers.

She squeezed his fingers before she slipped her hand from his to switch one light off, leaving the room like the lighting in a club.

The wind began to whistle. The glass of the windows was

suddenly splattered with droplets of rain. Shadows from the outside lights bounced off the walls, shrouding the room in a sense of mystery.

She set the radio from the clock at a low volume. Usher's "You Make Me Wanna ..." filled the room with R&B.

Monet returned to Jay, took his hand, and led him to the bed's edge. Then she put her hands on his shoulders and guided him to sit before her. She leaned her whole body into him, blew a warm breath into his ear, and then whirled around to grind on him, slowly, in a circular motion. She felt the hardness of him, his hands all over her body.

Monet turned back around to face him. She put her knee up on his thigh, then kissed his neck, his smooth jaw, and his silky hair.

He unhooked her bra, sliding the tiny straps down her shoulders.

She wiggled free and straddled his hips.

Jay kissed the fullness of her breasts, his tongue tickling her soft skin. When he took a nipple into his mouth and sucked hard, her insides tightened. Monet tangled her hands into his dark hair. He ravished her breasts with his mouth, his tongue, as if completely lost between them. She threw her head back, drowning in the sensation.

Pressure built to torment, and then he cupped her small, round bottom, unhooked her garter, and slid her stockings down her smooth legs. His fingers caressed the insides of her thighs.

With both hands, Jay helped her stand to remove her dainty G-string. Then she tugged his shirt over his head, tracing a trail with the tip of her tongue all the way down the center of his chest. She knelt down and found his belt buckle, unzipped his pants, freed him, and closed her hand around every solid inch.

He stood to shed his pants, resumed his position, and set her delicate body just over his erection.

"Jay," she murmured, pressing her weight against his strong hands. He held her up just enough to tease her. She could feel the head of his sex, straining, moist at the tip.

And then he set her down. His erection jutted against her thigh. Jay caressed her with his hand. With his fingers, he parted her inner lips and slipped two up into her damp heat. "You're so wet, so ready for me."

"I just want all of you inside of me—now," she murmured.

"Monet." His voice was rough. "I've never wanted anyone as much as I want you now."

His warm breath fanned her face.

And then he lifted her just high enough and set her right down on him, driving deep.

He groaned. "God, you're tight."

"You make me that way," Monet whispered, breathless. She didn't think she'd ever been so filled up. "Oh … God."

Their mouths came together hungrily. They kissed aggressive, the deeper he sank into her, with an urgent intensity that escalated into a raw yearning.

She gasped as she felt him stretching her.

"Oh God, Monet," he muttered, his breath heavy on her face. "You feel so good." He held her tiny waist, lifted her slowly, and with a long stroke of possession buried himself into her, forcing her to take all of him, soaking her up greedily.

She threw her head back. "Jay." She called his name over and over as she clutched and released, flexing her inner muscles tighter around him.

She felt him all the way to her stomach, and then she had a release so intense, she thought she might shatter.

Then she experienced his climax rip through him. Jay's body shook. His breath came out in small, hard gusts. She felt his release, like a heated waterfall, carrying her along.

* * *

The following morning, Jay answered a soft knock at the door.

"Room service."

"Come on in." Jay moved aside to let the server by.

The smell of strawberry waffles and blueberry scones instantly filled the room. Hearing Monet's stomach elicit a grumble, Jay gave her a quick grin. "Hmm … sounds like you've worked up quite an appetite."

Monet turned a slight shade of pink.

After the server wheeled out the cart, she said, "Last night was—"

"Amazing," Jay finished, thinking about the way her tightness surrounded him with a scorching heat.

She put her arms around him and leaned her head on his chest. "I'm hungry, but you must be starving."

He pressed his lips on her forehead. "I can take care of your hunger anytime … like right now." His hands slipped up her back.

She pushed her hips into his, teasingly. "How about breakfast first?"

"You got it," he said, and led her to the little, round table by the window.

Waves crashed on the beach, filling the background with the rhythm of the surf.

"This is so good," Monet said, licking a speck of pastry from her fingers. "I have to tell you something funny."

Jay couldn't keep his eyes off her lovely face. "What's that?" He sipped his coffee, watching her over the rim of his cup.

"Eating blueberry scones … it's what I dreamed of, being near the water with someone special … and that dream came true."

Jay stopped pouring syrup over his waffles to reach across the table and twine his fingers with hers. "I like the sound of that."

Monet squeezed his hand. "Tell me," she said, while a gentle breeze rattled the window screen, "what you enjoy. You mentioned going into real estate eventually. Besides your dad and his financial success, what else about it pulls you in that direction?"

Their hands untwined now, they resumed eating. Jay

enjoyed watching her dip each bite of waffle into a puddle of syrup on the side of her plate. He said, "I'd like to get into buying old houses and remodeling them. I think the sense of accomplishment would be very satisfying when they sell."

"Say, how about you do the remodel, and I'll do the interior decorating. We can be a team," she said, her eyes out-sparkling the water.

"I'd never be able to get away from work if you were there." He smiled slowly.

"Oh, sure you would," she teased. "You might get sick of me."

"Never." He took a bite of waffle drenched in syrup. After swallowing, he asked, "Do you miss dancing?"

"You know, it's interesting you asked." She dipped her scone in the remaining syrup on her plate. "I miss the movement, the sexuality of it, being able to feel the lyrics through my body and dance. Right now, of course, I dance in the privacy of my apartment when I can't stop myself, but it's not the same as dancing for someone. That's the part I miss." She looked out the window, then back at him. "Moving to the music, feeling it, challenging my own flexibility."

"Last night was incredible. You can dance for me anytime."

"I certainly will. You can fulfill that need of mine, replace the old one."

He narrowed his eyes as he ran his tongue along his bottom lip. "I look forward to it." Just the way her hair moved across her breasts and the way she flipped it behind her shoulders while she ate … He said softly, "I'm the luckiest guy in the world."

She smiled. "I'm the lucky one."

Jay felt a wave of warmth sweep through him, much like the ocean's waves—big,unstoppable, and everlasting.

An hour later, curled in each other's arms, Jay asked, "Shall we wander around the Old Historic Bayfront of Newport?"

She nibbled lightly on his neck. "That sounds like a plan."

He took her south of Lincoln City.

After a thirty-minute drive, he parked by the water. Before climbing from his pickup, Jay leaned over, pushed her back against the seat, and nearly devoured her. When he eventually pulled his mouth from hers, he couldn't take his eyes from her lips, full and wet.

"We'd better go," he said, his gaze moving to meet her golden eyes, shining like the sun.

Monet smiled. "I think you're right."

They climbed from his pickup, their hands laced together, and visited The Wax Works. Then they dined on the best fish and chips in town, and through a connected building, strolled, hand in hand, through the fascinating Ripley's Believe It or Not.

They made their way to Undersea Gardens across the street. Seagulls hovered above, waiting for someone to leave a scrap of food. The bright sunlight turned the bay into an endless mirror, highlighting Monet's lustrous hair. Jay reached out to brush a strand from her face, rubbing a finger against her warm cheek. It did unfamiliar things to his heart.

Entering the underwater aquarium beneath the surface of Newport's Yaquina Bay, they wandered through leisurely, feasting their eyes on everything from sturgeon, red snapper, Pacific salmon, and a wolf eel, to many more species of the sea, including the world's largest octopus gliding the reef. Then they settled in for a live show before leaving Newport to head back to the resort.

After a light dinner at the restaurant's surfside dining, they returned to their rooms. Jay draped a lightweight jacket around Monet's shoulders before they hit the beach. She said she didn't want to change, so they headed straight down the stairs and to the beach. He loved her spontaneity.

Holding her shoes in one hand, and his hand in the other, Monet said, "So tell me"— she gave his hand a light squeeze—"when you first came here?"

Side by side, fingers linked, they strolled on the seven-and-a-half-mile expanse of sand.

"It's been a favorite of mine since I can remember. Let me see." Jay looked up to the sky. "Probably the first time was when I was ten and my brother was seven."

"Tell me about your brother. I want to know everything about you," she said, flawless in her cream-colored sweater and silk skirt.

"Okay." He smiled. "Let's go sit on that log for a while." He gestured with his free hand.

"Sure," she said with delight.

They trudged through the sand, getting softer and deeper as they approached the log. Jay took off his coat and spread it out on the log. "There, that's a little better so you won't ruin your skirt."

"Thanks. You sure you won't be too cold?" she asked, and settled down onto the log.

"As long as I'm close to you, I could never be cold." He sat beside her, brushing her lips with his. "Okay, about my brother," he began. "You sure you want to hear about him? He's a strange one."

"Of course." She smiled. "He's your brother."

A cool breeze swept up from the water's edge. Seagulls soared overhead, calling to each other. The sky was growing dark.

"Well, let's see. He's three years younger than me and pretty much into himself." The ocean turned dark, reflective. Jay glanced out, took in the smell of the salty air, and continued. "I think Scott, we still call him Scotty, though, got a little perturbed at me when I bought out Dad's business, even though we both had a chance. He doesn't like that line of work anyway. When I try and explain how I do things, compared to some others in my line of work, he doesn't listen. He has in his head what he believes and that's the only truth. He's bullheaded and close-minded, but I love him. He's my little brother."

"It's tough when people don't understand, and if they're

family, it's harder yet." She brushed a wisp of hair from her eyes. "But you know what I think?" She turned into him, her eyes hopeful.

"What?"

"I think it's never too late to reconcile with family, or anyone, for that matter. With my parents, I never thought it would happen, especially with ... my dad."

Jay felt her shiver. He settled an arm around her and drew her close.

"I just never thought I'd know my dad, and then ... it's like, now I believe anything's possible. But hey, enough about me, we're talking about you."

Their eyes met and held.

"You're amazing, you know that?"

Monet shook her head. "Only with you."

Jay held her close. They watched the waves roll in and break on the shore. He laced his fingers through hers.

"Where does your brother live?" she prodded, content to lean against him.

"Downtown Seattle in some fancy high-rise. He has his own computer business and drives a Mercedes his girlfriend helped him buy. She works at a dealership downtown. That's how they met, I guess. According to my parents, her parents have money. Her dad owns the dealership. And I guess she's really high maintenance, has an attitude. You know the type." He gave her hand a squeeze. "I don't think my parents think much of her." He grinned. "You, they will love."

She dropped her gaze to their bound hands. "Where did you say your parents live?"

"In Duvall. They've been there all their lives. It's where I was raised."

"Duvall. I've heard of it. Isn't it near Monroe?"

"Yeah, between there and Carnation. It's pretty country."

"I bet. You're lucky to have grown up there."

"If it wasn't for my parents, I wouldn't be where I am today."

"You obviously think a lot of them." Monet smiled. "That's good."

Jay returned the smile. "I do, and I can't wait for you to meet them."

"Me, too. I also can't wait for you to meet mine, now that I've met them both." She laughed.

"I look forward to meeting anyone who's a part of your life. Family is important. Maybe you can help me out with my brother."

She smiled into his eyes. "I'd love to."

"Do you want a family of your own someday?" He held his breath as he waited for her answer.

She nodded yes. "I think I always have, but I wanted to at least get started with my career first. Like I'm doing now, I guess, or heading in that direction, anyway. I can hardly believe it. It feels really good working toward something I feel passionate about. I think I've always wanted a family of my own because I never had one growing up. And I missed that. You know what feels nice right now?" Her eyes sparkled into his.

His pulse quickened. "What?"

"To think that maybe I've found the person I want to have that family with."

A shiver went up his spine. "I feel the same way."

The silence between them felt right.

He squeezed her hand and she squeezed his back. He heard her swallow, saw her smile. He'd never felt so secure with anyone as he did right now with her.

A sea breeze tickled his nose, the loud slapping of the surf filled his ears, and Monet was heaven to his eyes.

She slipped her fingers from his to stretch.

He watched her in the moonlight. The thin fabric of her top fluttered in the breeze, exposing her hardened nipples that he'd lavished last night. Awareness shot through him, and then he drew her into his arms and held her, feeling as if he could stay like this forever. And he knew … he felt truly connected. They were linked now. It was something he'd never experienced before.

She was his destiny.

Without words, Jay pushed to his feet and helped her up. They headed toward the ocean. He felt like his life had finally come full circle. Monet had completed it. He took her hand at her side and laced his fingers through her delicate ones as the sea breeze picked up, blowing her hair back from her face and shoulders.

He stopped walking, turned toward her, and gently lifted her hair at her back to set it in front of her shoulders. She was so sexy.

Their eyes locked.

He caught his breath. His heart pounded.

And then … his breath was on her cheek and his lips were on hers, soft at first, deepening with passion, need, desire.

They kissed with the sound of the surf in the background, then slowly walked up the beach, hand in hand, Monet's head resting against his shoulder, the waves lapping behind them, all while the sun set in an unsurpassed sunset, enveloping them in the dramatic, night-lit beach.

"God, I didn't want this trip to ever end," Monet said when they were on their way home the following morning.

Jay blew out a sigh. "Me, either. Hey, I know," he said, his mind working.

"What?" She angled to face him, a smile growing on her pretty features.

"Let's not let it end. You don't have to be at school until morning, right?"

"Right."

"We'll extend it. How about I come in when we get to your place?" Jay cut her a glance and saw the disappointment in her eyes.

"My roommate is always home on Sundays."

"We'll go to my place then." He grinned.

"I'd like that."

"Trust me," he said with a reassuring wink. "I'll get you home in plenty of time for a good night's sleep."

The minute they set foot inside the house, he scooped her up and carried her into the living room, switching on lights along the way. Then he set her down in front of the marble fireplace.

"Believe me," he said, desire in his eyes. "I'll be right back."

In the guest bedroom, he grabbed a down comforter, then returned and watched her, growing more aroused with each beat of his heart.

She slipped out of her long, slitted skirt to reveal a purple, see-through bra and G-string, leaving silver high heels on. Her bare legs looked silky and smooth. She walked toward him with a bounce to her small, curvy hips.

Full throttle now, he dropped the comforter to the floor. It fell in a big heap around them.

She knelt before him, unbuckled his belt, and unzipped his pants, reaching in to free him. Then she looked up into his eyes, licked her lips, and touched the tip of him with her tongue.

He was in heaven.

Monet nudged him down onto the comforter, fell on top of him, and pressed her lips to his neck with soft, whispery kisses. She made her way down his chest, his stomach, and then with slow, lazy movements, ran her tongue around the wetness of his tip, spreading moisture all around and down the length of him. She caressed his balls with her fingertips before sucking them gently. He quivered. When she bounced his balls off her tongue, he damn near came.

Then, like a slow feast, she put her lips on him, taking him into her mouth, inching down his length, alternating with broad strokes all the way back up.

He fisted his hands into her silky tumble of hair. "Monet. Sweet Jesus," he muttered.

She took him deep now. Her throat squeezed him and her cheek muscles contracted around him, sending him farther, deeper into her mouth with a hunger so intense, it overwhelmed him. He felt himself all the way to her tonsils, past her throat muscles—and lost it.

Monet continuously swallowed while he trembled and emptied into her mouth. He finally felt the last of his release slide down her throat.

When he resumed breathing, he turned her over to lay on her back.

Jay unhooked her bra and devoured her breasts, taking her hardened nipples into his mouth, one at a time, sucking hard like a starved infant. Monet squirmed beneath him, ran her hands through his hair, and hugged his head to her chest.

He continued a trail of kisses down her sweet-smelling skin. Her stomach muscles quivered at his touch.

When he got to the heat between her legs, he slid her tiny G-string off and saturated his fingers inside of her.

"Your turn," he said against her slick skin.

Monet lifted her hips against his fingers. "Oh, Jay."

And then his mouth found her feminine core. He parted her inner lips and delved his tongue between her soft folds. She moaned, restless, as he licked and feasted on her, searching for that small, sensitive spot.

She caught her breath and tensed. "Jay."

Now his mouth and finger worked simultaneously, flicking back and forth and putting pressure on her clitoris. He pressed upward. She writhed in response, her hips pushing against him in time to the rhythm of his tongue and finger. She knotted her fingers into his hair, thrashing beneath him as his tongue devoured her with light, quick strokes, teasing and tormenting until her release danced through her body, over and over.

"Oh yes, Jay … oh … Jay, please." She gasped while he lapped up her nectar with his tongue, swallowing all of her sweetness until she was depleted.

When she quit trembling, his mouth found hers, their tongues colliding in a fevered rush.

"Now I need to be inside you," he whispered roughly against her cheek.

Still out of breath, she managed, "Over there," gesturing to the couch.

"Anywhere. I don't—"

Monet silenced him with a kiss, took his hand, and led him to the couch.

"You ready for me?" he asked, easing on top of her.

"Yes," she murmured.

He entered her slowly. She was very wet. Inch by inch he

filled her. She was so damn tight. Her thighs were hot around him. He felt her muscles contract, squeezing him. "Goddamn, you feel good," he said into her hair.

Her nails dug into his back. She arched up and into him, making him slide deeper into her.

Monet called out his name. "Jay, don't stop. Please." Her breathing was ragged, heavy.

He slipped his mouth over hers and swallowed her moans, working his tongue over hers while thrusting into the walls of her body, only to slide almost all the way out before fully bedding himself deep inside of her, stretching her to the limit.

"Oh God, Jay!" she screamed.

He pushed harder and found her mouth again. Their tongues mated in rhythm to their grinding bodies, sliding farther and farther off the couch.

When he tried to right their position, she said breathlessly, "I want it like this. I want the rush, the feel of you so far up—"

And then she did a backbend over the side of the couch, her butt just on the edge, her hands on the floor.

"Holy Christ!" He groaned in pleasure. "You're going to make me explode."

Clutching … releasing, he felt the explosion of her climax rip through him in shuddering waves as he came deep inside her, where she was slick, hot, tight. And when he pumped into her one last time, he knew he'd never get enough of her.

Peace and tension mingled into complete contentment.

He had to have her forever.

Chapter Twenty-Three

The following Friday slid into afternoon. Monet's heart picked up speed at the thought of seeing Jay again.

Just five days ago, he had taken her home after their incredible time together on the Oregon Coast. She never dreamed anything could feel so good, so real, so amazing.

And now, he would be calling any second.

She waited anxiously by the phone, her body on fire.

So, it came as no surprise when she heard the sound, picking it up before a full ring. "Hello."

"Monet."

The deep, sexy voice shot sparks through her. "Jay?" she said on a breath. "God, I've missed you."

"Me, too. I need to see you. Can you come over?"

"Of course."

"Right now?"

"I'm on my way."

"I'll be here," he said.

The urgency in his voice caused her heart to flutter, her loins to contract. They'd talked every night this week for an hour. It'd been heaven to her ears, and now she could hardly wait to see him.

Finally ready for him, Monet checked the mirror. She'd secured her long hair in a beaded clip, leaving a few tendrils dangling beside her face. Her low-rise, cream-colored pants and cropped, sleeveless sweater caused her to smile in satisfaction.

With a last glance to make sure all appliances and lights were out in the apartment, Monet closed and locked the door behind her.

By the time she turned into Jay's driveway, she ached for him.

At his door, she raised her hand and touched the bell. Seconds later, it opened.

"Monet."

The way he said her name tickled her skin with pleasure. "Jay, hi," she said and finger-combed a wisp of hair from her face.

"You look great." His blue eyes twinkled as he moved aside to let her in.

"So do you." She stepped inside, skimming his blue slacks, white dress shirt, and thick, dark hair.

"I'm glad you're here."

"Me, too." She followed him into the kitchen, instantly

greeted with the aroma of heavenly BBQ sauce drifting from the oven. The scent of food and sight of him made her mouth water. "I didn't know you could cook."

"You still don't know that." He chuckled, a deep, sexy sound. "It's my mom's recipe for BBQ chicken pot pie with a corn bread crust."

"You made all that for me?"

"It was easy. Everything's already prepared. I'll tell you about it later. How about some champagne first?"

At the thought of champagne, she felt exhilaration whirl through her. "Sounds great. I certainly didn't expect"—she hesitated—"something this perfect."

"Nothing's as perfect as you. Besides, tonight's special." He smiled into her eyes.

She felt a shiver go down her spine as she watched him retrieve a bottle of Dom Perignon from the refrigerator and take two champagne flutes from a cupboard.

Then he came to stand beside her, took off the thick, foil wrapping, held the bottle away from them, and pulled out the cork. A loud popping sound reverberated through the kitchen. He poured and handed her the filled glass.

"To us … and tonight," he said, raising his glass to hers.

Monet repeated, "To us … and tonight." She took a sip of her champagne. The sensation was smooth, wonderful, like bubbles made of velvet going down her throat. *How Jay had tasted.* The tingly sensation was electric on her throat and tongue. *Like Jay.*

Jay swallowed a sip of his champagne and set his glass on the counter. "I'd like to tell you something I've been thinking about lately."

The silence was deafening.

Her heart thudded in her chest as she anticipated his words.

"I love you, and I'd like to spend the rest of my life with you."

Her eyes moistened. A heartbeat later, she responded, "I love you, too. And oh God, Jay. Oh, Jay, I'd love to spend the rest of my life with you, too."

"Be careful," he warned with a wink. "Saying my name like that, you're going to make me strip you naked right here on the kitchen floor."

But instead, he pulled her into his arms and held her.

She drew back to smile up at him and blinked through a glimmer of a tear.

He brushed it carefully from her face before sliding his lips across hers.

Monet knew it was only the beginning of a lifetime of fulfilled dreams, desires, and love … together forever.

* * *

The doorbell rang at Ruby's parents' house. She rushed to answer it, expecting it to be the twenty-one-year-old car detailer she'd been seeing. Instead, she pulled it open to find two men in suits.

"Are you Ruby Wilkins?"

"Yes," she replied. "What the hell?"

"I'm Detective Rogers and this is Detective Price from the King County Sheriff's Department.

Ruby's face filmed with sweat.

"We're investigating an arson fire at Fantasy's Dance Club that happened on July 10th. You own a red Corvette?"

She blinked hard. "Yes."

"We have an eyewitness who described your car and says he can identify you at the scene of the crime."

Her body shook with terror. This couldn't be happening. Her biggest fear had come true.

Her knees weakened.

"You're going to have to come with us for questioning and to be put in a lineup for identification by this witness."

Ruby fainted.

Epilogue

Eight Months Later

Santorini was every bit as beautiful as Monet imagined it would be, and undoubtedly, one of the most extraordinary islands in the world. Oia, Santorini's second-largest town and nestled at the tip of the northern horn of the island, was where she and Jay would exchange their vows.

Monet stood in her long, white, satin-and-lace wedding dress. Her bare, lightly tanned shoulders emerged elegantly above rows and rows of pearls adorning a tight-fitting bodice. Her hair was swept up on top of her head in a small crown of pearls.

She gazed out over the land from their balcony at the Atlantis Villas in Greece to the breathtaking scene before her. Cubical, white houses tumbled down the cliffs toward a sapphire-colored sea.

She breathed in deeply and let it out slowly.

"Nice view," Jay said from behind her, wrapping his arms around her.

At the sound of his voice, the feel of his arms, Monet felt that familiar, sensual quiver shoot up her spine. "Yeah, but this one's even better." She turned into his arms and touched her lips to his.

The kiss began as a gentle one but quickly heated up as their mouths opened and their tongues met lavishly.

"If we start this, we'll never get there in time," Jay whispered in her ear.

"I know." She pulled back to look at him. He stole her breath in an elegant, black tuxedo, his dark hair combed back to perfection. "God, you look incredible."

"Look who's talking." He smiled, slowly and seductively.

He was so handsome that she could hardly breathe. She ran a hand down the front of her dress and tucked a stray piece of hair back in the giant, pearl comb.

"You ready?" he asked.

She blew out a breath. "Yes, I'm ready, but do you think they are?"

"You mean our parents?" Jay's eyes glittered the same bright blue as the sky.

"Yeah." Monet smiled, appreciating the warm welcome into his family.

"Oh, I'm sure they'll beat us there."

Monet laughed. "I'm sure they will."

They said "I do" on a veranda with the sunset casting shades of fuchsia and pale green on the moon-shaped cliffs rising a thousand feet from the caldera.

"You couldn't have asked for a more beautiful bride," Jay's mother said with pride. Short, mocha-colored hair framed her face.

His father, an older version of Jay, nodded in agreement.

Monet's heart overflowed. Real beauty went beyond the surface and lasted forever, and that's what she and Jay had found.

"You're so lucky, and I couldn't be happier for you." Monet's mother beamed at her.

"I agree," her father said, his eyes full of love for her.

Monet went to her mother and father, took a hand each, and squeezed. "Thank you so much for being here. It means the world to me."

She embraced each of them in turn.

As the newlyweds watched the sunset together from their balcony, they were already planning next year's reservations.

"We'll come back next year for two weeks, just you and me." Jay nuzzled her cheek as he spoke.

"I'd love to," Monet said, "but right now, I have plans for us." Her lips brushed the shell of his ear.

"Believe me," Jay whispered softly, "so do I."

THANK YOU FOR READING

Always Hope

A note from the author ...

If you enjoyed it and would like to know more about new releases, please join my mailing list for updates on my website at www.miastadin.com.

You can also reach me at miastadin@gmail.com, or facebook.com/MiaStadinAuthor.

I love to hear from my readers!

DID YOU KNOW THAT LEAVING A REVIEW IS THE BEST GIFT YOU CAN GIVE AN AUTHOR? I AM INVITING YOU TO LEAVE A REVIEW ON Amazon and Goodreads.

Thank you from the bottom of my heart.

Made in the USA
Coppell, TX
24 October 2021